PLEASURED
BY YOU

Also by Elle Wright

The Wellspring Series

Touched by You

Enticed by You

Pleasured by You

Published by Kensington Publishing Corp.

PLEASURED BY YOU

Elle Wright

Kensington Publishing Corp.

www.kensingtonbooks.com

DAFINA BOOKS are published by

Kensington Publishing Corp.
119 West 40th Street
New York, NY 10018

All Kensington Titles, Imprints, and Distributed Lines are available at special quantity discounts for bulk purchases for sales promotions, premiums, fund-raising, and educational or institutional use. Special book excerpts or customized printings can also be created to fit specific needs. For details, write or phone the office of the Kensington special sales manager: Kensington Publishing Corp., 119 West 40th Street, New York, NY 10018, attn: Special Sales Department, Phone: 1-800-221-2647.

Dafina and the Dafina logo Reg. U.S. Pat. & TM Off.

ISBN-13: 978-1-4967-1604-0
ISBN-10: 1-4967-1604-3
First Kensington Mass Market Edition: December 2018

ISBN-13: 978-1-4967-1605-7 (e-book)
ISBN-10: 1-4967-1605-1 (e-book)
First Kensington Electronic Edition: December 2018

10 9 8 7 6 5 4 3 2 1

Printed in the United States of America

For Jason, my husband and friend.
Your constant support means the world to me.
Love you!

Acknowledgments

Dreaming up Bryson and Jordan's journey was an unforgettable experience. *Pleasured by You* proved to be one of the most difficult books I've ever had to write. Tapping into Bryson's pain took the wind out of my sails often, but I'm so glad that he finally got his happy ending. I hope you enjoy it! I appreciate all of your love and support.

Giving honor to God, who is able to do anything. His Grace and Mercy brought me through. I am living this moment because of Him.

To my husband, Jason, I can't imagine my life without you. I'm still pleasured by you.

To my children, Asante, Kaia, and Masai. Every day you surprise me with your intelligence, your wit, your humanity, your courage, and your capacity to love. Keep being who you are. Keep God first. Love you!

To my family and friends, thank you for your unwavering support. My life is brighter because of you. Thanks for being #TeamElle!

To my Seester Sister, LaDonna, I'm just going to say that you're the BOMB! Thanks for rolling with me! Love you!

To my hairstylist extraordinaire, Stacie, thank you for your listening ear and your encouragement.

You have inspired me to create Stacyee and I can't wait for you to read her journey. I'm blessed to call you a friend.

To my lit sisters, and Once Upon a Series crew, Sheryl Lister, Sherelle Green, and Angela Seals; let's get it. I can't wait to do more. Love y'all!

To my Book Euphoria ladies, you are #SoDope.

To #EllesBelles, my street team, thank you so much for rocking with me.

To my agent, Sara Camilli, thank you for being in my corner always! Appreciate you.

To my editor, Selena James, thank you for your understanding and your encouragement. I truly appreciate you.

I also want to thank Priscilla C. Johnson and Cilla's Maniacs, A.C. Arthur, Brenda Kidd-Woodbury (BJBC), MidnightAce Scotty, King Brooks (Black Page Turners), Sharon Blount and BRAB (Building Relationships Around Books), LaShaunda Hoffman (SORMAG), Orsayor Simmons (Book Referees), Tiffany Tyler (Reading in Black and White), Naleighna Kai (Naleighna Kai's Literary Café and Cavalcade of Authors), Delaney Diamond (RNIC), Wayne Jordan (RIC), Radiah Hubert (Urban Book Reviews), and the EyeCU Reading and Social Network for supporting me. I truly appreciate you all.

Thank you to my readers! You're amazing! Nothing would be possible without you.

Thank you!

Love,
Elle

Chapter 1

I'm in town, staying at Casa Del Mar. We need to talk.

It had taken Bryson Wells years to find peace, to carve out his own path. Away from his father, away from Wellspring, Michigan, and Wellspring Water Corporation. And one text from his brother, Parker, had transported him back to the life he'd tried to put behind him. Sighing, he stared at his phone. The urge to ignore the text was fierce, but he couldn't do that to his brother. Instead, he'd thought of a suitable lie. Work. If Parker understood anything, it was work. But when Bryson had opened up the Messenger app to send his reply, he couldn't do it.

Parker Wells Jr. had done more for Bryson than anyone. He'd taken a lick for Bryson more times than Bryson could even count. As far as big brothers went, Parker was the best. So, he'd simply typed out "give me a few hours," left work, and hopped on the I-10 to Santa Monica. Now, he was sitting in the restaurant at a luxury hotel waiting on his brother.

It had been several years since he'd seen his siblings, Parker and Brooklyn. By design. For his own sanity. Life in Wellspring, Michigan, had been a nightmare. One that still haunted him. And only because of Parker Wells Sr., his father. Senior, as they called him, was a monster, plain and simple, with no redeemable qualities.

Bryson knew early on that he wouldn't survive another minute in that house with his father. He'd been subjected to horrors that made his skin crawl, beatings that seemed to last hours, verbal tirades that made his ears bleed. Even now, Bryson had sometimes awoken with a soundless scream in his heart, sweat seeping from his pores, sending silent prayers to God to help him forget.

A waitress smiled as she approached his table, and he greeted her in kind, ordering a cognac, neat. Several minutes later, Bryson was holding the balloon glass in his palm, letting it warm, before tasting it. *Damn good.*

He nodded to the waitress, signaling he was satisfied with the pour, and she strolled away. Bryson watched the sway of her hips as she departed, and wondered if he could go there. It had been a while since he'd had the company of a woman, and he was wound tight, ready to burst.

Over the past few years, Bryson had spent an inordinate amount of time throwing himself into work. When he'd left Wellspring, he'd given Senior the middle finger, throwing his acceptance letter to

Michigan State University in his face and hightailing it out of the house.

Bryson could still hear the shrill shouts of his father as he walked out of that house once and for all. *"You'll be back. You're nothing without me."* The last words from his father had stayed with him long after he'd hopped in a cab and left Wellspring with nothing but a small suitcase and the clothes on his back.

The satisfaction that he thought he would feel didn't come, but it hadn't dampened his resolve. He'd worked hard in high school, busted his ass to win a coveted scholarship to University of Southern California, far away from Michigan and Wellspring and Senior. Bryson had used Senior's words as a stepping stone to get what he wanted. He majored in civil engineering and minored in construction planning and management, and had recently completed his graduate studies in planning. And he loved his work, he loved his life. *I did damn good.*

Still, Bryson found himself missing his siblings more and more as the days flew by. He was accomplished, and he yearned to share that with the people who'd loved him through the hardest time of his life. But he knew that stepping foot in that town would be a huge setback for him, and he couldn't bring himself to do it yet.

Bryson sighed, and finished his glass of cognac. He glanced up, intent on waving the waitress back over to refill it, when he saw her.

He blinked. But when he opened his eyes, she was still there. Jordan Clark.

It couldn't be a coincidence that Parker was in town, staying at the same hotel as Jordan. Bryson let his gaze wander over her form. Her curly mane was swept to the side, exposing her long neck. Her skin was sun-kissed, golden brown. Jordan wore a pale pink and white strapless dress that fell just above her knees and she carried a small clutch in her hand. Bryson shifted in his seat, unable to stop the groan that escaped. She was stunning, soft, regal. She was everything he remembered about her, and pink was definitely her color. Always had been.

At eleven years old, Senior had yanked Bryson out of his life with his mother in Detroit. After a nasty court battle for custody, his mother had packed him up, kissed him on his forehead, and told him to "be brave" before Senior had dragged him out of the only home he'd ever known. Bryson had known who his father was, had even spent time in Wellspring, mostly because of Brooklyn and Parker's mother, Marie. But he'd never imagined or expected to *live* in Wellspring. In fact, it wasn't until Marie died that Senior decided to pluck him out of his life.

Bryson had cried the entire trip, and the days after, until his first day of school. The playground had been filled with kids, playing and enjoying one another. Brooklyn had assured him that she wouldn't leave him to fend for himself, but his sister had been called to the office during lunch and Bryson had to sit alone. It was Jordan who had joined him at the table that day, and handed him a piece of her apple. She had been one of his first friends in Wellspring. And although their lives were so far apart now, he would never forget that day. Bryson could never forget her.

Bryson smiled to himself when he thought of Jordan at eleven years old. She was an athlete, a star softball player in middle school and high school. But she was also smart and funny. And she'd loved pink, even back then. He was happy to see that hadn't changed.

Jordan slid onto a barstool and smiled at the bartender. Bryson noted the wide grin on the bartender's face, and narrowed his eyes on him. The man had to be at least fifty, probably married with a family. *So why the hell is he flirting with Jordan?* Bryson was just getting ready to find out when Parker walked into the restaurant.

His brother, dressed in a blue three-piece suit and no tie, walked right up to Jordan and pulled her into a hug. Bryson frowned. *What the hell?* Parker was grinning from ear to ear and Jordan was . . . Well, Jordan was her usual glowing self. And all of her black girl magic shined on his brother. His married brother, at that.

Bryson couldn't help the surge of jealousy that filled him as he watched his older brother and Jordan interact on the other side of the bar. It definitely wasn't a coincidence that they were staying at the same hotel. The only question he had now was why. Was it a tryst? Was his brother cheating on his new wife, Kennedi, already?

Bryson had learned early on that there weren't many people more popular than Parker. His brother had been a football legend in the town, helping Wellspring High place in several divisions and even winning Most Valuable Player titles for three of his four years in high school. Parker was not only popular with the girls, but his stellar grades and community-minded personality made him a favorite with teachers and school administrators.

While Bryson could give Parker a run in academics any day of the week, he could admit that sports weren't his thing. The only "sport" he'd excelled at was bowling, if that could even be considered a sport. That simple fact had been a bone of contention between Bryson and Senior often, and he had the scars to prove it. And women? Let's just say Bryson wasn't voted "Most Likely to Get a Date" in school. But he didn't care about just any date, either. Back then, he'd only had eyes for Jordan. And judging by the way his body had responded to just the sight of her, he would say that hadn't changed.

Bryson grumbled a curse under his breath when Parker leaned forward and whispered something to Jordan, which in turn, made her laugh out loud. It was a beautiful sound, melodic. And once again, it was reserved for Parker. *Asshole.*

A few more torturous moments of watching them, and Bryson wanted to break that shit up. He pulled his wallet out and grabbed a fifty-dollar bill, all the while cursing his brother to hell and back for being so damn charming all the time.

"Bryson."

Bryson glanced up, surprised that Parker was now standing in front of him. "Parker." He stood and gave Parker a tight man-hug.

"Good to see you, man," Parker said.

"You, too." For some reason, Bryson was overcome with emotion, but he swallowed it down and pulled back. "Have a seat."

Parker took the seat opposite Bryson, a wide smile on his face. "I see you already started, huh?" Parker motioned to Bryson's empty glass.

"Long day," Bryson murmured.

Parker nodded. "I have a lot of those."

"I bet." The waitress approached again and took Parker's order quickly before rushing away. "So how long have you known where I was?" Bryson asked.

Parker shrugged, tapping his finger on the table lightly. "Honestly, I've known for months where you were."

"And you're just now coming to see me?"

Bryson couldn't help the tinge of hypocritical hurt that had settled in at Parker's admission. Sure, Bryson had done a lot to hide his whereabouts from his family, but the knowledge that his brother had known where he was for a while and never attempted to come see him still stung.

"Trust me, brother, I wanted to. But you don't answer your phone or call, and I'm not too keen on forcing you to do anything you don't want to do. Good job, by the way, of hiding your tracks."

Bryson had enrolled at MIT for undergrad, and had even flown to Cambridge as if he was really going to attend the prestigious university. Then, he'd changed his last name and moved to California. He didn't want to sever *all* ties to his siblings, so he'd given them a Google Plus number to reach him.

"How did you find me?"

"Carter's business partner, Martin, helped me."

Bryson knew that Carter was Brooklyn's husband. He'd yet to meet the man, but Bryson had Googled him. Everything he'd read about him led him to believe she was in good hands. Which is what mattered to him at the end of the day.

With a new drink now on the table, Bryson took a sip and allowed himself a glance over to Jordan. She still sat at the bar, head down, her barely touched drink next to her.

"I get it," Parker said, drawing Bryson's attention back to him. "If you remember, Cali was my goal for a while, too."

Bryson did remember. He also remembered that he and Brooklyn were the reasons Parker never made the move. "I know. For what it's worth, you would love it here."

His brother chuckled. "Looks like the California sun is treating you well. I'm proud of you."

Smiling, Bryson thanked Parker. High praise from Parker made him feel good. "What brings you here?"

"Jackson Clark got married today here."

Ah, that explains it. "Really?"

"Yeah, his daughter Jordan is sitting over there at the bar." Parker turned and pointed to Jordan. "I know you remember her. Y'all were cool back in the day."

Bryson cleared his throat and tried to pretend he hadn't noticed her. "Oh right. That's her? I didn't even recognize her," he lied.

Parker smirked at him, almost as if he wanted to cry foul on Bryson's statement. "Yeah, she's all grown up. Beautiful woman."

"I'm sure not as beautiful as your wife," Bryson said.

"You're right about that, brother," Parker agreed, a smile on his face. "And now she's even more beautiful now that she's pregnant."

"Wow, congrats, big brother. I'm happy for you. I know you'll be a good father."

They fell silent for a moment, before Parker said, "I want you to meet Kennedi. She's in our room, freshening up. The reception is in one of the ballrooms. They should be getting started there soon, after pictures and everything."

"When are you leaving?" Bryson asked.

"Tomorrow morning. I have a fund-raising event to attend tomorrow evening." Parker looked outside. "It's beautiful out here. Weather's nice, not like the snow and ice in Wellspring."

Bryson glanced at the beach. March in Santa Monica was usually rainy, but it was sunny and warm. Perfect day for a wedding on the beach. "Was the wedding outside?"

Parker shook his head. "No. Apparently, Jackson's new wife is from this area and didn't want to chance the weather."

"Makes sense. Where's Brooklyn? Why didn't she come?"

Parker explained that Brooklyn was in Detroit celebrating Carter's stepfather's sixtieth birthday.

"How is Brooklyn?" Bryson asked.

"You know Brooklyn." Parker smiled. "She's something else, but she's happy."

Every so often, Brooklyn would send Bryson a selfie making a funny face or a picture of her and the crew shooting pool at Brook's Pub. And although he rarely replied back, he appreciated her attempts to stay in touch.

Hearing from Parker that his sister was happy felt good, but to see the proof of it in her eyes was even better. After her wedding, she'd sent Bryson a file with tons of wedding pictures. His sister was a beautiful, vibrant bride, and her love for Carter was plain to see.

If anyone deserved happiness, it was Brooklyn. She was giving and sweet and funny. Senior had tried to dull her light many times, from shipping her off to boarding school for three years to yanking her out of boarding school just when she'd found her footing in Massachusetts, to announcing her engagement to Sterling King without her knowledge.

Bryson studied Parker. His brother was happy, too. And Bryson wanted to thank Kennedi personally for making that happen. *Still doesn't change the fact that Parker was flirting with Jordan, but he's not dead and he does have eyes.*

"I want you to come home," Parker said.

Bryson stretched his neck. He knew it was coming, but he'd hoped they'd be able to talk about other things before he had to tell him no. "That's not going to happen."

Parker leaned forward. "Look, Senior is not going to survive this."

Several months ago, Senior suffered a severe heart attack and had been comatose, kept alive by a machine. "Good." That one word was all Bryson could muster for the man that made his life hell. Senior didn't deserve his concern after the way he'd treated him. Hell, he didn't deserve anything from any of his children. Bryson wasn't the only one who'd suffered.

"I know how you feel, brother," Parker said. "Trust me, we've all been through the ringer when it comes to Senior. But even if he were to live, he'll be going to jail."

"I heard." Bryson knew of the scandal that had rocked Wellspring after Senior had his heart attack. Corruption, deceit, lies . . . all in a day's work for Senior. Bryson was just glad it had finally caught up to his father.

The news that Senior had been indicted on multiple charges, even while in a coma, had been music to his ears. Senior had forged his first wife's will and conspired with others to grab land from Wellspring residents and others in surrounding counties. Several of Senior's friends and longtime associates had been arrested as well. Although his father would never stand trial for the many crimes he'd committed, Bryson took solace in knowing that Senior wouldn't be able to worm his way out of trouble like he'd done for years.

"It's been crazy, Bryson. But things are turning around in Wellspring. I have control of the company. We're cleaning house, getting rid of all of the Senior loyalists. The entire town is brighter without Senior's reign. Many who moved away are returning to town."

Dead or alive, Senior's horrible treatment of Bryson had made an indelible mark on him, one that wouldn't soon be forgotten. "I hear you, Parker. And I believe you. I'm happy that things are turning around. But . . . I can't do it, man. I can't come back there."

"I told you Brooklyn thinks Senior is holding out for his kids."

Bryson frowned. "Seriously, Parker. You really think Senior is holding out for me?"

"At first, I wasn't sure I agreed with her, but he's holding on for something."

"Maybe it was Veronica." A few months ago, Parker had told Bryson about a long-lost sister who'd been living in Indiana.

"That doesn't explain why he's still alive. Veronica has been to see him, several times."

"I don't know, Parker. You know as well as I do that Senior didn't care about me. He only brought me to live with him because he could and he had some warped idea in his head that I could make you fall in line."

Parker sighed, and Bryson knew he'd hit a nerve. Senior had tried to pit Parker against Bryson from the moment he'd stepped foot in the big house for the first time. "Except, he never succeeded with that," Parker said through clenched teeth.

"Not because he didn't try."

"No, because *we* didn't let him."

Bryson swallowed hard. "I don't think I've ever thanked you for being the brother you were to me. You protected me more often than not."

"That's not necessary. It's what I do."

"It's who you are. And I'm glad that you've finally done something for you. Look at you . . . married? And happy?"

"Look at you, little brother." Parker pointed at him. "You're doing your thing. Everything you've accomplished since you left Wellspring is all you. You didn't need Senior's money or his name to get where you are."

"Thanks for that. It means a lot coming from you."

"It's not too late to show him that he was wrong about you."

Bryson shook his head. "Nah, I don't need to. I know it, and that's all that matters."

"You're right. You don't have anything to prove to him. But you're still a Wells. Together, we can take Wellspring Water Corp. to new heights. Your background in planning and environmental science is the key to our continued success."

Parker had done his homework. Bryson had concentrated on environmental and civil engineering topics in his studies, from maintaining air quality to providing safe drinking water. Parker wasn't wrong, and Bryson knew he could make a difference in Wellspring. But going back there wasn't safe for him, and he needed to maintain his peace.

"Just think about it." Parker finished his drink. "I won't push you. I just wanted you to know that I need you on our team. More importantly, I miss you. You're my brother, and family is everything."

Except for Senior. "I'll think about it."

Parker stood. "How long can you stay? I want you to meet Kennedi."

Bryson smiled at his brother. "I can't wait to meet her."

"Give me a few minutes."

Bryson watched Parker head off in the direction of the elevators and stood. *Now or never.* He dropped a fifty-dollar bill on the table to settle the bill and walked over to the bar. Jordan was still sitting there, looking lovely as a summer day.

He'd kept an eye on her throughout his conversation with Parker, letting his eyes wander over her petite frame periodically. She hadn't moved much since she'd arrived. Jordan looked like she had the world on her shoulders, and he wanted to help ease her burden in some way.

Leaning against the bar, he motioned for the bartender to bring him a drink. Her scent wrapped around him. She smelled like fresh rain, water lilies, and flowers. Turning to her, he said, "Hi, Jordan."

Jordan glanced up at him, a frown on her face and her mouth pulled in a tight line. But then recognition lit her green eyes, and she reared back. "Bryson Wells. What the hell are you doing here?"

Chapter 2

Jordan Clark had expected her father's wedding to go exactly as it had. She'd expected his new bride to gush about how she couldn't wait to get to know her. She'd expected her father to tell everyone the story of how Jordan had sprained her ankle sliding into home base during a softball tournament, yet continued to play, helping the team win the divisional title. She'd even expected her stomach to roll with disgust when the officiant announced the happy couple.

What she didn't expect was to hear the bridesmaids whispering to each other that Rebecca had "finally snagged a rich one." She didn't expect to be sitting at the hotel bar, nursing a half-full glass of cognac, while the reception was under way a few hundred feet away. And she definitely didn't expect to be staring into the brown eyes of Bryson Wells.

Damn. Jordan gazed up at Bryson. Gone was the nerdy, shy boy he'd been in high school. In his place was a man. She allowed herself another appreciative glance, taking in his broad, hard shoulders, lean and powerful legs, bald head, and the hint of sexy stubble on his defined jaw. *Oh yeah, he's a hottie.*

Swallowing, she tried to formulate a coherent sentence. *Something other than babbling would be great.*

"Wow." He stared at her as if he expected her to say more. "It's been a long time," she added.

Bryson smiled, giving her a glimpse at his pretty white teeth. A big departure from the braces he wore for years. And that damn dimple on his right cheek? Adorable. *Did he always have that?*

"Too long," Bryson said. "It's good to see you."

Then he pulled her into a hug, one that made Jordan forget her train of thought. He was warm and smelled like sage and ginger. Finally he pulled away and Jordan wanted to pull him back to her. Instead, though, she sat back down on her stool and told herself she only sat down because she was tired. Not because he made her feel woozy.

Jordan picked up her glass and gulped down the rest of her drink. The cranberry and Hennessy did nothing to calm her nerves. When she peered back at him, he was watching her intently, his smoldering eyes probably seeing more than she intended to show. "Do you live here?" she asked.

"In L.A. Parker texted me and told me he was here, so I drove down for a quick visit."

"Oh good." Jordan knew that Bryson had been missing in action since he'd left Wellspring. She also knew that his siblings had been looking for him. Her best friend, Madison, had an on-and-off relationship with Parker's best friend, Trent. Maddie was Jordan's Wellspring connection and often gave

Jordan updates on the goings-on in their hometown. "I'm glad to hear you and Parker are talking."

Bryson frowned "Why? What have you heard?"

She shrugged. "Just that you were MIA."

"That's it?"

"Bryson, you left town and essentially fell off the face of the earth. Well, at least as far as we were concerned. You deleted all of your social media accounts, and changed your phone number."

"Did you try to call me?"

Not really. *Well, not after a while.* But Jordan had often thought about Bryson. They'd been good friends at one point in time. "I'm guilty, too. But at least I have Facebook."

Bryson laughed. "Touché."

"How have you been?"

She watched as Bryson took a sip from his glass. The years had been good to him. Not only did he grow up fine, he looked happy—at peace. And that was something she'd rarely seen in him while they were in school.

"I'm well. I've lived here for nine years now. I love the area."

"Really? So no MIT?"

He shook his head. "Nah. I had to change up my plans. I graduated from USC."

"That's pretty awesome."

"What about you? Are you finishing up law school?"

Jordan was surprised he'd remembered her law school ambitions. "Well, I took a detour and joined the military after graduation."

"Like father, like daughter."

"I guess you could say that. I thought it would be a great opportunity to travel, pick up valuable skills."

Jordan had surprised everyone when she'd announced that instead of attending Howard University like she'd planned, she had enlisted in the army. Her grandmother had nearly fallen out of her chair and her grandfather was stunned silent. Her father, though . . . He was happy, proud of the decision she'd made, albeit a little concerned because of the world climate at the time.

"I did four years," she explained. "Then I enrolled in college. Just graduated actually."

"Congrats," he said.

Does he know his voice is like fine wine? "Thanks."

"What are your plans now?"

"I was accepted to Yale, and had every intention of starting in the fall. But I'm going to defer enrollment for a year."

"Why? Is everything okay?"

Jordan sighed. "Yeah, I'm going to Wellspring to help my grandparents out for a while. Me and my father are the only family they have, and they're getting older."

"That's understandable. Parker told me your father got married."

"Yep, that's why I'm here." Jordan couldn't help but roll her eyes when she thought of her father's wedding.

"Right. But you're at the bar, and I'm assuming the reception has started by now. Shouldn't you be celebrating with him?"

"I should be, but I had to step away for a while."

"What? You don't like your new stepmother?"

Jordan shoved Bryson lightly. "Don't play me."

Bryson held her hand against his chest. "I'm just kidding with you. But you don't look like someone who's happy for her father."

"Jury is still out on that."

"Ooo. That's not good."

Jordan didn't want to get into the reasons why she wasn't #TeamJacksonAndRebecca. "Well, I only call it like I see it."

Bryson finally let go of her hand and she gripped the fabric of her dress. "I know how you feel about your father. So this new wife must have pissed you off."

That was the thing. Rebecca hadn't pissed her off. For all she knew, her messy bridesmaids could have been lying. *But they could be telling the truth.* "I don't want to talk about it right now."

Bryson's gaze dropped to her cell phone, lying on the bar top. He picked it up and held it out to her. "Unlock this, please."

Confused, Jordan used her thumb print to unlock her phone. "Why?"

He slipped the phone from her palm. Jordan should have railed against him for being so bossy, but she was too busy swooning from the command in his tone, the confidence that spilled from him in waves. He was so unlike the Bryson that she knew. "I'm saving my number in your phone. And I want you to go back into the reception and try to enjoy yourself."

"But I—"

"If you still feel like escaping, give me a call and I'll come rescue you."

Jordan eyed him suspiciously. "What makes you think I need you to rescue me?"

He laughed. A damn sexy, deep sound that made her toes curl. "I wouldn't presume you needed me to rescue you. You always have been stubborn."

Jordan rolled her eyes. "Whatever."

"Hey," Parker said, approaching them with his wife, Kennedi, at his side.

Jordan watched as Parker introduced Bryson to Kennedi, and noted the way Kennedi shooed away Bryson's attempt at a handshake and pulled him into a hug. Jordan had met Kennedi earlier and had been immediately taken with the woman who'd stolen Parker's heart. Kennedi was intelligent, funny, and generous. They'd chatted about fashion, fried fish and potatoes, and life in Wellspring. Kennedi had also offered to help Jordan in any way she could with law school.

Deciding it was time to excuse herself and let Bryson catch up with his family, she squeezed Bryson's arm. "I'm going to go into the reception."

Bryson smirked. "Good. Remember what I said."

Jordan hugged him, and said her good-byes before she strolled away. She wished she didn't have to go back into the room, but Bryson was right. She loved her dad beyond words. She didn't want him to feel like she wasn't supportive of him or his new life. He deserved happiness. He deserved love. Especially after her mother had disappeared on him after five tumultuous years of marriage.

Even though Jordan had only been five when her mother left, she remembered the arguments, the screech of her mother's voice through the walls. It had been obvious to her, even at that young age, that her mother hadn't been happy. At all. Then, one day her mother had gathered her up in her arms and told her that she was going to the store and never came back.

The only thing she had of her mother's was a note she'd found years later in her mother's journal. The letter had read:

Dearest Jordan, I love you, but I can't do it. I am not mother material and it's better that I leave now before you grow up and resent me for it. Your father will take care of you.

Her mother hadn't even signed the letter. It had just ended, just like their relationship. Jordan had never seen her mother again, never received a phone call from her, never had a birthday gift or Christmas gift delivered from her. Jordan had learned a long time ago to never hope for any sort of a meaningful relationship with the woman who'd birthed her and then abandoned her like she was an old doll. For all she knew, the woman was dead. But she suspected the woman was still alive and well.

The party was in full swing when Jordan entered the ballroom. Jackson Clark was a well-respected general in the army. He'd done successful tours in the Gulf War, and Afghanistan. He had friends everywhere in the world. And today, he looked happier than she'd ever seen him. Her father loved his new bride. And Jordan hoped the woman he married was worthy of that love.

Jordan had spent the last hour trying to convince herself that maybe the bridesmaids didn't know what they were talking about, that Rebecca didn't view her father as some sort of "come up." From everything her father had told her about Rebecca, his new wife had come from money. Her parents had paid for the luxury wedding, after all. And Rebecca was an older woman, in her late forties. So, it wasn't like she was some young broad looking for a sugar daddy. Still, Jordan couldn't shake off the negative thoughts about Rebecca. The fact that Rebecca was a white woman didn't bother her. Hell, her mother was white. Yes, her father had a type it seemed.

Jordan's protective instinct had kicked into full gear and she couldn't help but give the woman a side-eye as she walked past her father and Rebecca swaying to the music on the dance floor.

"Hey, Jordie."

Jordan turned and smiled. "Hi, Grams." She hugged her grandmother. Diana "Dee" Clark was short, but mighty. As a child, Jordan knew to stay away from her garden, to not open the refrigerator without asking, and to mind her manners *and* her business.

"I've been holding your seat for you," Grams said. "Your father has been looking for you."

Jordan followed Grams to the table where her grandfather, Will Clark, was seated, bobbing his head to the music. Earlier, Jordan had noticed that he was moving a little slower than usual, and it made her feel sad. "Hi, Granddad." She leaned down and kissed his forehead.

"Where you been? We thought you got lost!" He laughed, and she joined in. "You don't look too happy to be here."

"I'm fine. I just needed a break," she said.

Grams placed the back of her hand against

Jordan's forehead. "Are you sick?" Her grandmother's hand felt cool against her skin. "You don't have a temperature."

To this day, Jordan had no idea how a person could determine if someone had a fever with a simple touch. But her grandmother had it down to a science.

Jordan rubbed her stomach, much like the way she would have when she was a kid. "It's my stomach." That was partly true. Her stomach had been doing somersaults since she'd arrived in California the night before.

"Aw, baby." Grams motioned to the empty seat next to Granddad. "Sit on down next to your old granddad."

"Old?" Granddad scoffed. "If I'm old, you're old."

Jordan laughed and took the seat next to her grandfather. Leaning her head against his shoulder, she said, "I love you, Granddad."

He kissed her brow. "Love you, too, Punchkin."

Jordan giggled. Her grandfather had called her Punchkin since she was a little girl. Her first trip to the apple orchard had seemed more like a nightmare, because Jordan had been deathly afraid of pumpkins for some reason. Except she couldn't pronounce the word correctly. So she'd run to the car screaming, "No punchkins!" After that day, her grandfather had christened her his little punchkin. He was the only one who could get away with calling her that.

"Granddad, are you feeling okay?" Jordan asked.

"I'm fine, Punchkin."

Jordan swallowed. Two weeks ago, her grandfather had been diagnosed with prostate cancer. The bad news had knocked the wind out of Jordan, and she'd immediately broken down in tears.

Although Jordan was proud of her father's service record, his commitment to the military took him away more often than not. Her grandparents were everything to her, the only people in her life who'd never disappointed her. Their presence alone had made her childhood bearable. They'd attended recitals, spelling bees, and softball games. They'd nursed her back to health when she was sick, held her in their arms when she'd had a nightmare. Grams had taught her how to cook, how to decorate, and how to kick a man in his sweet spot if he was getting too fresh. Granddad had taught her how to hit a softball, how to change a tire, and how to elbow a boy in the nuts if he got too grabby. She learned how to count money, balance a checkbook, and how to work because she'd watched their example every day.

Jordan knew she could never repay them for the sacrifices they made for her, for stepping in when her father couldn't be there. They'd raised her to be a confident and assured woman. And Jordan would do anything, drop everything to be there for them. Because she loved them, she needed them, and she didn't know what she would do if anything happened to Grams and Granddad.

Jordan peered into her granddad's eyes. "I'm coming home with you."

His eyes widened. "What? You can't. You have a job. You have to get ready for law school."

"Nothing is more important than you. I can take a year off." Jordan had already made the decision and told Grams. But she'd asked Grams to let her tell Granddad. "I know what you're going to say but I've made up my mind. I have to do this."

Granddad patted her hand, before he squeezed it. "I know better than to try and change your mind. Stubborn as your grandmother." He shook his head, a wistful smile on his lips. "You know I'm going to be okay, right?"

Jordan nodded. "I know. I just want to be there with you."

"Baby girl, you're back." Jordan's dad approached them, a wide smile on his face.

"Yes, I'm back. I had to get some air."

Jackson Clark was looking mighty fine in his heather gray tuxedo, with his salt-and-pepper beard trimmed and his head freshly shaven. "Care to dance?" he asked her.

Jordan took her father's offered hand, and let him pull her to her feet. He led her out to the dance floor. As they swayed to the music, Jordan considered telling him what she'd overheard. But she couldn't bring herself to burst his happy bubble.

"Are you okay, baby girl?" he asked.

Swallowing past the lump in her throat, Jordan told him, "I am, Daddy. I'm just tired. It's been a long week."

Jordan had given her resignation at the law firm where she worked when she'd received the grim news about Granddad and had spent the past two weeks training her replacement.

"You're worried about Dad, aren't you?"

And you. "Yeah, I guess I am."

"I think it's noble of you to go back to Wellspring to stay with them for a while, even though you know you don't have to do it."

"Somebody has to," she muttered, before she could stop herself.

The last thing she wanted to do was make her dad feel bad for not being around. He'd built an impressive career that had allowed him to travel all over the world fighting for the country. She loved that he was so committed, so loyal. But sometimes she wished he would have been around for those small moments, like her learning how to ride a bike, slide into home base, or drive a car.

"I'm sorry, Daddy," she whispered. "I shouldn't have said that."

"No need to apologize, baby girl. One of my biggest regrets in life is the time I spent away from you."

She met his gaze, saw the tears in his eyes. "I just wish we had more time together."

Jackson would be leaving for eight months on a top secret mission for the army. He wasn't on the front lines anymore, but he played an integral role in the military. "We will. I was telling Rebecca that I wanted this next assignment to be my last."

"Really?" Jordan asked, too afraid to hope it was true. In that moment, she felt like the little girl who'd cried for her daddy every time he had to leave. "That's wonderful. You served with honor. You can retire and start a new career."

"I know. That's my plan."

"I love that plan." Jordan smiled at her dad. Off to the side, she heard a roar of laughter. Turning toward the sound, she watched as her father's new wife twerked on the dance floor. Mortified, she met her father's gaze. "She twerks?"

He laughed softly, his eyes soft with adoration for

his new wife. "She really is a good woman, Jordan. I wish you would make the effort to get to know her."

Jordan eyed her father. She was sure her mother twerked, too. And look where that got him. From all accounts, it appeared her mother had been a party girl and a compulsive spender. She'd spent her father's money like water and liked to hang out with her friends. According to Grams, she'd even cheated on her father numerous times throughout the short marriage.

"I think you should go get your new wife, Daddy." She smoothed the lapels of his jacket and patted his shoulder. "I'm not feeling well. I think I'm going to go and lie down."

"Are you sure?" he asked, worry in his eyes. "Do you need to go to an urgent care?"

She shook her head. "No, I just need sleep."

They stopped dancing and her father kissed her brow. "Love you, baby girl. Breakfast tomorrow before your flight?"

Jordan nodded. "Sure. Enjoy the rest of your night."

When her father joined his wife and her gyrating bridesmaids on the dance floor, Jordan sighed. Pivoting on her heels, she returned to her grandparents' table and told them she was going to go to her room. They each gave her a kiss on the cheek and bid her farewell.

As she stalked toward the door, she pulled her phone out of her clutch and typed out a text. It was simple, and to the point.

Jordan: "Rescue me."

Chapter 3

Sending that text to Bryson earlier, asking him to rescue her, hadn't been in her plans when Jordan had initially decided to leave the reception. But she was sure glad she'd sent it. Bryson had met her in the hotel lobby and whisked her away to the Santa Monica Pier. It was still early, so they'd strolled along the pier, taking in the attractions.

He'd bought tickets to the huge Pacific Wheel, treating her to a breathtaking view of the Southern California coastline. Under different circumstances, she might have been able to stay a few extra days, just to do the tourist thing. She wanted to spend some time seeing the sights or simply lying on the beach under the sun and taking in the salty ocean air.

Now seated on a bench, she observed Bryson. She had so many questions, but wasn't sure if he would be forthcoming with his answers. Jordan dipped her spoon into the Brass Ring sundae they were sharing from a place called Soda Jerks.

"This was fun," she said. "Thanks for bringing me here."

"I still can't believe you've never been to Cali before."

"Why not?"

He shrugged. "I imagined you traveling all over the world when you told me you enlisted in the army."

"I did some traveling, but it wasn't what I thought it would be." After basic training, Jordan lived in Germany for a few years before ending her career at Fort Hood in Killeen, Texas.

"What did you expect?"

Jordan didn't want to tell him that she'd hoped to be stationed near her father at some point during her stint in the army. But her many requests had been denied. Still, she made the most of her time in the military. While on active duty, she'd trained as a paralegal and continued the work when she finished her tour of duty.

"When I enlisted, I didn't expect much of anything," she replied. "I just knew that it was something I had to do at that moment in time."

"That makes sense."

They ate in silence for a few minutes, until Jordan couldn't take it anymore. She had to know. "Why aren't you married?" she asked.

Jordan laughed when Bryson choked on the gob of ice cream he'd just eaten. After several tense seconds, he finally told her, "I don't know. Why do you ask?"

In school, Bryson was the only boy she knew that wanted to marry and have kids. It was like a dream of his. Back then, she'd suspected it had a lot to do with his parents. It must have been hard to be the son of an ogre like Parker Wells Sr. and his mistress.

"I just remember you announcing that your goal was to get married as soon as possible."

The admission had branded Bryson a punk for a few months, as the other boys clowned on him for daring to want to be tied down to one woman. But Bryson had held firm, and didn't seem to care what others thought of him. It was one of the things she'd always admired about him. He marched to his own beat, and was laser focused on achieving his goals.

"I don't know." She forged ahead when he grew quiet again. "Maybe that was someone else."

"No, it was me. I still feel the same way about marriage. Not so sure about the 'soon as possible' part. And of course, I'd have to find someone I want to marry."

Jordan wondered if Bryson was being truthful. It was hard to believe that he hadn't found one woman that he'd want to commit to. Especially since it had been something he'd wanted for years.

"Have you been looking?" she asked.

He paused, his spoon midair, as he pondered her question. "Honestly? Not really. I figure when the time and the woman is right, it'll happen organically."

She eyed him. The important parts of Bryson were still there—he was kind, smart, and focused. But there was also an edge to him that hadn't been there when he'd left Michigan. "I guess you're right."

"What about you? You're not married either."

"It's not because I haven't been asked," she muttered under her breath.

Bryson tilted his head to the side, his eyes boring into hers. "Really? You've been proposed to?"

"Three times, actually."

With raised eyebrows, he asked, "Three? Same guy?"

Jordan shook her head. "No."

Bryson grinned. "Look at you, playa playa. So, what? They ask and you turn them down right away, or you start to plan a wedding and they disappoint you?"

Talking to Bryson about her failed relationships was not something she wanted to do. But she had nothing to hide. In every single case, the man had proposed out of the blue, at the wrong time. She had no choice but to say no because she didn't want to get married for the sake of getting married.

"You know . . . I just think marriage is sacred. If it's not right, it's not right."

Bryson observed her, a pensive look on his face. "When was the last proposal?"

"Well . . ." She scratched the back of her neck. "About six months ago. It was a long-term relationship. He was my teaching assistant in college. We got to know each other, and eventually things blossomed from there. But I wasn't ready for forever, and he was older and ready for a commitment."

"And you broke up with him?"

Shrugging, she said, "Not really. But you can't come back from a declined marriage proposal, right? I knew that if I turned him down, he would walk away. And he did."

"Wow. That's brutal."

"How is that brutal?" She swatted him playfully. "And how does that make me a playa playa?"

He laughed. "Hey, you definitely know how to dis someone."

Jordan's mouth fell open and she closed it. Frowning, she asked, "What are you talking about?"

"You played me several times in school."

Giggling, Jordan dropped her gaze. "Stop. I didn't do that."

"Yeah, right. Remember the middle school dance?"

She knew he was going to bring up the annual Valentine's Day dance. During their eighth-grade year, Bryson had asked Jordan to go steady with him, and she'd accepted. They'd made plans to meet up at the dance. But Jamari Coleman had made a grand overture in the hallway on the day of the dance, complete with a huge bag of candy, a little white teddy bear, and balloons. And she'd dumped Bryson like a hot potato. It wasn't her finest moment, but she was only thirteen years old.

"You would bring that up, Bryson," she said.

He raised his hands in surrender. "I'm compelled to speak the truth, Jordie."

Jordan felt warmth pool in her belly at her school nickname on his lips. He made something that seemed so juvenile sound erotic. She closed her legs tight at the ankle.

"You were a heartbreaker in that damn pink dress," he continued, seemingly oblivious to his effect on her. "You thought you were all that."

"I was thirteen," she argued. "I didn't know any better. I was all about who gave the best candy."

Bryson barked out a laugh, that dimple on full display. "I gave you a huge heart thing with chocolates."

"Yeah, but that was nasty, old people candy. I wanted Nerds and Mike and Ikes. The fruity candy."

He waved her off. "You were cold-blooded. Just admit it."

Jordan nodded. "If I admit it, will you never bring this up again?"

Bryson held up three fingers. "I promise."

"Okay, I was wrong. Please forgive me for my wayward thirteen-year-old, candy-focused brain."

"All is forgiven."

"But you have to admit something, too."

He leaned forward, his eyes on hers. "What's that?"

"At the dance, you told me my dress was ugly. And you know you liked that pink dress."

Bryson chuckled. "Fine, I'll give you that. The dress was pretty fly. But not as fly as the girl wearing it."

Jordan let out a slow breath, and relaxed in her seat. "Thank you," she breathed. The man was good. If she wasn't careful, he'd be able to talk her right out of her panties. "I should probably get back to the hotel." Rising to her feet, she smoothed her dress.

He stood and tossed their trash into a nearby waste bin. "Sure. I figured we'd take the scenic route back to the hotel, along the beach."

"Sounds good to me."

Bryson wrapped his jacket around her shoulders. "It's chilly by the water. Don't want you to get cold."

"Thanks." His suit coat smelled like him, and she brought the lapel up to her nose and inhaled his scent. When she peered up at him, she was struck by the depth of emotion in his eyes. The heat in them made her inch closer to him.

He leaned in, brushing his lips against hers and

tracing her bottom lip with his tongue before fusing his mouth against hers in a searing kiss. It was electric and not enough. Jordan crushed her body against his, needing to feel his heat against her skin. *Oh goodness.* His tongue was like magic, turning her inside out, reaching every part of her body and soul. It was unlike any kiss she'd ever had before. It made her feel somehow inexperienced, like she'd been doing it wrong this entire time.

Then . . . reality crashed into her, and she pulled back. She immediately missed his mouth on hers and had to force herself not to go for more. Because after tonight, she'd probably never see him again and it didn't make any sense to start something neither of them could finish.

Her intention was to insert a quirky line, make a joke about the swagger that seemed to spill out of his pores. But she couldn't pull together a string of coherent words at that point. Not when he was looking at her like she was his savior and his muse all in one. So, instead, she just asked, "Ready?"

Bryson traced the line of her jaw with his thumb. "I'm ready when you are."

When Bryson made the decision to meet Parker today, he had no idea he'd be spending his evening with Jordan Clark. He'd had fun with her, reminiscing about school, and showing her the different attractions on the pier. Then, he'd kissed her. And he wanted more. No, he needed more. It was everything he'd ever imagined, and then some.

Jordan had been there in the moment with him,

too, taking everything he had to give her. She had responded to him in a way that made him want to strip her naked and worship her body for hours.

As they entered the hotel after a stroll on the beach, he couldn't help but think about how the evening would end. As it was, he couldn't stop looking at her full lips, the sway of her hips, her deep dimples. He was tempted to lay all of his cards on the table, put everything on the line with her. The fact is, he'd dreamed of kissing her, of being with her, for years. And he didn't want to waste any more time stepping around it.

Bryson eyed Jordan as they exited the elevator on her floor. She was quiet, pensive. "You all right?"

"Are we going to talk about that kiss?" she asked. He met her gaze and she gave him a lopsided grin. "I mean . . . you did kiss me like we've been doing this for years."

He noted the way she tugged at her earlobe and couldn't help but smile. "It did feel like that, huh?"

"Yeah," she said with a chuckle. "What was that about?"

He leaned into her as they continued to walk. "Do you want the honest answer or the PC answer?"

She stopped in her tracks and turned to him. "How about both?"

Bryson knew he couldn't tell her every X-rated thing that had been running through his mind since he'd spotted her at the hotel bar. She said she wanted honesty, but he didn't think she was ready for that. Hell, he didn't know if he was ready to voice it out loud, because then he'd really want to act on the impulse he had to pick her up, carry her into her room, and take her against any hard surface.

Meeting her gaze, he said, "I've wanted to kiss you since that first day in the lunchroom."

She sucked in a sharp breath. "Really?"

"Is that so hard to believe?"

"It's just . . . We're friends. Well, we were friends in school. I didn't know you still felt that way."

"I didn't know I did either, until I saw you today."

Bryson wasn't sure why he was baring his soul to Jordan. She could very well walk away from him again, leaving him wanting her just like she had all those years ago at the Valentine's Day dance.

After that dance, they'd remained friends, but he'd never stopped hoping she would pick him. Every time she'd graced him with her smile, his world was a little brighter. And in his world, living in that house with Senior, that tiny bright spot had meant the world to him.

They'd never even gotten close to "going together" again. Jordan had been popular, while he'd been content to do his own thing. But they'd still shared pure friendship. In middle school, he would walk her home from school on most days. In high school, he'd drive her to work at her family's restaurant, the Bees Knees. They were in many of the same classes, so she was his study buddy. And they'd spent many a Saturday at the library quizzing each other and going over notes for midterms and final exams.

"Bryson, that's . . . I don't know what to say." She pointed to the door behind him. "This is my room."

He moved aside and watched as she pulled out her keycard. "You don't have to say anything, Jordan. We're adults, and I made an adult decision to kiss you tonight."

"Is that all it is?"

He wasn't sure what she was asking him, and he was tired of trying to analyze it. For once, he just wanted to go with this feeling, to let himself be free to touch her. "Jordan, if you're asking if I want more, I would have to say yes."

Jordan backed up a step. "Bryson," she whispered. "I'm not sure this is a good idea. We haven't seen each other in years, and I—"

"Jordie, there's something going on here between us. It feels like more than just two friends reconnecting."

She visibly swallowed. "What are you asking me, Bryson?"

"I'm telling you that I don't want this night to end outside your hotel room."

"Where do you want it to end?"

"Inside you."

Jordan blinked. "What?"

"Can I be honest?"

Frowning, she nodded. "Of course."

"I'm not asking for a commitment. We live in different states, and we both know that would be a stretch. But"—he reached out and traced her bottom lip with his thumb—"I do want you, Jordan." And Bryson would take her any way she'd let him. On the floor, against the wall, on a bed, in a tub.

Slowly, he moved toward her. She was nervous and Bryson couldn't be happier. Up until now, she'd had him squarely in the "friend" category. She'd regarded him as one of her besties. But this . . . today? He could feel the electricity crackle between them and he could see the wheels spinning in her head.

Jordan Clark wanted him, and he was going to make his move. Now.

He placed his palms against the door behind her, on either side of her head, caging her in. They stood like that for a few moments, him staring into those moss-colored eyes, daring her to let him in. He ran a finger down the side of her face to her neck, where he felt her wildly beating pulse. Smirking, he leaned against her ear. "It's okay. You can say it, ya know?"

"Say what?" she whispered.

"Tell me you ache for me. Tell me you need me to soothe that ache." He lifted his index finger and placed it against her lips. "One word. And you know what it is."

Another inch forward and they were touching, her breasts against his chest. She let out a ragged breath and a tiny whimper when he pressed his hardening erection into her belly.

"Yes," she whispered, so low he wasn't sure he'd heard it. But he'd heard it, and his body felt it. Then . . . he broke, kissing her so hard, so long, he couldn't breathe. His hand tangled in her hair and the low moan she let out went straight to his groin. He prayed she didn't change her mind. He was hard. Impossibly hard. Out-of-this-world hard.

Cupping her ass in both of his hands, he pulled her closer, groaning when she ground her wet heat against him. *Shit.* They were in the hallway, in a public hotel. Anybody could walk up on them. Her grandparents, or even her daddy, could decide to check on her at that very moment.

His heart pounded in his ears, his brain was foggy. He needed to get her inside the room. But Jordan

Clark was writhing against him, her soft body against his hard one. She was kissing him with a passion that stole his breath. He'd wanted her since he was eleven, and she always seemed just out of reach. But not now, not tonight. And he was going to make the most of it.

Chapter 4

Jordan couldn't be sure if she was in heaven. Or on the fast track to hell. Because she'd basically skipped her father's reception and spent the evening with Bryson. She was a horrible daughter.

But his hands . . .

The way he was touching her . . . *Oh God.*

Her body was on fire, her nerves tingling. And it was hot. She was hot. Every reservation she had about inviting him into her room seemed to melt away with her skin under his touch. Jordan should have thanked him for keeping her company, for making her laugh, for taking time out of his Friday evening to show her around. That was the right thing to do. But . . . he'd issued a challenge. And she'd never been one to back down from a challenge. One word. *Yes.* Which she'd said in a breathy whisper, a sound she'd never heard come from her own mouth.

"Open the door," he grumbled against her skin. "Now. I need you now, baby."

Jordan pulled back and turned to the door,

shaking as she attempted to swipe her keycard. Of course, that damn thing didn't work. She tried again several times to no avail, and froze when she felt his hand wrap around hers. Slowly, he helped her swipe the card and the green light lit, signaling the door was unlocked.

He laughed and placed a kiss against the back of her neck. "You can open it now, Jordie."

Once inside the room, his mouth on hers was like a heat-seeking missile, and Jordan was holding him to her, kissing him back with an equal demand. *Yes.*

The bite of the hard wall against her back made her lose her train of thought. The same train that was heading to hell. Could she really do this? Could she throw caution to the wind and let Bryson do her and then walk away like it never happened? Jordan knew how to categorize sex. But did he know this could only be a one-night thing? He'd kissed her like his life was on the line, like she held the key to something he desperately needed. And that gave her pause.

"Bryson?" Her mind was hazy with desire and her body burned with need. When his fiery gaze met hers, he blinked. She read the question in his eyes, and swallowed. "Is this a good idea? Can we do this?"

The corner of his mouth quirked up. "We can. And we will," was his reply as he trailed hot kisses down her neck.

Before she could say anything else, he captured her lips with his again, pushing his jacket off of her shoulders and unzipping her dress. When the thin fabric fell to the floor, he brushed his lips over hers again, deepening the kiss. *Damn, he can kiss.* Who was she kidding? She was going to do it. Because he was fine and she was horny.

Jordan couldn't get enough of his mouth. He tasted like vanilla, cognac, and sin. He stepped back, raking his gaze over her body. His eyes were soft, reverent. "You're beautiful, Jordie."

Grateful that she'd thought to put on matching undergarments, she smiled. She felt beautiful under his gaze, and the anticipation of his touch made her want to reach out and pull him back to her.

"I need you. Let me taste you," he murmured, dropping to his knees before her and easing her thin, lace panties down her legs. "Let me feel you on my tongue. Do you want that?"

"Yes, please," she purred.

She heard his soft chuckle before she felt his tongue against her heat. Her orgasm built faster than it ever had before, almost lightning speed. So fast, so hard, that it zapped her strength as it overtook her and caused her knees to buckle. She gasped as she imagined toppling over and losing all of her cool points, but his arms wrapped around her waist and held her steady. Soon, she felt like she was flying as he lifted her into his arms, carried her over to the bed, and lowered her to the mattress.

Perching herself up on her elbows, she watched as he unbuttoned his shirt, revealing his hard body to her so slowly Jordan had to fight the urge to sit up and rip it off. But once the shirt was off, Jordan wanted to shout, "Hallelujah." He was glorious. Young Bryson had been stick thin, but this Bryson . . . the grown man Bryson was all lean muscle and hard thighs. She traced the black tattoo that wrapped around his bicep, and brushed a fingernail over the one above his heart. It said BE BRAVE and she wanted to ask why he'd chosen that specific phrase.

Her gaze dropped to the hard ridge of his dick, visible through his black slacks. He was splendid, sexy, and hers. For the night, anyway. When she peered up at him again, he smirked as if he knew what she was thinking.

Bryson slid his belt off and made slower work with his pants. Jordan fell back against the mattress and closed her eyes. With a loud groan, she said, "You're killing me, Bryson."

"Patience, Jordie. I've got you."

Bryson placed wet kisses along the column of her throat, between her breasts, over her belly button. Soon, she felt his breath over her core again and she shuddered. "Bryson," she moaned.

"Can't get enough of you," he said, before he took her in his mouth again, sucking on her clit until she climaxed again. She squeezed her legs shut, trapping his head between her thighs. But he didn't stop. He continued to taste her, laving her core relentlessly until all she could do was lie there and let the pleasure wash over her. Jordan felt boneless, sated. She should be tired, but she was anything but.

When she opened her eyes, he was above her, a smile on his lips. "Hi," he said.

"Hi." She felt a blush snake up her neck to her cheeks.

Bryson placed a kiss on her nose. "I can't stop looking at you."

Burying her face in his chest, she said, "You make me feel . . ." *Crazed?* No, she couldn't tell him that.

But that's how she felt. She was desperate for him. It didn't matter that he'd made her come so much, she could barely catch her breath; she wanted more. She *needed* more of him. Her body was on fire, hot with longing.

"Use your words, Jordie," he teased.

"Please," she whispered.

"Tell me," he murmured against her mouth.

Lying underneath him, his erection so close to her core was doing crazy things to her. She arched her back off of the bed, pushing herself onto him, silently urging him to fill her up. Instead, he plunged a finger inside, then added another. She cried out as another orgasm ripped through her. Still shaking with pleasure, she watched as he quickly shed his boxer briefs and pulled a condom from his wallet.

Jordan smiled at her first glimpse of his bare erection. *Magnificent.* He didn't give her enough time to ogle him, as he slid back up her body, laced his fingers through hers, and pressed his length against her.

"Jordan," he groaned against her ear, before biting down on the skin beneath it.

"Oh God," she said, lifting her hips to take him in. "You're making me crazy."

Bryson closed his eyes and muttered a filthy curse under his breath. He bent to kiss her, sweeping his tongue in her mouth and mating with hers. Then he pushed inside her, burying himself to the hilt. And she accepted him, willingly and gladly.

He pressed their joined hands into the mattress, squeezing her fingers tightly. Slowly, he began to move, allowing her time to adjust to his size. Soon, they were in sync, thrusting against each other to their own rhythm. Jordan had never felt so connected to another man before. Everything about him called to something deep and primitive inside of her. Jordan clung to him, held him close to her as they moved closer to release.

Bryson kissed her jaw, sucking it into his mouth until she cried out his name in surrender and she exploded around him. Pleasure, hot and blinding, rolled over her. Vaguely, she heard him cry out her name as he joined her.

Several seconds later, he rolled over, pulling her with him until she was sprawled on top of him. It took moments for her to catch her breath, but she felt good. Jordan wrapped her arms around his waist and snuggled into him. She felt his lips press against her forehead.

Silence descended between them, and she wondered what he was thinking. Instead of asking, she decided to leave well enough alone and sat up, intent on climbing out of the bed, getting a shower and . . . Well, she didn't really know what was supposed to come next.

She turned to Bryson and found him staring at her. "What?" she asked, wondering if the smirk on his lips was because he'd enjoyed himself or because she looked a hot mess. Jordan raked a hand through her curls.

"I hope you don't think you're leaving?"

Jordan couldn't form a response if she tried. "I thought—"

"Just so you know . . ." Bryson tugged her back to him. "I'm not the one-and-done type."

"Oh," she said, breathily.

"And I'm definitely not finished with you, Ms. Clark."

Bryson reveled in the feel of Jordan's naked body in his arms, the sound of her heart beating against his chest. There was no fear, no second thoughts, no regrets. Only peace.

He had made love to Jordan, thoroughly. And he'd loved every minute of it. For once, they were both in sync with each other. Bryson had spent years wanting her, and he'd finally had her. Everything was different with her. The way her body felt custom-made for his, the way her eyes seemed to see pieces of him he hadn't shown anyone, the way she'd screamed his name as he sent her over the edge multiple times.

They hadn't talked much, and he wondered if that had been a mistake. A conversation was probably needed, but he didn't know if it would help or hurt. As much as he wanted her, he knew the odds of them extending this beyond that night were slim to none. Relationship, commitment, love . . . That wasn't what this was. *Right?* He'd learned a long time ago that good sex was not an indicator of good love. And despite the close friendship they'd had in the past, they hadn't seen each other in years. They barely knew each other anymore. He'd had an amazing night with a woman he'd crushed on for years, and that was enough.

Bryson picked up his cell phone. It was the middle of the night, and it had been years since he'd spent an entire night with a woman. Admittedly, he was torn between leaving or snuggling into her for the rest of the night. And there was the pesky little fact that he was seriously starving. He hadn't eaten a meal since lunch. All he'd had was cognac, ice cream, and Jordan.

And having Jordan again wasn't a bad idea. He shifted, and Jordan bolted upright.

"What's wrong?" she asked, smoothing her hand over her wild curls.

She looked so good, so damn sexy, he couldn't bring himself to tell her good-bye yet. "Nothing," he said. "I was just going to find some food."

She fell back against the bed. "Okay."

Bryson was glad that things weren't awkward, and she hadn't closed up on him yet. He didn't know when that moment would come, but he knew it would. "Want anything?" he asked.

She burrowed into the pillow. "No. I'm too sleepy to eat."

Pulling on his pants and his shirt, Bryson took off in search of food. Several minutes later he was back in the room with a candy bar because that was the only thing he could find.

Jordan was sitting up in the bed, her eyes on him. "Did you find anything?"

He held up the candy bar. "Just a Snickers bar."

"Oh. You have a thing with chocolate, don't you?" She shot him a wicked grin.

"Ha ha." He wouldn't presume she was okay with him climbing back into bed with her. "When are you flying out?"

"Early afternoon. My father wants to have breakfast in the morning."

"How do you feel about that?"

"Well, I don't know. I guess I should. I did basically skip out on his reception."

"I can leave, Jordan. I know you probably want to rest."

She sighed. "I kind of wanted to talk to you."

Taking a seat on the small sofa in the room, he opened the wrapper to his candy bar and took a bite. "About what?"

"This?" she said, a question in her eyes. "Us."

Bryson knew what she wanted to say, but he didn't particularly want to hear her try to "let him down easy." He didn't need to talk, really. As far as he was concerned, he'd had the best sex of his life with a woman he'd crushed on for years. That was enough.

"Listen," she continued. "I enjoyed myself with you, and—"

"And it was an amazing moment in time, one where we were both on the same page. Jordie, we don't have to have this conversation. I know what tonight was. We're good."

Jordan observed him, an unreadable expression on her face. Sighing, she muttered, "Okay."

Bryson stood. "I better get going."

"I have a better idea." Dropping the sheet, Jordan beckoned him to her with her forefinger. "Why don't you come back to bed?"

And that was all it took. Her sexy eyes and her husky voice and her naked body were too much to resist. Hunger forgotten, he tossed the candy bar on the table, stripped, and climbed back into bed with her, taking her mouth in an intense kiss.

Jordan pushed him on his back and straddled his

legs. He reached for his wallet and let out a terse curse when he realized he didn't have any more condoms.

"What's wrong?" Jordan asked, wrapping her hand around his length.

Wrapping his hand around hers to stop her movements, he told her, "I don't have any more condoms."

Jordan winked. "No worries. I got you." She leaned over and dumped the contents of her purse on the bedside table. He saw the gleam of the condom wrapper and sent up a silent prayer of thanks.

Bryson grunted as she put the condom on. It was snug, but he could handle it. She wiggled against his erection and he hissed. It felt so good. *She* felt good. Threading his fingers through her hair, he pulled her to him and kissed her sweet mouth. The whimper that came from her spurred him on, and he flipped her over, pushing into her with one swift move.

A possessiveness filled Bryson, slamming into him and catching him off guard. And despite what he'd told himself, as they moved together, raced toward completion, Bryson realized that one night would never be enough. He was convinced he would go to his grave wanting Jordan, craving her touch.

Jordan fell over first, milking his orgasm from him. Bryson rolled off of her, struggling to catch his breath. "Shit," Bryson grumbled.

Jordan sat up, her eyes dark with lust and her hair mussed. "What? What happened?" She kissed his jaw, and he fought the urge to take her again. Because they were in trouble.

Bryson looked down at the condom he wore, then back at Jordan. "Please tell me you're on birth control."

With a frown on her face, Jordan shook her head. "I can't take them. They make me sick. That's why I had the condom."

Bryson had been distressed once he realized that he only had two condoms in his wallet. When Jordan had assured him that she had it under control, pulling out a condom from her purse, he'd considered it a sign. Except her condom was a size too small, and he knew it the moment she'd slipped it on him. Still, he couldn't stop. Not when she was so open, so ready for him. And now . . . "The condom broke."

"Shit," she murmured, jumping away from him as if he had a disease.

Bryson rolled out of the bed, and headed into the bathroom. He disposed of the condom and peered at his reflection in the mirror. He'd gone into a situation without being prepared, and that was something he never did. He'd prided himself on his ability to plan, and he'd dropped the ball.

Jordan walked into the bathroom and stared at him. She was wearing his shirt, and it looked damn good on her. "It's okay." She rubbed his back.

He met her gaze through the mirror. "Jordie . . ."

"No, seriously. It's fine. I'll go get emergency contraception before breakfast. I just did a quick Google search, and I will be fine as long as I take it within twenty-four hours."

Bryson let out a deep breath, pulled her to him,

and embraced her. "Good. You should know I'm clean."

She reared back and looked up at him. "I never had any doubt. I'm clean, too."

He buried his face in her neck. "How are you feeling?"

"Well, my muscles are sore," she admitted with a wink. "I need a shower." Jordan turned on the shower, took off his shirt, and handed it to him. "Care to join me?" She winked again and stepped into the shower.

Bryson knew he should've said no. He should have backed out of the bathroom, gotten dressed, and left. But . . . he was only a man. And although he wouldn't chance sex without the proper protection, there were other things they could do that were just as good.

Dropping his shirt on the floor, Bryson told her, "I don't mind if I do."

Chapter 5

The next afternoon, Bryson stared down at the text message Jordan had sent. It was a selfie with her smiling, holding the Plan B One-Step emergency contraceptive package in her hand. Another text came through with her holding a huge bottle of water. A few seconds later, another text appeared and he opened it to find her grinning and giving a "thumbs up" sign. He smiled, prepared to type out a response, when his phone dinged again.

Jordan: It's done. See, I told you not to worry.

Bryson thought about that for a minute. Aside from the initial shock that shot through him at the sight of the ripped condom, he hadn't really been that worried. If it were any other woman, he probably would have insisted *he* buy the morning-after pill, and sit there while she swallowed it, even checking her mouth in case she was up to no good. But with Jordan? He wasn't at all concerned. He knew she was a woman of her word. She wouldn't lie about something so serious. She'd also always been up front, honest even if it hurt. He doubted that had changed over the years.

Bryson: I'm not worried.
Jordan: Good. Bryson?

The bubble indicating that she was still typing appeared, and he waited. There was more he wanted to say, but they'd agreed to keep things casual, even though the word didn't seem to fit what had transpired between them.

Jordan: I had a good time.
Bryson: Me, too.
Jordan: Thank you. For everything.

Bryon stared at the screen for a moment. He didn't have any idea how to respond to that. Was she thanking him for taking her around town, or thanking him for rocking her world? In order to keep it simple, he typed a simple "You're welcome."

"What's up with you, son?"

"Nothing, punk." Bryson greeted his boy, Remy, with some dap. "You're late."

Remy set his bag on the bench next to Bryson and pulled out both of his bowling balls. The alley was packed with the usual teams, practicing for league night on Monday.

Bryson peered at his phone. Jordan hadn't responded again, so he set it on the table. "I paid for an hour to start."

"I got the second hour."

Standing, Bryson picked up one of his balls and wiped it with the small towel he kept in his bowling bag. "Cool."

"Who's the woman?" Remy asked.

Bryson frowned. "What the hell are you talking about?"

"In all the years I've known you, I've never seen you smiling at your phone the way you were just now."

I was smiling? Bryson had been so focused on the exchange between him and Jordan, he hadn't realized he was smiling. "Shut the hell up. I wasn't smiling. And there is no woman." *Anymore.*

"Whatever, man. It has to be somebody. I mean, we were at the bar waiting on your ass for hours."

Bryson barked out a laugh. Driving to Santa Monica had been a spur-of-the-moment decision, and he'd forgotten to let Remy and Tez know he wasn't going to make it for drinks. "My bad. My brother was in town, and I went to meet him."

"Brother? I haven't heard you mention your family in a minute."

That's because Bryson rarely brought up his family or his past. Remy knew the details, though. When Bryson had moved to California, Remy had been his freshman year roommate. Ironically, they didn't hit it off at first, and had even got into a fist-fight over after-shave and dirty drawls. Bryson was a neat freak, and Remy was not. It wasn't until Remy had invited Bryson home with him over the Thanksgiving holiday that the two forged a lasting friendship.

"It wasn't a planned meeting," Bryson told Remy.

Remy stepped up and aimed his ball before shooting it down the lane. Pins clattered at the end of the lane and Remy did a small fist pump before he walked back to the ball return. After he rolled his second turn, Remy turned to Bryson. "What made you decide to actually see him?"

Bryson stared at the arrows on the lane. He'd been bowling since he was a little kid, on Detroit's east side at The Garden Bowl on Woodward Avenue. It was something he continued to do when he'd arrived in Wellspring, often spending hours at the bowling alley. Being in the alley had been an escape for him, a way to blow off steam.

"It was time," Bryson said simply. He rolled his ball, cursing when he split the pins.

"How was it?"

Bryson shrugged. "It was good. There was a wedding in Santa Monica. He introduced me to his wife."

Remy nodded. "So you spent the night catching up?"

Bryson scratched the back of his neck. "Something like that," he murmured.

Remy snickered. "I told you a long time ago that lying was not your strong suit. So, I'm going to ask again. Who is she?"

"Jordan Clark," Bryson admitted.

His friend frowned. "Jordan Clark? You mentioned her before." Remy looked like he was putting the pieces together. Snapping his fingers, he said, "The girl in the pink dress."

Bryson didn't understand why he'd ever told Remy about the Valentine's Day dance. He remembered the moment he made his mistake. They'd been drinking, talking about the girls who'd dissed them.

That was when Bryson had made his confession, and Remy had promptly clowned on him. His best friend had laughed so hard, Bryson had ended up pushing him off of his chair.

"Man, this is why I don't tell you shit," Bryson said with a mock glare.

Remy held his hands out at his sides. "Hey, you know I have to tell you the truth at all times."

Bryson dismissed Remy with a wave, and took his turn. Once he finished, he said, "Parker asked me to come home. He thinks Senior is holding out for me."

"He may not be wrong," Remy said. "Maybe you should go back."

Bryson glared at Remy. "Hell, no. I meant what I said before about never going back. I've worked too hard to distance myself from that town to step foot in the city limits again."

"But Senior is dying. And your siblings are there. It's obvious you miss them. Why not go back?"

"Because my life is here. There's no reason to go back."

Shrugging, Remy said, "Well, if Jordan is the reason you're making googly eyes at your phone, I'd say you have a good reason to go back."

Bryson thought back to the way Jordan had looked beneath him. If he went for a visit, he might be able to convince her to spend another night with him. Just the possibility made his dick twitch.

"Think about it," Remy continued. "A trip back to Wellspring will accomplish multiple goals. You can finally speak your piece to Senior, visit Brooklyn and Parker, meet Veronica, and *smile* at Jordan."

Bryson tossed his towel at Remy. "Man, get out of here. I wasn't smiling."

"Whatever. Yo ass was grinning from ear to ear. Looking like Arsenio Hall up in here."

Bryson barked out a laugh. "Roll the damn ball, man."

While Remy took his turn, Bryson picked up his phone and dialed Parker. When his brother picked up, Bryson said, "Hey, brother. I thought about what you said. I have a project I need to finish at work, and then I'll think about a visit."

Jordan set a plate with a peanut butter and jelly sandwich on it in front of Granddad. "Here you go," she told him. "I don't know why you don't let me just cook you something."

Granddad chuckled. "This is good enough for me."

Jordan arrived in Wellspring late Saturday night, and had promptly fallen asleep and proceeded to sleep Sunday away, too. Monday morning, Grams had nudged her awake and told her that she was heading to the Bees Knees, and asked her to make Granddad breakfast.

"You know Grams is going to kill me for this," she told Granddad. "This is not a suitable breakfast, Granddad."

"Oh, Dee will be just fine."

Jordan picked up a mug of hot coffee she'd made, and held it in her hands. It was cold as hell outside. When she'd first stepped out of the airport, she was immediately hit with that Michigan "Hawk," another name for cold wind. "You need anything else, Granddad?"

Granddad bit into his sandwich. She knew her

grandfather was used to getting up and going into work with Grams, but he hadn't been able to do as many hours at the diner since his diagnosis.

Tears pricked her eyes as she thought about how thin and frail Granddad looked. It seemed like he'd lost weight overnight. The last time she'd visited, he'd been his same big, strong self. Now, he looked like he was wasting away. Jordan prayed that the doctors were right, and his cancer was curable. She didn't know what she would do if he weren't around anymore.

Sighing heavily, she sipped her coffee and watched her granddad eat. "When do you want me to drive you over to the restaurant?"

Granddad peered up at her and shrugged. "I think I'm going to stay home today, Punchkin."

"Well, I'll stay with you. Want to watch a movie?"

He shook his head. "No, I think I'm just going to lie down. But I'll be fine. You can go out if you have to."

"If you're here, I'm here."

Grams walked in through the back door, a brown paper bag in her arms. "I'm here," she announced.

Jordan walked over to her and took the bag from her. "What are you doing here? I thought you were going to be at the Bees Knees all day."

"I thought I was, too. But when I got there, I could barely keep my eyes open, so I decided to let my competent staff handle things. I'm tired. Long gone are the days when I can travel across three time zones and bounce back so fast."

Grams kissed Granddad on his lips and looked at the now-empty plate in front of him. Looking at

Jordan, she asked, "Did he trick you into making a peanut butter and jelly sandwich?"

Jordan's eyes widened. "Grams, I—"

"Aw, leave her alone, baby," Granddad told her grandmother. "We raised her to do what we said and that's what she did."

Jordan laughed. "I told him it wasn't a good idea, but he got me with those puppy dog eyes, Grams."

Grinning, Grams took the plate and set it in the dishwasher. "Whatever you say. Your grandfather will eat these sandwiches all day if he had his way, for breakfast, lunch, and dinner." She looked at Granddad. "I'm going to make you a nice, hot breakfast. How about steak and eggs?"

"That's too heavy, baby," Granddad replied, before he stood up and shuffled to the family room.

Jordan's stomach growled at the mention of her grandmother's steak. She'd had some delicious food in her life, but nothing topped Dee Clark's cooking. Jordan was no slouch in the kitchen herself, but she couldn't touch Grams's steak or her fried catfish or the famous Denver omelet that had people coming from neighboring towns to sample.

The Bees Knees was a Wellspring staple. Her grandparents had opened the diner almost forty years ago, and had made a living serving up delectable food to the residents of Wellspring. Granddad's family was one of the original founding families of Wellspring, along with the Wells family, the Walkers, and the Hunts.

Jordan was proud of her familial history, and didn't hesitate to tell people who she was and whose she was. Although the Clark house was small, it was situated on one of the largest acreages in Wellspring.

"Jordan?" Grams asked. "Any plans for the day?"

"I promised Stacyee and Maddie I'd meet them later."

Grams smiled. "That salon is doing big things. I'm proud of her."

Jordan's friend Stacyee ran the best salon in Wellspring, and arguably the best on this side of Michigan. It seemed no matter where she'd lived, Jordan couldn't find anyone that did her hair like her friend. She couldn't wait to have her whip her do into shape.

"I can't wait to see the remodel," Jordan said. "I saw the pictures, but I need to see it in person to get the full effect."

For the past few years, Jordan had lived in Detroit and attended Wayne State University. Even though she'd met wonderful people there, she didn't have the same feeling of home in the "D" and she was happy to be back.

"You don't have to hang out here with us, girl," Grams said. "Why don't you get on out? It's chilly, but not too bad."

"Grams, it's thirty degrees and windy. It's freezing."

"Stop acting like you didn't live in Detroit a few days ago."

Jordan giggled. "The cold in Detroit was nothing compared to the cold here."

"Girl, bye," Grams pulled a cast-iron skillet from the bottom cabinet and set it on the stove. Jordan recalled how her grandmother had shown her how to clean and season the pan. At the time, Jordan didn't understand the need to go through the trouble, but as she'd grown into adulthood, she could admit that nothing tasted quite like it did when cooked in a cast-iron skillet.

"Did you want steak and eggs, Jordie?" Grams asked.

Grabbing her coat off the hook behind the door, Jordan tugged the heavy wool coat on. "I think I'm going to take your advice and get out of the house. I need to run a few errands, and then I'll head over to the salon early." Granddad had been sitting in his favorite seat, his eyes glued to the television. Jordan met her grandmother's worried eyes before she walked over to her grandfather and gave him a tight squeeze from behind. "Love you, Granddad."

"Love you, too, Punchkin."

Jordan kissed Grams on the cheek. "Love you."

Grams gave her a watery smile. "Love you, too."

When Jordan entered Stacyee's salon later, she couldn't help the grin that spread across her face. It was beautiful. Turquoise, purple, gray, and gold accents set the tone of the salon. As she walked through the foyer into the main area, she felt like she was stepping into a safe haven. She smiled when she saw her friend talking to a client in hushed tones. Off to the side, she noticed Maddie lounging on one of the plush sofas, magazine in hand.

Maddie spotted her first. "Jordan!" She ran over to Jordan, pulled her into a tight embrace.

Stacyee screamed and dashed over to them. "Group hug!"

The three friends shared an emotional reunion, a tear or two, and a few giggles before breaking apart. Once Stacyee rejoined her client, Jordan turned to

Maddie, who was dabbing her eyes. "Girl, don't you know crying is for chumps?"

"I'm not crying," Maddie said. "I had something in my eye."

Madison Thomas had been Jordan's friend since first grade, after they were both pulled out of their regular class for an advanced reading workshop. They'd been inseparable as kids. They'd graduated from kitchen sets to jump rope to hide-and-go-get-it to grown-ass women ready to make their marks on the world.

Jordan nudged Maddie. "I miss your face, girl-friend."

Maddie was a classic beauty with flawless ebony skin, beautiful brown eyes, pretty white teeth, and gorgeous big hair. Her friend walked as if she were royalty. With her calm demeanor and a singsong voice, Maddie had talked Jordan off the ledge more times than she dared to admit. "I missed you, too. I'm so happy you're back."

"I'm glad you're on vacation this week. I had perfect timing, huh?"

"You always do," Maddie said. "I have so much to tell you."

"I'm almost finished," Stacyee said, as she flat-ironed her client's hair. "Sit your ass down somewhere and stay a while."

Stacyee and Jordan became friends while singing in fifth-grade choir. They bonded over their mixed race, hair, and the fact that neither of them could sing. Jordan wasn't exactly the most talented when it came to hair, and Stacyee had given her valuable tips on how to style her mane. Even as a child, Stacyee charged fifty cents to braid hair on the playground during recess. By the time they'd made it to middle school, her friend had amassed a small fortune.

"I love your place, Stace," Jordan told her. "You did good."

"Thanks, J." Stacyee finished up with her client and escorted her out of the salon. A few minutes later she returned with a bottle of champagne, orange juice, and three paper cups. "It's time to get it in. Mimosas for everyone. We have so much to catch up on."

Jordan took the offered cup. "I was actually surprised you wanted me to meet you here today. I thought Monday was your off day. Do you have any more clients today?"

"Girl, no. Monday is my day off, but I did her hair as a favor today because she is leaving the country for work."

"In that case"—Jordan held out her cup—"fill this up then." Once her cup was full, she leaned her head back against the cushion. "Man, I'm tired."

Stacyee burped. "Shit, we're getting old."

Giggling, Maddie threw a pillow at Stacyee. "Speak for yourself. I'm not old."

"Right," Jordan agreed. "Twenty-something is not old."

"So why do I feel like my body is going to give out?" Stacyee asked.

"Because you're on your feet all day," Maddie told her. Maddie was a physical therapist, and worked for the Wellspring Health Center. "I'm glad you decided to slow it down some days. That's what you have staff for."

Jordan looked around, took in the colors and the slate gray ceramic tile. "I love the sound of that. You have a staff, girl! That is so awesome."

"I know, right? It's exciting because they're so eager to learn. I actually sent them to a class today. Have to make sure they stay abreast of all the new techniques. I want the best of the best in here."

Not only was Stacyee a gifted stylist, she was also an educator and worked for one of the top hair care lines in the country teaching other hairstylists the latest techniques. She was wicked with the scissors and her coloring game was unrivaled.

"That's great, Stace. I'm so proud of you. You're doing your thang, girlfriend."

"I'm trying. I want to make my first million by age thirty."

"You can do it; I have no doubt. Just don't blow up and stop doing my hair." Jordan smoothed a hand over her hair.

"And judging by that hot mess of a ponytail on your head, I need to squeeze you in sooner than later."

Maddie fell back on the couch in a fit of laughter. "I was going to say the same thing."

Jordan feigned offense. "Don't play me."

Stacyee grinned. "As a matter of fact, get your butt in my chair. I'm going to hook you up."

Standing up, Jordan shuffled over to the chair and sat down. "You're the best, Stace. Thank you."

Stacyee picked up a strand of hair. "What the hell did you do in California? Besides the wedding, of course."

A blush worked its way up Jordan's neck, and she averted her gaze. "Nothing."

Maddie sat in an empty chair next to them and observed her. "How was the wedding?"

Jordan told her friends everything about the wedding. Well, everything except the part where she had sex with Bryson.

"Damn," Maddie said. "I don't know what you should do about your new stepmother."

"She should do nothing." Stacyee glanced at her in the mirror. "You need to stay out of it. Besides, you don't know for sure that she's out to get his money. All you have is the messy whisperings of her trifling bridesmaids. Who does that anyway? If y'all heffas wanted to marry someone for their money, there is no way I would say anything about it at the wedding and risk someone overhearing me. That's crazy."

It was just like Stacyee to simplify something that seemed so complicated. "Good point," Jordan said.

"I don't know . . ." Maddie eyed Jordan curiously. "There's something you're not telling me."

Oh Lord. Jordan never could get anything past Maddie. If she didn't know any better, she might think her friend was psychic or something. "What?"

Then Stacyee peered at her, all in her face.

Jordan laughed, and pushed her away playfully. "Move, girl."

A slow grin spread across Stacyee's face. "You're right, Maddie. Jordan doesn't even look that stressed. And the Jordan I know would be a bundle of angst about her daddy."

Maddie threw her hands up in the air. "Exactly. She's glowing."

"I'm still in the room," Jordan deadpanned.

"Not just glowing," Stacyee said. "More like freshly fucked."

Jordan gasped. "Stacyee!"

"Bingo," Maddie cosigned. "See, you told us just enough to try and throw us off the scent, but when I seed you—I know'd there is a God."

Jordan laughed at Maddie using the phrase from their favorite movie, *The Color Purple*. "Girl, you're a mess."

"So who was it? Did you meet him at the wedding?" Stacyee asked.

"A groomsman?" Maddie tossed out.

Stacyee frowned. "That's lame. A guest? One of your fine daddy's friends?"

Maddie pushed Stacyee. "Ew."

Jordan shook her head at their antics. They were a handful. "That is so nasty, Stacyee. I told you about ogling my daddy."

"I'm lost. Was it a random guy at the bar?" Maddie asked, her finger on her chin.

Jordan choked on her drink. "Oh God."

"Come on, girl." Stacyee shook the seat. "You're killing us. We need a name."

And Jordan needed to tell someone about her night with Bryson. Taking a deep breath, she said, "It was Bryson."

Maddie and Stacyee exchanged confused looks.

"Bryson? Who the hell is Bryson?" Stacyee asked, plopping down on a chair.

Jordan rolled her eyes. "Bryson Wells."

Maddie's mouth fell open. "What?"

After giving her friends a quick synopsis of her time with Bryson, she finished off her drink. Both of her friends were silent for a few moments, but she knew the explosion would come. So she waited.

Sure enough, Stacyee blew first, jumping out of her seat and doing a little dance. She held up her hand, giving Jordan a high-five. "Damn, girl, I'm so proud of you. I feel like you're my kid and you just walked across the stage! You're back in the game."

"You know we need details, right?" Maddie said. "That brief, shitty storytelling you just did won't cut it."

Jordan made a motion signaling her lips were sealed. "Nope. No details."

Maddie groaned and slid off the chair. "I can't even with you . . ."

"Really?" Stacyee asked. "You're just going to leave us hanging like that? I mean, Bryson was Mr. Nerd in school. And suddenly he shows up on the scene with enough game to make you break all your damn rules and do him?"

Jordan smiled, remembering the way he'd handled her. He'd told her he wasn't the one-and-done type. She wasn't either. She knew what she wanted and she'd ordered a mind-blowing orgasm, which he'd served up multiple times that night. It would have been smarter to stay far away from him, but her body had been on some traitor-shit. She'd been open for him, ready for his brand of loving. But he'd done things to her body that made her shudder. Memories of that night had plagued her thoughts, made her want more.

"I'm telling you, he's not the same guy," Jordan told them. "I mean, he is. But . . . he isn't."

"So would you see him again?" Maddie asked.

Shaking her head, Jordan told them both no. "He

lives in Cali. Besides, what do I look like asking for a repeat? It's best that we leave things as they are. I'm not necessarily looking for love, and he's still firmly running from his past. And that's all I'm saying, so let's change the subject."

Several hours later, Jordan was giving good-bye hugs to her besties. They'd spent the rest of the day sitting on the plush couches in the salon laughing, drinking, and enjoying each other's company. Stacyee had even ordered in dinner. Jordan couldn't remember the last time she'd laughed so much. Life for her had been so serious lately. It felt good to kick back with two of her favorite people in the world. It was so good to be home.

Chapter 6

Eight weeks later

It was a busy day at the Bees Knees, and Jordan felt like the walking dead. There seemed to be a re-volving door of customers and she hadn't had a chance to sit down. For the last several weeks, she'd worked with Grams, helping run the diner. She usu-ally enjoyed it, but today . . .

The smell of greasy bacon in the air mixed with fried fish, onions, ketchup, and syrup made her want to throw up. A wave of nausea washed over her and she rushed to the bathroom, barely making it in time to empty her breakfast into the toilet. Ugh. It was the second time she'd vomited that day.

Back in the dining room now, Jordan gulped down a large glass of water and used a napkin to wipe her brow.

"Are you okay, Jordan?" Grams asked, concern in her eyes. "You look like you're coming down with something."

Jordan swallowed. "I might be. I just feel queasy."

"Had any good sex?"

Jordan spit out the water she'd just ingested. "What?"

"I said how long have you been sick?"

Jordan blinked. Her mind was playing tricks on her, and she didn't like it. Two days ago, she'd dreamed that Michael Myers was chasing her, but he didn't have a knife or an ax. He'd been carrying a Jimmie John's sub. And the sad part? All she remembered thinking in the dream was that she wanted that sandwich. It looked good, too. It was her favorite.

"Um, Grams, it's been like this for a few days. Not sure what's going on."

"Why don't you go to the urgent care? You might have the flu. It's late in the season, but you can still get it."

"Maybe."

"What are your other symptoms?"

Jordan shrugged. "I just feel tired, nauseous. I'm hungry, but every time I eat something, I feel like I have to throw it up. And then . . ." She grimaced as a whiff of something unpleasant floated to her nose. "Everything smells bad, like really bad."

Grams frowned. "Like what?"

"Meat."

"Chile, you need to go to bed."

That was her grandmother's answer to everything. In Grams's mind, sleep was the cure to everything. That and baking soda. Tummy ache? Put a little baking soda in water. Back ache? A teaspoon of Arm & Hammer. Have a cold? Six doses of baking soda in a glass of cool water.

Gagging, Jordan rushed into the back. Jordan

gasped for breath as she dry heaved over the toilet bowl. She felt soft hands on her neck, pulling her hair back into a ponytail. Then she felt a cool rag on her neck.

"Thanks, Grams," she said.

"I'm worried about you, Jordan. I think you should go to the doctor."

"Grams, I can't. It's busy here today. You need the help."

"What I need is for you to be okay, babe. Matter of fact, I'm going to drive you. Give me a second."

"No, Grams. I'm good. I'll just drive myself. I'll be fine."

Jordan finally stood and gave Grams a quick hug. "I'll let you know what the doctor says."

"You'd better."

Jordan grabbed her coat and her purse and left the diner. She arrived at the health center in ten minutes and was immediately escorted into an examining room. They'd instructed her to put on a face mask in case she was contagious and asked her to give a urine sample.

The doctor knocked on the door and stepped into the room. Dr. Martin was a petite African American woman with kind eyes and a wide smile. "Hello, Ms. Clark." The woman took a seat on a stool and set up her tablet on the docking station. "What brings you here today?"

Jordan explained her symptoms, all the while praying that she didn't hurl on the nice white linoleum. Or worse, the doctor's shoes. Once she was finished, she swallowed past a lump in her throat and waited.

Dr. Martin looked at her, and gave her a small smile. "We got your urine culture back."

Jordan perked up. "Is everything okay?"

The doctor grinned. "Everything is fine. You're pregnant."

She shook her head. "No."

The doctor frowned. "When we get a positive pregnancy test, we usually run it twice. Both tests came back positive."

"That can't be true. It's impossible."

Crossing her legs at the ankles, Dr. Martin asked, "It is possible to get a false positive. That's why we repeated the test."

Jordan couldn't wrap her brain around the news. Logically, she knew that no form of protection was 100 percent effective, but damn.

"Have you been sexually active?" Dr. Martin asked.

A lie would be counterproductive, but damn it if Jordan didn't consider it. Because . . . *this can't be happening to me!*

She nodded slowly. "Yes," she murmured, even though she suspected the good doctor already knew the answer to that question. "But we used protection."

Jordan rolled her eyes as the doctor spouted out some worthless statistics. Dr. Martin also threw out "the only birth control 100 percent effective is abstinence." Suddenly, Jordan wished she could throw up just so the woman would leave her alone.

"I know there's a slight chance that a method of birth control will fail, but I . . . I also took a morning-after pill." She'd followed the directions to the letter. It hadn't even been six hours between sex and the pill. There was no way she was pregnant.

"I understand that, but even that isn't a guarantee, Ms. Clark."

Jordan took a minute to try to compose herself before she said something she'd regret. It wasn't the doctor's fault, after all. She was just the messenger. The perky, too happy messenger, but still. She counted to ten. Then counted to ten again. Nothing helped. She was screwed.

"Although the urine sample indicates a pregnancy, I still want to have your blood drawn."

Jordan hated blood work, she hated needles, she hated doctors, she hated the stupid oversized poster of Wellspring hanging on the wall . . . She hated everything. But she didn't have anyone to blame but herself. *And Bryson's ass.* She should have said no. She should have turned him away. Or she could have walked her happy ass back to her room like she'd told her father she was going to do—but alone. *Damn.*

An hour later, Jordan walked into her grandparents' home. Granddad was lying on the couch, snoring lightly. She brushed a hand over his brow, over the slight frown lines in his forehead. He'd been sleeping more lately, tired from the treatment he'd been receiving. He'd also been withdrawing from her and Grams.

They'd made it a point to try to engage with him whenever they could, but he would often just sit there staring off into the space. Jordan couldn't understand why, though. Because the doctors were still saying his prognosis was good.

She wiped her eyes. They burned from the tears she'd shed the entire way home from the urgent care. She didn't know what the hell she was going to do. Jordan didn't consider herself irresponsible. It was just the opposite. She did what she was supposed to do 98.9 percent of the time, and the one time she didn't, the one time she'd thrown caution to the wind and done something she wanted . . . *Ugh.*

Pregnant.

Jordan spread the blanket on the back of the couch over Granddad and went to her room. The house she'd grown up in was cozy, but there wasn't a lot of privacy. Grams and Granddad were minimalists. They believed in tithing to the church and having money in the bank. They didn't care to keep up with the Joneses with fancy cars and houses. Her grandmother still drove the Honda Accord she'd bought when Jordan was a senior in high school.

It was because of them that Jordan had saved her own stash. And even though she didn't have a church home, she'd still sent money to her childhood church for the perpetual building fund.

A baby?

Jordan had never thought much about being a mother. She wasn't all that fond of little kids. And she had no idea what to do with a baby. When Maddie had brought her doll over, Jordan would inevitably drop the damn thing on its head. The diaper always fell off and she'd often fought the urge to toss it in the trash can. *And don't get me started on those creepy eyes that blink like the demented doll in that horror movie.*

She'd baby-sat for the neighbor a few times, but she'd spent all of her earnings bribing the kids to go to sleep. The only good thing she did was cook for them, but when it was time for bed, Jordan botched the storytime voices and failed at cuddling.

And Bryson.

What the hell was she going to tell him? She'd promised him she had everything under control. There was a strong possibility that he could think she'd lied when she told him she took the pill. He could think she tried to trap him.

They didn't know each other anymore. Being friends in high school was vastly different from being adult friends. What if he was a jerk in real life? What if he had a girlfriend? It wouldn't be the first time she'd dated someone who lied about being in a relationship.

Or worse? Would he propose to her out of obligation? It was no secret that he wanted to be a father. He'd made that very clear in school. He was voted "Most Likely to Procreate," for heaven's sake. Jordan knew his reasons were tied to his own relationship with his father, but still . . . The last thing she wanted to do was marry someone because of a baby. Her mother had done that, and look where that got her. Abandoned and rejected by the one person who was supposed to have her back no matter what.

I'm not ready.

Obviously, her mother wasn't ready either. Could Jordan bring a kid into the world anyway, knowing that it was the last thing she wanted to do at her age? Yes, she had choices, but she wasn't sure she could go through with any of them.

Jordan fell back on her mattress. A temper tantrum wouldn't help, but she sure wanted to punch a pillow or scream. She curled up into a fetal position, hugging her pillow as tears streamed out.

"Babe?" Grams walked into her room and over to the bed.

Jordan looked up at her grandmother. "Grams?"

The bed bowed beneath her and Grams smoothed a hand over her brow. "You okay?"

She nodded. "I'm pregnant," she blurted out.

Grams blinked. "What?"

"They did a urine test at the doctor's office. It's positive."

The doctor had told her that the blood test would be more reliable, but Jordan knew she was pregnant. The minute the words came out, she knew. The hCG test was just a formality at this point. She'd fucked up, and now she had to prepare to deal with the consequences.

"Oh babe." Grams squeezed her hand. "I didn't know you had a boyfriend."

Jordan rolled her eyes. "I don't."

"But—"

"It was a one-night thing. In Santa Monica."

With wide eyes, Grams reared back. "Santa Monica? What? Who?"

"It was Bryson Wells."

"Oh dear," Grams muttered. "Oh my."

Jordan wasn't shy when talking to her grandmother. She'd always been able to share things with Grams, from trying her first joint to trying her first dick. "He was at the hotel visiting with Parker when we ran into each other. Long story short, we spent time together."

"Well, you have to tell him, babe."

"How am I going to do this? We haven't talked since then. It was just supposed to be a fling. Not forever."

After his last text the morning after, they hadn't chatted. Not even a quick hello or a funny GIF. It had been radio silence between them, and that had been okay with her. Even though she'd thought of him often. Even though she'd dreamed about that night several times.

"Listen, Jordan. You have no choice. In less than nine months, you are going to have to take care of a baby. It's better if you have the support and help of its father."

Jordan knew Grams was right. Her father had struggled in the beginning to take care of her, before he'd brought her to live with Grams and Granddad. She didn't want that for her child. The best thing she could do was make sure it felt the love of both parents.

Wiping her face, Jordan nodded. "You're right. I'll try to get a hold of him."

And then what? Bryson had made it clear that he had no intention of even coming to Wellspring for a visit. And she was not leaving her grandparents, not when Granddad was so sick.

"Good," Grams said, standing to her feet. "I'm going to start dinner and check in on your grandfather. If you need me, holla."

Once Jordan heard the click of the bedroom door, she picked up her phone and typed out the text. She'd started and deleted over ten texts in one minute, deliberating with herself over whether to even reach out to him so soon. The doctor had explained that the urine test was only the first test. She would get the results of the blood work tomorrow, and then she would know for sure. But he did need to know. Sighing, she hit the send button.

Jordan: Hey. Can you give me a call when you get a minute? Important.

Setting the phone on the table, she took a deep breath. A few minutes passed, and he hadn't texted her back. She looked at her screen, noting an error message. Unlocking it, she shook her head. The text had come back undeliverable. Did he change his phone number?

Her thumb hovered over the green phone icon for a minute, before clicking on it. She scrolled to his contact and paused. It was still early in Cali and he was probably at work.

"Jordan!"

Her grandmother's scream caught her off guard and she dropped her phone to the ground and bolted out of the room, racing toward the front of the house. "Oh God!" she screamed. Grams was on the ground, holding Granddad in her arms, rocking him back and forth. *No.*

Jordan froze. She couldn't move. She could barely breathe. "Is he . . . ?" she croaked, her eyes filling with tears.

"Call an ambulance!" Grams yelled. "Now."

Chapter 7

"I'm glad you came, brother."

Bryson embraced his sister, Brooklyn. Uncomfortable, apprehensive, and cold were only a few of the many things he felt when he stepped outside of the Gerald R. Ford International airport that morning. "That makes one of us," he murmured.

Brooklyn pulled back and gave him a sad smile. "I know. But you sure are a sight for sore eyes."

For four days of the year, he and Brooklyn were the same age. They'd shared a lot in the years he'd lived in Senior's house, and he couldn't deny seeing her was like a balm to his frayed nerves.

He muzzled her short hair. "I like you natural, sis. I'm glad you stopped wearing that damn weave."

Brooklyn swatted his hand away. "Thanks for messing up my whip, brother. I paid good money to get it done."

"Stacyee still doing your hair?" he asked. He knew that Jordan and Stacyee were thick as thieves.

"Every week. Carter loves my hair spiky," Brooklyn said with a wink.

"Well, judging by that glow on your face, you love Carter."

Brooklyn smiled, her teeth on full display. "I do, Bryson. I never thought I could love someone like this. He believes in my dreams, and he even loves me on my 'stank' days."

Bryson barked out a laugh, recalling those times of the month when he'd tease his sister about her "stank" attitude. "Well, that's good to hear because I didn't love those days. You were a nightmare."

She smacked his arm. "I wasn't that bad."

He nodded. "Yes, you were."

"Shut up. Anyway, it fills me up with hope for the future. Even now, with everything going on, I feel at peace. And it's because of him."

His sister reached for one of his bags, and he pulled it out of her reach. "Now, you know that's not how this works," he told her. "I can carry my own bags."

Brooklyn elbowed him. "Whatever. Just because you came back all buff and stuff . . ." She gasped, and did a little dance. "Hey, that rhymed."

He shook his head and followed her to her car. "You're still crazy as ever." When she popped her trunk, he shoved his suitcases in it and pulled her into another hug. "I missed you."

She shoved him away. "Ugh, stop. I spent an hour on these smoky eyes today."

"You spent an hour on that?"

Her mouth fell open, in faux offense. "Really? I look damn good."

Bryson smirked at his sister. She did look good, and he wasn't ashamed to admit that his sister was hot. "You do look good, sis. But it's not because of that eye makeup."

"I hate you," she said with a giggle.

"I hate you," he mimicked.

"Ugh. In town for only a few minutes and you're already on my nerves. At least I don't have a big head . . . Big Head. Your muscle work didn't do anything for that big-ass noggin."

Bryson thumped his sister on her arm. It felt good to fall back into that sibling banter that made his days a little less dim while he was in Wellspring. "Is that all you got, sis? You're seriously out of practice."

"Give me a few hours." She winked, and embraced him again. "I missed you, too. I have so much to tell you."

Once they were buckled up in the car, and on their way, Bryson turned to his sister. "Are you sure Carter is cool with me staying with y'all?"

Initially, Bryson had planned to book a room at the Wells Hotel. But Brooklyn had insisted he stay with her and Carter, stating they needed time to catch up.

"He's fine with it. Actually, he wanted to come with me to pick you up, but I told him I needed some brother-sister time."

"If I see a naked anything, I'm checking into the hotel," Bryson warned.

His sister was still a newlywed. And so was Parker, having only been married a few months to Kennedi. The last thing he needed was to walk in on his sister and his new brother-in-law getting it on on a piece of furniture.

Brooklyn laughed. "Trust me, that will never happen. I would be mortified."

"You? My eyes would never recover." Chuckling, Bryson pulled out his phone and sent Remy a quick text to let him know he arrived.

"So . . ." Brooklyn said in a singsong voice. *Oh shit.* It was never anything good when his sister started a sentence in that voice. More often than not, that same "so" got him into trouble. Like when he'd been caught stealing candy from Mr. Mays's market, or when they'd been arrested for vandalism by Sheriff Walker for spraying graffiti on Senior's beloved Porsche. Then there was the time Brooklyn had convinced him to take her friend Nicole to the prom, and his face had ended up on the other end of Nicole's boyfriend Kyle's fist. "How long are you staying?"

He shot her a wary glance. "Not long. I don't want to be here any longer than necessary."

"Planning on seeing anyone special?"

She was still singing, and Bryson was curious. "Why?"

Brooklyn shrugged. "No reason."

Yeah, right. "What is it, Brooklyn?"

"Kennedi just told me something, so . . ." She sighed. "I heard you and Jordan were flirty in Santa Monica."

Telling Brooklyn about Jordan was a no-go. Because if he did, Brooklyn would have his wedding planned before he left. Back in high school, he'd made the mistake of telling his sweet sister that he was attracted to Jordan and Brooklyn had never given up on a future hook-up and cute nieces and nephews with dimples.

"I saw Jordan in Cali while I was at the hotel, yes." Bryson kept his voice intentionally even.

"Apparently, Jordan looked smitten."

Smitten? Hmm. Bryson wanted to know more. "How so?"

"Kennedi *and* Parker said they saw the sparks."

Bryson highly doubted Parker used the word *sparks*. His brother was not the waxing-poetic type of guy. "We just talked." *And fucked 'til the wee hours of the morning.* "Then, she went back to the wedding reception."

"But you gave her your phone number?"

Bryson had forgotten Parker and Kennedi were there for part of his exchange with Jordan. "Yeah, so?"

"So . . . did you call her?"

"No." That part was the truth. He hadn't called Jordan—not that night or the day after. She had called him the next morning, and that was it. He'd thought of her over the past couple months, but he'd never picked up the phone to call her.

"Fine," Brooklyn groaned. "What are your plans while you're here?"

"See Senior. Spend time with you and Parker and your new spouses, and meet Veronica. Then, home." And he wouldn't tell Brooklyn, but Bryson hoped he did see Jordan while he was in town. And if she should happen to fall on his dick, he'd be okay with that, too.

"Okay, good. I have tons planned. I can't wait."

"On a serious note, what are the doctors saying about Senior?"

Although Bryson had told Parker he would plan a visit, he hadn't expected to come so soon. And, honestly, the more time had passed, the less he'd thought about it. He hadn't even requested time off for the trip yet when Brooklyn and Parker called him to give the grim news. Senior's organs were failing and it was time to call in the family.

Brooklyn glanced at him out of the corner of her eye, but quickly turned her attention back to the road. "They call it a persistent vegetative state. He's unresponsive, and the only thing keeping him alive is medical intervention. Last week, he developed pneumonia. Now, his kidneys are failing. He's losing weight, even with the feeding tube."

Bryson nodded. "And because of the advanced directive, they can't pull the plug." He'd read up on the medical terminology before he arrived. The doctor's hands were tied, and Senior had left strict instructions that he be kept alive.

It seemed off to Bryson, knowing his father, that Senior would want to be kept alive, breathing only because of a machine. Just the thought of his father choosing to live this way, unconscious for months and cared for by strangers, seemed wrong. Senior was a lot of things, but helpless wasn't one of them, and being in a coma on life support was as helpless as one could get.

"I wonder why he chose this?" Bryson mused.

"I have no idea," Brooklyn said. "It's not like him. At all. Me and Parker were talking about it the other day. It makes no sense. The only thing I can think of is that he is holding out for someone."

"Or something," Bryson muttered. It wouldn't surprise him if Senior was holding out because there was some secret, some crime that would only be revealed upon his death.

"Could be." Brooklyn reached out and squeezed his hand. "Hell if I know why Senior did anything."

Bryson used to sit in his room and ponder the same

thing. There was no explanation for the atrocities
that his father committed, no reason to be so vile.
"Too bad we'll never find out."

"Do we even want to?"

He turned his attention to the road. A part of him
wanted—no, *needed*—to know. He'd spent years wondering why Senior had yanked him away from his
mother only to treat him like shit. Bryson thought of
his first night in the house. Senior had scheduled a
big dinner under the guise of welcoming Bryson
into the home. The house hadn't been unfamiliar
to Bryson, since he'd spent summers and long
weekends there, so he'd trekked off to his favorite
hideout spot: the attic.

Bryson could still remember the smell of wood as
he'd climbed the stairs and made a pallet in the un-
finished space. He'd started to write a letter to his
mother when Senior interrupted him. Bryson recalled the feeling of trepidation he'd felt when
he'd been alone in the attic with Senior. His father
had been silent, assessing at first, looking him over
as if he were chattel.

Senior had asked him what he was doing in the
attic. When Bryson had explained he was writing a
letter to his mom, Senior snatched the paper from
his hands and ripped it into pieces. Then, Senior
had yanked Bryson to his feet and told him to stop
acting like a pussy, that no son of his would be weak.
That was the first time Senior had punched Bryson—
right in the gut. It had knocked the wind out of him.

If you cry, I'll beat your ass some more.

Those were the words his father had said to
Bryson before he stormed out of the attic. From that
moment on, Bryson knew he'd never win as long as

he was under that roof. And that's why he'd made it his mission in life to never return to it once he was old enough to decide for himself.

"Bryson?"

He blinked, and turned to Brooklyn. "Yeah." The car had stopped in front of the hospital, and Bryson couldn't believe that he'd zoned out the way he had.

"We're here. The valet will park the car."

Opening the car door, Bryson started to slide out when he felt Brooklyn's tight grip on his wrist. His gaze dropped down to her tiny hand, her brown skin against his dark skin.

"Don't go there," Brooklyn told him. "Don't go back there."

She didn't have to elaborate for him to know what she meant. His sister was urging him to stay in the present, to stay in the light. Because the only thing in the past was darkness.

"Good to see you, bruh." Parker pulled Bryson into a strong hug. "'Bout time your ass came home."

Bryson took the comfort Parker gave him, and said, "It didn't sound like I had an option. You do know where I live."

His brother chuckled. "Smart man. I would have been on your doorstep in four hours."

Kennedi gave him a tight hug. "Good to see you again, Bryson."

"Same to you." Bryson pointed at her baby bump. How's my niece or nephew?"

"Your nephew is doing great. I'm just tired."

Brooklyn grinned as she led a man, whom Bryson

assumed was Carter, over to them. "Bryson, this is Carter . . . my husband."

Carter gave Bryson a firm handshake. "Good to finally meet you. I've heard the stories."

"Then, you know it was all her fault, right?"

His brother-in-law laughed. "No doubt."

"Hey," Brooklyn shouted. "Don't do me like that, babe." She kissed Carter and Bryson felt a surge of happiness for his sister.

Bryson scanned the area. The hospital had been remodeled since he'd last been there. Instead of drab brown everywhere, there were bursts of red, orange, and blue. The family waiting area they were in was quiet. Another family sat on the other end of the large, open room.

"Hungry?" Parker asked. "We were just about to head to the cafeteria. Or do you want to go in and see Senior now?"

Bryson wasn't ready quite yet to see his father. Truthfully, he wasn't sure he would ever be ready to see Senior. The last time they'd seen each other was the day he'd walked out of the house never to return. There were no letters, no telegrams, no nothing. And Bryson had preferred it that way.

Nodding, he said, "Yeah, let's grab something to eat. Plane food is not what's up."

Parker squeezed his shoulder, much like the way he used to do when they were kids. Bryson soon realized that it was Parker's way of lending him some of his strength, or letting Bryson know that he had his back no matter what. "If I've never told you before, I just want you to know that I love you," his brother told him. "And there's not much I wouldn't do for you, or for any of my siblings."

Hearing the words was good, but Bryson knew how Parker cared because he'd shown it, day in and day out. It was Bryson who'd disappeared out of their lives and barely kept in touch. And yet, they'd still welcomed him home with open arms. "Love you, too, man." And then in an effort to veer away from the emotional stuff he added, "But if marriage is going to make me all sappy like it's done you, I'll pass."

Kennedi laughed then. "Hey, lay off my man, brother-in-law. I know your secrets."

Bryson frowned and wondered what Kennedi thought she knew. While Parker, Brooklyn, and Carter walked ahead, he turned to his sister-in-law and leaned in. "What do you know?"

With a smile as wide and as mischievous as a Cheshire cat's, she said, "Let's just say, I get up early every morning to run. And I'll leave it at that."

Damn. Bryson hadn't seen Kennedi, but it was obvious she'd seen him leaving the hotel the morning after his night with Jordan. He scratched the back of his neck. "Yes, let's leave it at that. And I hope you left that little tidbit in Santa Monica, sis."

Kennedi grinned. "I did. No worries. I don't see and tell."

"But you did tell Brooklyn there were sparks," he muttered.

"She talks too much." Kennedi hooked an arm in Bryson's and whispered, "But rest assured, that's pretty much all I told her. Your secret is safe with me."

He gave Kennedi a fist bump, surprised at the level of comfort he had with her. Bryson wasn't the type to let people in, but he'd immediately been taken with Parker's wife. She was genuine, funny, and definitely loved his brother.

"Veronica?" Brooklyn called. "You made it."

Bryson looked up to see a petite woman walking toward them. She looked a little like Brooklyn from afar, but as she drew closer, the differences became apparent.

Veronica smiled as she approached. "Yes, I made it." She hugged everyone, and when she made eye contact with Bryson, she reached out to shake his hand. "You must be Bryson. I've heard a lot about you. I'm glad to meet you."

Bryson shook Veronica's hand. "It's good to finally meet you, too." There was an awkward silence for a moment, as he struggled to find something else to say.

Veronica slipped her hand from his grasp. "When did you get in?"

"I just came straight from the airport."

Crickets.

"Wow, that was awkward," Brooklyn announced. "Ya know, it's okay to say more than one stilted sentence at a time."

Bryson hooked an arm around Brooklyn's neck in a faux choke hold. "You always have something to say."

Brooklyn wrenched herself from his grasp. "Seriously. I want you two to get to know each other. At the end of the day, we're all we have."

She was right. They didn't have a lot of living relatives. He was sure there were some distant cousins somewhere, but he didn't know how to get a hold of them. Senior hadn't associated with extended family much. In fact, Bryson could only remember going to a family reunion one time in all the years he lived with Senior.

"Right," he relented. "Veronica, it's good to meet you. Let's start again."

"Yes." Veronica gave him a hug. "It's been a crazy year. But I hope to be able to get to know you."

"We will," he told her.

Parker joined them. "The doctor just called me. He'd like to talk to us."

A few minutes later, they were all crowded into a private consultation room with Dr. Justice Slone. As the doctor talked, Bryson watched the faces of his siblings. Brooklyn was the only one with tears in her eyes, but he wasn't sure they were for the Senior that was lying in the hospital bed. She'd shared with him a few times that she had fond memories of Senior when she was a little girl so Bryson assumed that's the Senior Brooklyn was crying for.

"As you know," Dr. Slone said, "the living will your father submitted is very specific as to how he would like this situation handled. And we've done everything we can to honor his wishes. However, there is only so much we can do once the organs begin to fail. The longer he remains in the coma, the greater the chance more issues will develop."

The doctor was professional, clear, and concise with his explanation of Senior's prognosis. Bryson appreciated that he didn't sugarcoat anything. Since Senior was in a coma, and hadn't designated a health care power of attorney or patient representative, the hospital had chosen to follow the living will on file.

"Dr. Slone, we've had this conversation before. I was hesitant to say anything that would override my father's wishes, but now that his kidneys are failing,

I have to assume his other organs will follow. I see no reason to continue to prolong his life. He's being kept alive by a machine." Parker sighed, and met each of their gazes. "I think we're all in agreement that it's time to pull the plug."

Bryson watched as Kennedi wrapped her arms around Parker, at the same time Carter pulled Brooklyn in his arms. For the first time in a long while, Bryson wished he had someone at his side, offering him silent support. Yes, he had his brother and sisters, but he couldn't deny there was an emptiness in his life that he knew would only be filled by the woman he fell in love with. *If that woman exists.*

Veronica cleared her throat, and asked, "Are you okay?"

He nodded. Before he could talk himself out of it, he pulled Veronica into a quick hug. "Are you?"

"I guess. I just worry about you all. I didn't know him. But you three did."

Bryson resisted the urge to tell Veronica that she should be glad she didn't know Senior, or have to be raised under his roof. No sense in bringing her down even further. "Yeah" was all he could say in response.

"Bryson?" Brooklyn wiped her cheeks. "I think you should go see Senior. It's time."

"She's right, bruh," Parker said. "It's time to make peace with him."

Make peace? Somehow he doubted that would ever happen at this late juncture. But he agreed anyway, and told Parker and Brooklyn to lead the way to the hospital room.

They passed by the emergency entrance on the way to Senior's private room. He noted several nurses and staff members rushing toward the doors.

Seconds later, he heard someone yell at them to move back and watched as they wheeled a patient in. But it wasn't just any patient. It was Will Clark.

He heard Brooklyn gasp next to him. "Oh no," she cried.

Bryson knew that Brooklyn and Parker had a special relationship with Will and Dee Clark, as their mother was good friends with the couple before she died. He hated to see his sister cry, but he knew that if something happened to Will Clark, Jordan would be devastated.

He had just reached for his phone when Dee Clark rushed into the hospital, with Jordan right on her heels. She looked worried, scared for her grandfather's life. Her eyes were swollen and her cheeks were blotchy, like she'd been crying.

Bryson wanted to go to her, but he didn't want to overstep or even assume she'd want his comfort. He deliberated with himself on what he should do, and just when he'd made the decision to go to her, he heard his name on her lips.

When their gazes met, he stepped forward.

"Jordan"—Dee Clark pulled on Jordan's sleeve— "let's go. We have to go to the back."

He thought that Jordan might say more. Instead, she rushed off behind her grandmother.

Chapter 8

The only sounds in the room were the whoosh of the ventilator and the soft beeps of the machines. Senior's room didn't have any get well cards displayed on the table or balloons swaying in the air. It was cold, dark. And Bryson couldn't help but think it fit the man lying in the bed.

Sighing, Bryson stepped closer. Brooklyn had wanted to come in with him, but Carter had told her to let Bryson handle it on his own. Bryson appreciated Carter stepping in. It was in Brooklyn's nature to be the nurturer, but he needed to do this alone.

He'd expected to feel some sense of relief when he saw his father. The man had put him through hell with no apologies. Instead, he just felt sad, empty. When he was a kid, Senior seemed so big, larger than life. For a long time, Bryson had thought his father was a giant, a mountain of muscle that stood tall at six feet three inches. And although Bryson got his height from his father, he hadn't had the same stature in school. In fact, he was so thin and clumsy, the kids used to make fun of him.

Bryson's mother used to tell him tall tales of his father, and he'd build Senior up to be this invincible, courageous man. He'd wanted to know him, had dreamed of one day being able to meet his daddy. But once he'd met him, that had all changed.

From the minute he'd laid eyes on Senior, at the young age of five, his father had rejected him. After building the man up in his mind, his father had taken one look at him and told his mother that Bryson was not his son.

That one rejection had not only stuck with Bryson for years, it gave him a complex about his looks and his worth. Compared to his siblings, Bryson was dark skinned. He wasn't sports inclined like Parker. And he wasn't funny and outgoing like Brooklyn. He was just him, and that made him an outsider. And Senior took every opportunity he could to point that out to anyone who would listen.

Bryson snickered when he wondered what Senior would say to him now. He wasn't the skinny, scary boy that his father remembered. He'd put on a good fifty pounds of lean muscle in the years since he'd left Wellspring. Even if Senior was alive and kicking, he doubted the old man would step to him now.

"You . . ." Bryson swallowed, pressing a fist to his chest. He hadn't expected to feel the crushing weight of grief that seemed to fill him up in that moment, but he guessed it only signaled that he was in fact human and he had a heart. And that was the one thing he could say for certain he didn't get from Senior.

"You sucked as a father." Those weren't the words he'd planned to say, but they worked for the time being. "So I don't even know why I'm here. A parent is supposed to make their child's life better. But the only thing you did for me is make my life worse."

Bryson's heart pounded in his chest as he stepped even closer. Several emotions vied for dominance in his mind, but he chose to embrace the one that would fuel him. Anger.

"I survived despite your attempts to break me. You spent so much time trying to beat me into submission, whether with your fists or your words. But I'm still here. And I'm smart, I'm successful, and best of all, I'm nothing like you. I didn't need your money to get where I am, I didn't need your name."

Bryson had taken his maternal grandfather's last name when he'd moved out. Legally, his name was Bryson Parks. It had been his last act of defiance, and effectively wiped out any visible connection to his father. Leaving Wellspring, leaving his siblings had been for one reason—survival. He had one goal, and that was to make it without his father. And he'd done that. He lived a comfortable life, free of bullshit.

Bryson heard the click of the door behind him, signaling he was no longer alone. He knew Brooklyn wouldn't be able to resist coming to him, even though he'd told her he would be okay. She was like a mother bear, always in protective mode when it came to her brother.

"Hi."

It wasn't Brooklyn. Bryson turned to find Veronica standing next to him, her eyes on Senior's still form. "Hey," he said, shoving his hands in his pockets.

"I don't even know why I'm here."

"Me either." Bryson could feel her eyes on him,

and imagined she was trying to figure him out. From the outside looking in, he wasn't exactly emotional on the impending death of his own father. That was bound to create questions.

"I've always known about him," she continued. "But I didn't know him. I don't know what his voice sounded like, how he smelled. He's a stranger."

Bryson wanted to tell her to consider herself lucky she didn't know Senior. But instead, he said, "Sometimes things work out for the best."

Frowning, Veronica said, "I would ask you to elaborate, but something tells me it's not a pleasant story."

He shrugged. "It's not. But it is what it is at this point."

"True. My mother used to always tell me to not question God. So, I won't. I have just always wondered why my father didn't want me, or why I didn't matter to him."

It was a million-dollar question that Bryson had asked himself on many occasions. But he'd realized that it was a waste of time to try to figure out Senior. "Just so you know . . . Senior may have acted like he didn't want you, but I can tell you that we're nothing like him. Parker and Brooklyn will never treat you like you don't matter, and neither will I.".

He caught the glimmer of unshed tears in Veronica's eyes. Bryson understood all too well the emotions his sister might be feeling, and he wanted to offer her support. Holding her hand in his, he gave her a reassuring squeeze.

"Thank you," she told him.

* * *

"The cancer is stable. Mr. Clark has pneumonia."

Jordan slumped against the wall. For the first time since they'd arrived at the hospital, she felt like she could breathe. Seeing her strong grandfather splayed out on the floor earlier had nearly brought her to her knees. And Grams . . . Her grandmother had been trying to hold it together, but Jordan knew she was a wreck.

Grams and Granddad had been together for over half of their life. Dee and Will Clark had met in their late teens, while he was vacationing in Colorado. Grams had been working in a diner, serving up what was now her famous Denver omelet.

Jordan remembered her grandfather telling the story of their meeting in his gregarious way, complete with sound effects and sweeping hand gestures. It had always been one of her favorite stories. Her grandfather had fallen in love at first sight and they were married soon after.

"Dr. Troy?" Grams's voice sounded so small, so soft, Jordan had to strain to hear her. "How did he get pneumonia?"

"More than likely, it developed from a simple cold or the flu. With your husband's age, he's at high risk to develop complications from the disease. I'm glad you got him in here when you did."

"We didn't have a choice," Grams told him. "He toppled over when I tried to help him to the bathroom. I should have insisted he go to the doctor."

Jordan wrapped an arm around her grandmother. "Grams, you know Granddad is stubborn. It's not your fault."

"There was a buildup of fluid in his lungs," the doctor explained. "We had to drain it, and now he should feel more comfortable. With his cancer diagnosis, we want to keep an eye on him so we're admitting him to our intensive care unit. But we expect a full recovery."

"Is he awake?" Grams asked.

Dr. Troy nodded. "When I left, he was asking for you."

Grams's chin trembled and she covered her mouth with a shaky hand. "Thank you," she whispered, her voice filled with emotion.

After the doctor shook their hands and walked off, Jordan turned to her grandmother. "See, he's going to be okay."

Grams fell into her arms, her shoulders shaking as she sobbed. They stood like that for minutes, Jordan soothing her grandmother, rubbing her back, and whispering nonsensical words of comfort to her.

When she pulled back, Grams shot her a wobbly smile. "Thanks, Jordan. Love you, babe."

Jordan swiped her thumbs under her grand-mother's wet eyes, and grinned back at her. "Love you more."

Squeezing Jordan's hand, Grams leaned in. "Are you okay?"

"I'm fine, Grams. I'm just relieved the cancer hasn't spread." That had been Jordan's biggest fear. It had taken every bit of strength she had to focus on the road ahead as she sped behind the ambulance to the hospital.

"I saw Bryson," Grams said. "My guess is Senior is getting worse."

Jordan hadn't allowed herself to think about seeing Bryson. Seeing him again earlier had brought

a flood of memories to mind, ones that she'd tried
to forget over the past two months. Ones that she
shouldn't have been thinking about with her grandfather being dangerously ill.

She'd stopped herself from texting him because
she didn't know why he was there. If her grandmother was right, and Senior was getting worse, he
was probably busy with his family. She didn't want to
interrupt any time with them.

Everything in life always seemed to happen fast,
but she had no choice but to live through it slow.
Being pregnant, while important, wasn't life threat-
ening. The news could wait. Yes, they had a lot to
discuss, but it just wasn't the right time.

They hadn't talked about seeing each other
again. In fact, she felt that it was unspoken that they
would enjoy each other for the one night and move
on with their lives. Apart. It helped that he didn't
live in Wellspring and had no intention of ever stepping foot in town again—until he did.

Grams tucked a strand of hair behind Jordan's
ear. "I think you should definitely talk to him, babe."

"Not now. But I will. Listen, don't keep Granddad
waiting. I'll give you two time alone. I'm going to
head to the café to grab a cup of tea." *Even though
coffee would be better.*

Jordan watched Grams disappear around the
corner and headed to the café. Although the café
was closed, she noted a vending machine that served
hot beverages and walked over to it. She shook her
purse, hoping she had cash with her. She hated to
use her credit card on vending machines. Digging
inside her bag, she pulled out a few pennies and

grumbled a curse. She tried again, this time only pulling out a piece of lint and a nickel. *Damn.*

Sighing, she pulled her wallet out, hoping she had a few singles. Unfortunately, there was nothing in there but a twenty-dollar bill and a Starbucks punch card. If Jordan was a lesser person, she would have kicked that vending machine and screamed in frustration at the unfairness of it all.

Out of the corner of her eye, she saw a hand reach out and insert a dollar into the machine. Rolling her eyes, she turned to the person, intent on cursing them out for one, invading her personal space, and two, cutting in front of her while she was standing at the vending machine. Her curses died on her lips, though, when she was face-to-face with Bryson.

He smirked. "I figured you needed some help."

Jordan leaned against the vending machine. Either it was hot in there or his mere presence was warming her from her head to her toes. She chose to go with the actual temperature in the room and not the temperature in her panties as the explanation for the sudden hot flash she was having. They were in the damn hospital and her attraction to him had reared its inappropriate head.

Swallowing, she said, "Thanks. I didn't have any change."

She made her selection and waited for the machine to prepare her herbal tea. A few hours ago, she'd been attempting to contact him and now he was standing next to her, his eyes boring into her.

"I called you," she blurted out, before she could think better of it. Why the hell she said that when she had no intention of telling him why she'd called at that moment was beyond her. She reasoned with herself that she had to do whatever it took to stop him from staring at her like that.

He lifted an eyebrow. "You did?"

Avoiding eye contact, she said, "It was nothing."

"You're sure?"

"Yeah," she croaked.

Jordan didn't know what kind of cologne Bryson wore but "smelled good" didn't even do it justice. More like smelled amazing, smelled tantalizing, smelled like heaven. *Yeah, that's it.* "What are you wearing?"

He looked down at his outfit and shot her a confused look. "Clothes?"

She giggled. "I mean cologne. You smell good." Because apparently she couldn't bring herself to tell him exactly what she thought of his scent.

"Oh." He smirked. "Tom Ford Noir."

"Hmm." She grabbed her cup and walked over to the counter where the sugar was.

"How's your grandfather?" Bryson asked.

Jordan busied herself opening two packets of sugar and pouring it into her tea. She stirred it with a coffee stirrer. "The doctor told us he had pneumonia." She turned to face him. "Bryson, I was so scared. I didn't know what was going on." She gave him a quick explanation of the events leading up to their arrival at the hospital, leaving out her morning sickness and pregnancy.

"Wow, that is scary. I'm glad he's going to be okay."

"He'll probably have to stay here for a while. So that means my grams will be here, too."

"That's understandable. They've spent a lifetime together. I'm sure they hate sleeping without one another."

Jordan nodded. "That's true. Granddad always told me he couldn't sleep without my grandmother. Not sure how they handled her trips back home to Colorado."

Grams used to go back home to visit her mother in Denver often before she died. Jordan had joined her quite a few times. Each time they left, Jordan remembered how distraught Granddad looked at the airport when he'd dropped them off. And each night while they were away, she would listen to Grams and Granddad chat on the phone until they both fell asleep.

Seeing her grandparents happy and in love after so many years of marriage should have reinforced the power of love and marriage to Jordan. But Jordan considered them the exception, not the rule.

"I'm sure he managed somehow," Bryson said. "But I bet your grandmother didn't go more than once a year."

Jordan thought about that for a moment. He was right. Every year, they'd visit on the Fourth of July, which was also Great-Grandmother Yvonne's birthday. "You know what? You're right."

"That's love right there."

She sipped her tea. "So, I'm surprised to see you here. Is Senior . . . ?"

Bryson nodded. "Yeah. Come have a seat with me?"

Jordan followed him over to a secluded table in the corner. Once they sat, he leaned forward, perching his muscular arms on the table. "Are you okay?"

she asked, trying hard not to look at the way his biceps pushed against the fabric of his shirt.

"I'm fine. We're pulling the plug today."

"Oh no. I'm so sorry, Bryson. I figured that was why you were in town."

His tongue darted out to wet his lips. "I . . . I don't know how to feel." He smoothed his hand over his bald head. "On one hand, I feel like it's time, and the other . . . I just wish things happened differently."

"Does that mean you wish you would have had a chance to repair your relationship with him?"

"No. That would never happen. But I do wish I'd been able to tell him how I feel. Talking to his still form didn't seem to be enough. Brooklyn told me that he heard me, but we just don't know that."

"They do say that comatose patients can hear what's going on around them. Why don't you just assume that he heard you?"

He stared at her again, his eyes sweeping over her like he was seeing something deep inside of her. "I guess I can think about it like that."

"You should."

"Are *you* okay?" he asked.

Even with everything going on in his own life, he seemed to be genuinely concerned about her. Smiling, she said, "Now that I know he's fine, yes. And you?"

"I'll be all right. You know you can tell me, Jordan."

She blinked. "Excuse me?"

For a moment, Jordan thought he might know something, but she quickly realized that was impossible because the only person she'd told her little secret to was Grams. She hadn't had time to tell Maddie and Stacyee yet.

"You seem like you want to say something," he said. "Even when I saw you in the hallway, you looked like you had something on your mind."

Jordan closed her eyes tight, and took a deep breath. "Bryson, I—"

"Bryson!" A frantic Brooklyn ran over to them.

Both Jordan and Bryson jumped up from their seats. "What's going on?" he asked his sister.

With a hand over her heart, Jordan awaited Brooklyn's answer. It couldn't be good news. She wrapped a hand around Bryson's arm and squeezed. It wasn't much, but she hoped it would offer him some support.

"It's Senior. You have to come now." Then, Brooklyn raced out of the café area.

Bryson turned to Jordan. "I have to go."

Jordan nodded. "Okay. Bryson?"

His gaze met hers. "Yes?"

"Please let me know if I can do anything for you."

He gave her a sad smile and dashed out of the area, leaving Jordan alone with a cup of cold tea and her loud thoughts.

Chapter 9

"Come on, son. Have a seat with me."

Bryson glanced at his mother and then back at the open casket in front of him. Senior had finally died. But it wasn't the way they'd expected. Instead of dying, after the doctors shut off the machines keeping him alive, Senior had gone into cardiac arrest.

He'd made it back to the room just in time to see the doctors pull the tube out of Senior's throat. From that point on, it had only taken a few minutes for Senior to pass away. When the doctor had called time of death, there were no hysterical cries or theatrics. They'd all simply stared at the bed, at the lifeless body of their father, Parker Wells Sr.

"I'm fine, Mom." Even now he still couldn't believe Senior was dead. He'd half expected him to jump out of the casket and make some sort of scene about how they weren't sad enough, or he'd picked the wrong suit for the occasion.

His mom wrapped her arm around Bryson and squeezed. "I'm worried about you, Bry."

"No need to worry, Mom," he told her.

Bryson's mother was the only person that called him Bry. It seemed he would forever be her little "Bry Bry" no matter how much he hated the nickname. He smiled down at his mother. Adrienne Moore was a slender woman, with skin the color of blackstrap molasses and eyes the color of cinnamon.

After Senior had taken custody of him, his mother would come and visit him in Wellspring. Bryson remembered the men in town following them down the street, staring at her as she walked. He also remembered wanting to kick all of their asses. But his mother wasn't studying any of them. Even now, he'd noticed the older men, and some of the younger ones, watching her when they'd entered Mason's Funeral Home earlier.

She patted his hand and kissed him on the cheek. "Okay, son."

It wasn't long before he felt Brooklyn's hand on his, gripping it tightly in hers. She leaned her head on his shoulder. "It doesn't seem real," she said. "I still can't believe we're here."

Bryson rested his head on hers. "I know."

His father hadn't wanted a public funeral, but they'd decided to have a viewing where residents could come and pay their respects to the family. A private ceremony would take place at Wellspring Cemetery the next morning.

People had been pouring in and out of the funeral home since the visitation started, offering condolences, giving hugs, and smiling sadly at all of them. Ever the big brother, Parker had spent his time making sure they were okay, while Bryson and

Brooklyn stood near the casket receiving the visitors. The visitation had been too much for Veronica, and she'd decided to leave early. Bryson didn't blame her. Not only had she been forced to deal with Senior's death, she'd had to deal with the curious looks from visitors just finding out that she was the love child of Senior and another of his mistresses.

"Do you think it's weird that no one is crying?" he asked Brooklyn.

"Nah. I didn't expect it. I think half the people in town just came to make sure he really is dead."

Bryson chuckled softly. "You might be right."

At some points of the day, it had almost seemed like a party of sorts. Instead of solemn silence, there was laughter and lots of chatter among the guests.

During the day, Bryson had caught up with several classmates from school and met many Wellspring Water Corp. employees. He'd also met Carter's family, who'd come from Detroit to support Brooklyn.

"Carter is a good guy," he told Brooklyn. "I like him."

Since he'd been staying with Carter and Brooklyn, he'd gotten a chance to talk to his brother-in-law. They'd bonded over technology and growing up in Detroit.

"That makes me happy," Brooklyn said. "I just wish we could spend more time together."

Initially, Bryson hadn't planned to stay past the weekend, but when Senior died, he'd changed his ticket. There was a lot to take care of, and he wouldn't leave Parker and Brooklyn to handle Senior's affairs by themselves. He'd done that enough already.

"I talked to my boss and I'll be here for a little while longer. Not sure how long, but I'm not leaving tomorrow."

Brooklyn squeezed him. "I love you. Thank you."

Parker joined them and wrapped his arm around both of them, pulling them into a group hug. "Hard to believe, huh?"

Bryson and Brooklyn laughed because Parker's statement had just confirmed they were all on the same page. They stood there for a few minutes, each of them lost in their own thoughts as they stared at the man who'd impacted their lives in different ways.

"You two take a break," Parker said. "I'll stand at the casket for a while. Go get some air."

"You don't have to tell me twice," Brooklyn said, squeezing them both one more time before she excused herself.

"I mean it, Bryson," Parker said, his voice a stern warning. "You need to get out of this area for a while. You've been standing here for hours."

"Fine, bruh. I'll step outside. I have a call to make anyway."

On his way out, Bryson ran into Remy, who'd just arrived. The two friends shared a man hug. "I'm glad you came, man," Bryson told Remy.

"I'm sorry for your loss, son. I'm glad you made it here for a visit before . . . ya know."

"Yeah. You were right. I needed to come."

The two of them stepped outside. Remy looked around. "You weren't lying about your hometown. It's like a black Mayberry."

Bryson barked out a laugh. "I told you."

Wellspring, Michigan, was a town situated on the

western side of the state between Kalamazoo and Grand Rapids. It was a small, mostly African-American town with a quaint little downtown area that had small shops like Mr. Wilder's Ice Cream Shop and Margie's Soup Kitchen.

Bryson had been surprised to see the new businesses that had come into the area, though. Although he wasn't too sad about the new Jimmie John's that was now in the town. But the new businesses hadn't changed the feel of his hometown. Over the last several days, he'd been running around with his siblings, reacquainting himself with Wellspring. Admittedly, he was proud of the strides the town had made to remain viable.

Mason's Funeral Home was on the outskirts of Wellspring, close to Hunt Nursery, which was Kennedi's family's business. There was nothing else around but a McDonald's, which had been there since Bryson was a little kid.

"How are you holding up?" Remy asked.

Bryson shrugged. "Honestly, I don't know how to feel."

"I get it. Death can be a numbing experience."

Remy had personal experience with death. His mother had died right before college graduation from breast cancer. Bryson had loved Ma, as he'd called Remy's mother. She'd been nothing but kind to him since he'd shown up with Remy during Thanksgiving all those years ago.

"Yeah," Bryson agreed. "But I didn't think it would be like this."

Bryson couldn't describe how he felt, he just knew he felt some type of way. In the last few days since

Senior had died, he'd gone through all the stages of grief multiple times. Now, although it was still hard to believe, he was in the acceptance phase. Navigating the world, knowing Senior could no longer find him, would be his new norm.

"Thinking of changing your name back to Wells?" Remy asked.

The thought had crossed his mind, but only because Parker had asked him about it the other day. The reasons he changed his name were no longer valid. And he was a Wells. That was a fact. Bryson opened his mouth to respond to Remy when he saw Jordan walking toward the building with her grandmother.

"Who *is* that?" Remy asked.

"Jordan," Bryson called, drawing her attention toward them.

She smiled and walked over to him. "Bryson." Pulling him into a hug, she whispered, "I'm so sorry."

Locking his hands together behind her waist, he said, "Thank you. I'm glad you're here."

When they pulled apart, Bryson hugged Dee. "Hello, Mrs. Clark."

Dee waved a hand, dismissing his formal greeting. "Boy, you know not to call me Mrs. Clark. I've been feeding you since you were skin and bones."

All of Jordan's friends called Dee "Grams," like she did. "Hi, Grams. It's good to see you."

Bryson gestured toward Remy and introduced them. "He flew in from California."

Grams smiled warmly. "That's nice."

"Brooklyn and Parker are somewhere around here," Bryson told Grams. "How is Mr. Clark?"

Grams went into a quick explanation about Jordan's grandfather's recovery. The doctors were planning to release him in the next few days. When his gaze met Jordan's he noted the soft smile on her lips. They hadn't talked since that evening in the hospital, so he was glad to hear that her grandfather was on the road to recovery.

"That's good to hear," he told Grams after she'd finished talking.

"Thank you for asking. I'm so sorry for your loss, Bryson."

"Thank you, Grams."

Grams looked to Jordan and said, "Ready to go inside? I can't stay too long. I need to get back to the hospital."

Jordan smiled at her grandmother and Bryson's stomach clenched. "Sure, Grams." Jordan turned to Bryson, grabbed his hand, and squeezed. "Talk to you soon."

Bryson watched her retreat, noting the way her black dress fit her petite form. Every time he saw her, she took his breath away. It seemed she grew more beautiful by the hour.

When she'd disappeared into the building, Remy said, "That's Pink Dress?"

Throwing his friend a side-eye glare, he said, "Yes, and don't get any ideas."

"Damn. Are all the women in Wellspring that fine? 'Cause she is lovely."

Bryson stared ahead, his mind still on the sway of Jordan's hips and her toned legs in those black heels she wore. "Yeah," he muttered. "She is."

* * *

Jordan flattened a hand over her belly. It was officially official. The presence of the baby's heart-beat on the "dating" ultrasound she'd had yesterday had confirmed that there was in fact a life growing inside of her. Her baby already had tiny arms and legs, too. When she'd spotted the fetus on the tiny screen in the doctor's office, she'd immediately teared up. Grams had teared up as well, as she'd stood next to her holding her hand.

The past few days had gone by in a blur. Bryson's father was dead. And she hadn't seen or talked to him since that night at the hospital. Her stomach churned in anticipation as she watched him walk back into the crowded funeral home with his friend. He was so tall, so male.

"I can't get over how fine Bryson is," Grams whispered to her.

Jordan's eyes widened. "Grams, you do realize the whole world probably heard you." Her grandmother might as well have shouted it from the rooftop.

With her low chuckle, Grams said, "I have nothing to hide."

Maddie had joined them in the corner. She and her boyfriend, Trent Lawson, had arrived shortly after her. "Grams isn't lying, Jordan. Bryson is definitely fine as hell."

Jordan shot her friend a wary glance. No one had to tell her Bryson was a hottie. She had eyes. She swept her gaze over him. Today, he was dressed in a mid-blue suit. He wore a light blue shirt underneath and a tie, looking good as sin. Bryson was on the other side of the room, at least ten people and ten chairs away from her, but she felt his presence in the room. It did crazy things to her body, made her feel off-kilter. Their eyes locked, and she averted her gaze, turning to Grams.

"Let me know when you're ready," she told her grandmother.

"I'm okay, babe," Grams told her. "We can stay a bit longer."

Jordan nodded. Unable to resist, she glanced over at Bryson again and found him watching her, heat in his brown orbs.

"Look at the way he's looking at you, J," Maddie muttered under her breath. "You should go talk to him."

Jordan scratched the side of her neck, and shook her head slightly. "No, he's busy with his family and his friends."

"Maddie, can you please grab me a bottle of water, sweetie?" Grams asked.

"Sure thing, Grams." Maddie excused herself and headed over to the table that held several bottles of water and mints.

"Jordan, you need to tell Bryson about the—"

"Don't say it here, Grams," Jordan said. "It's not the right time. I'm going to talk to him."

"When?"

Jordan shrugged. "Soon. Grams, he's grieving. I can't very well go over there right now and tell him I'm carrying his child. That wouldn't be okay."

"Is that the only reason why you're hesitating?"

"Yes." That, and Jordan had a sneaking suspicion that Bryson would find out about the baby and take the opportunity to try to swoop in and marry her or something crazy. "I'll tell him, Grams."

"Tomorrow. The sooner the better. It's best to rip the Band-Aid right off."

"What if he doesn't want the baby?"

"Then you'll deal with it then. No matter what, this baby will be loved. But you don't know how he's going to react. Give him the benefit of the doubt, babe."

Maddie rejoined them with three bottles of water. Jordan took the offered bottle, opened it, and guzzled it down in seconds. When she finished, she looked at Maddie, who was staring at her with her mouth agape. "What?" she asked Maddie. "Why are you staring at me?"

"Thirsty?" Maddie asked, handing Jordan her own bottle of water.

Jordan took it and smiled. "Not really. I need to get my water in for the day," she lied.

"Oh, that's good. I'm glad you're paying attention to your water intake. That's important."

Grams shot Jordan a knowing look before she excused herself to talk to Kennedi's aunt, Angelia Hunt.

"Trent told me everyone is gathering at Parker's house after the viewing. Do you want to come with us?"

"I hope you consider it."

Jordan jumped at the sound of Bryson's voice. *Where did he come from?* She scanned the area, wondering how she'd missed his approach. She really was a nervous wreck. "Bryson," she breathed.

"That's why I came over here, actually," he said. "I was going to invite you over tonight. A few of us are gathering to kind of kick back. I'd love for you to come. Maybe we'll get a chance to talk?" Bryson asked.

Feeling faint, she pressed the tips of her fingers against her forehead and willed her body to stop reacting to the nearness of him. *Jordan, get a grip.* She had no business feeling the way she did, not when everything was complicated and his dead father was less than fifty feet away from them. *Who does that?*

"Sure," she said. "I'll drop by later."

When Jordan arrived at Parker's house, the house was packed. Music played from a Bluetooth speaker and a card game was going on in the kitchen. Jordan scanned the room, trying to find Maddie in the crowd. Spotting her friend talking to Trent and Parker, she made her way over to the sofa.

"You're here," Maddie said, standing and giving Jordan a hug.

"I'm here," Jordan said. She greeted Trent and Parker with hugs and took a seat next to Maddie.

"Drink?" Parker asked.

Sure, a cognac neat. And make that a double. "Water is fine. I have to drive."

Maddie wrapped an arm around Jordan's neck. "My friend is so responsible, Parker. I'm so proud of her."

Jordan cringed when Maddie placed a kiss to her cheek. It was obvious her friend was more than a little tipsy. Turning to Trent, she asked, "Did you give this girl tequila?"

Maddie and tequila didn't mix. Hell, Maddie and

anything not wine didn't go well together. Her bestie could not hold her liquor to save her life.

"You know that's a no-no," Trent said. He was one of the best mechanics in the area, and owned Lawson's Garage. He and Maddie had been dating, off and on, for years. Tonight, they were on.

"Hey, Jordan," Brooklyn said, hugging her. "I'm so glad you came. Are you looking for Bryson?"

Brooklyn was only a year older, and they'd hung out together more than a few times. Jordan knew Bryson's older sister to be smart and giving, easy to talk to.

"Not really. Is he here?" As soon as Jordan entered the house, she'd decided tonight wasn't going to be the big reveal. There were too many people around.

"He's over there somewhere." Brooklyn gestured behind her in no particular direction.

It was then that Jordan realized that Brooklyn was a little tipsy as well. And since Parker hadn't moved to get her drink, she decided to go get it herself. She stood. "I'm going to grab a bottle of water."

On her way toward the kitchen, she waved at Carter, who was sitting at the card table playing Spades with three other people. Inside the kitchen, she greeted Kennedi with a hug. "Hey, Kennedi."

"Jordan. Good to see you. I'm glad you stopped by."

"I'm looking for the bottled water."

"We're out in the kitchen, but there is a cooler outside on the deck. I'll grab you one."

Kennedi opened the door, but Jordan stopped her. "No need. I can grab it myself. Could use some fresh air."

Nodding, Kennedi turned back to what she was doing. Jordan stepped out on the balcony. The view of the Grand River from the back of Parker and Kennedi's house was stunning at sunset, and she took it in, stepping farther out onto the deck.

"Beautiful, isn't it?"

Jordan yelped, whirling around to face Bryson. "Oh my God. You have to stop walking up on me like that."

"I'm sorry."

With her hand over her beating heart, she said, "I'm just jumpy."

"Which is so unlike you."

When he wrapped his arms around her in a long, tight embrace she relaxed into him, taking in the male scent that had filled her dreams. They stood like that for a moment before Jordan forced herself to pull away. Peering up at him, she said, "How are you?"

"I don't know. I had expected to feel a lot of things, but mostly I just feel sad. And then I get angry with myself for feeling this way."

"Do you have to identify the feeling?" she asked.

He gripped the wood railing of the deck, and peered out at the setting sun. "The day he died, I actually shed a few tears, which surprised me because I've spent my entire adult life running as far away from Senior as I could."

Jordan joined him at the railing, leaning forward and taking in the scene before them. The sound of the gentle water trickling reached her ears. "Bryson, you're still allowed to grieve. For all of his faults, Senior was still your father."

Bryson glanced at her, before averting his gaze. "Our relationship was so complicated, and I don't want to sit here and pretend that I will miss him, but—"

"How about you give yourself permission to just feel how you feel? Whether it's relief, sadness, anger, you have a right to all of those feelings. Unfortunately, your relationship with Senior wasn't one to write home about, but he did impact your life good or bad. You have committed yourself to not being like him, and I'd say you succeeded. You're nothing like your father."

Jordan hadn't spent a lot of time with Senior, but she'd been around when he'd been on the warpath and had witnessed the harsh way he'd treated Bryson. She'd never forget the time Senior came to the high school and embarrassed Bryson in front of their advanced chemistry class. She couldn't even remember why he'd been there that day, but she did remember the dejected look on Bryson's face. After school that day, she'd asked him to drive her to the bluff overlooking the river. They'd sat for hours in silence, watching the waves crash against the riverbank and listening to the birds chirping overhead, until he was ready to go home.

Placing her hand on his shoulder, she said, "You can be sad for not having the relationship you wanted with your father, Bryson. You can be angry that he did the things he did to you. You can be hurt that you never got to tell him how you felt about him. And you can be relieved that you'll never have to face him again, you'll never have to deal with his overbearing, manipulative ways again." Bryson's head fell, and she wrapped her arm around his shoulders. "You're allowed to feel everything, even if your emotions seem inconsistent with one another. Just feel them."

While Jordan had never experienced the loss of a parent to death, she'd grieved for her mother her entire life. Not that Grams hadn't been a mother figure to her, because her grandmother had given her everything she imagined her mother would if she'd been there. But it still hurt her to her core to know that her mother had just walked away and never looked back. As the years flew by, she'd ceased to remember her mother's voice, her smell, her smile. She had pictures, but they were locked away in a box because it gutted her to look at them.

"And know that I'm here for you if you need to talk," she added.

Bryson stood to his full height, and turned to her. He brushed the tips of his fingers over her mouth. Jordan wanted to push him away, because there was still so much they had to talk about. But she couldn't even think, let alone move. His smell wrapped around her, and her body—*that traitor*—had responded to him.

"Kiss me," he said.

"I don't think that's a good idea."

But she still didn't step away, or even push his hand away. Bryson leaned down and sealed his lips over hers, and she opened for him, letting him explore her mouth with his tongue and his teeth. She'd dreamed about his kisses, his hands, his . . .

"Jordie," he murmured against her lips, his voice raw with emotion, husky with desire.

The sound of the patio door opening behind them jerked Jordan from her haze and she backed away from Bryson. It was Carter.

When he noticed them standing out there, he froze, letting his gaze travel back and forth between them. "Oh, shit. I'm sorry."

"No, it's okay," she said. "I better go in and check on Maddie."

She started to walk away, but Bryson grabbed her arm. "Jordan, wait."

The soft plea in his eyes nearly did her in, but she gently pulled her arm from his loose grasp. "Bryson, I have to go."

He cleared his throat, and nodded. "Okay."

Jordan glanced at Carter, who was digging into the cooler, then back to Bryson. "I wanted to ask if you would mind stopping by the Bees Knees tomorrow morning. I want to talk to you."

A soft smile flashed across his face. "I can do that," he said.

"Okay. See you tomorrow."

Jordan hurried inside without looking back. She needed to breathe. She needed to get herself together because when they did finally talk, nothing would ever be the same again.

Chapter 10

"You need a joint."

Jordan blinked. "What?"

Stacyee had come into the Bees Knees for breakfast and to check on Granddad's progress. Her friend had been talking for about fifteen minutes about Lord knows what because Jordan hadn't been listening. Because all she could think about, *had* been thinking about, was Bryson.

"J, you know weed can be used for all types of medicinal purposes, including anxiety." Stacyee leaned in closer and added under her breath, "You know I have a hook-up. One of my clients is a—"

Jordan clapped her hand over Stacyee's mouth, and scanned the immediate area, grateful that none of the customers seemed to be paying attention. The last thing she needed was Grams or Granddad asking her if she was lighting up.

"Stace, you can't say stuff like that here. This is a place of business."

Her friend shrugged and took a sip of coffee. "Shoot, this is real life. And Wellspring is pretty

progressive. They even have a dispensary over by
Mr. Taylor's dry cleaners. And between me and you,
I think old man Taylor goes in there and gets him
some product every now and then."

Jordan laughed, covering her mouth when one of
the older gentlemen in the diner looked their way.
"Shut up, crazy girl. You are too much."

"I'm so serious. Anyway, you know I'm just kidding with you. I know you don't smoke. I *was* right
about you, though. What is going on? What are you
so anxious about?"

"Just a lot on my mind," she told her friend.
Jordan guessed her behavior would seem rather odd
to Stacyee. Since she'd arrived at the diner that
morning, she'd spent an hour cleaning already
clean surfaces, moving things around that didn't
need to be moved.

Stacyee gripped her hand and squeezed. "I know.
I hate that Granddad is sick like this. When will he
get to come home?"

Initially, the doctors thought her grandfather
might be able to come home today, but she'd received a call from Grams that morning stating it
would be another few nights. Shrugging, Jordan
said, "At this point, we don't know. They tell us one
thing and then a few hours later, it's another thing."

The primary concern was treating the pneumonia. Because of that, the treatment for his prostate
cancer had to be postponed. From everything
Jordan had read about cancer, it was important to
treat it quickly, and she worried that the longer they
delayed treatment for the cancer, the greater the

possibility that it could grow and spread to other areas of Granddad's body.

"I swear, these doctors like to keep people dangling on a string," Staycee said. "It's a conspiracy. Keep people sick so they can get paid. I told you HIV was man-made, and the food we eat is contributing to the rise in cancer."

Stacyee was a bona fide conspiracy theorist, and a voracious reader. She knew a little about everything, had read the Bible and the Koran many times, and could speak to anything from the Illuminati to the probable Russian interference in the 2016 presidential election to the medicinal uses of marijuana.

"J, I told you that it's important to think holistically," Stacyee continued. "I have a book I want you to read. It talks about the food we're eating and how it contributes to the increase in documented mental illness. It's deep."

No, thanks. Not that Jordan didn't believe Stacyee. She actually did. But she wouldn't be able to read about it to save her life.

In high school, they'd started a book club and each of them got to pick the book of the month. Maddie had picked some smutty romance novel, complete with a smoldering couple on the front wrapped in flowing garments. Jordan had picked a thriller about a family of assassins trying to escape the life. And Stacyee? She'd picked a five-hundred-page book about the conspiracy surrounding the attack on the World Trade Center.

"I'll pass." She grinned at her friend and batted her eyelashes. "But I love you and your 'woke' self. Stay woke, girl."

Stacyee laughed. "You got jokes."

Jordan stuck her tongue out at her friend before she stepped over to the register to cash a customer out. Since Grams was spending most nights in Grand Rapids, Jordan had picked up the slack at the Bees Knees. The transition had been pretty seamless because she'd worked there since she was old enough to hold a broom. The cooks and waitstaff were loyal and loved her grandparents.

"So are you going to tell me why you're so anxious?" Stacyee asked when Jordan made her way back over to her.

Jordan thought about telling Stacyee about the baby. She needed to talk to someone other than Grams. She loved her grandmother, but if she had to hear about another home remedy to combat morning sickness or listen to her wax poetic about Jordan and Bryson getting married and walking off into the sunset, she was going to scream.

Sighing, Jordan leaned forward. "I hope you're ready to be a godmother come December."

Stacyee choked on the coffee she'd just sipped on. "What the . . . ? You're pregnant?"

Jordan nodded. "Yep. The doctors have confirmed it and I even saw the little one on an ultrasound."

Her obstetrician had given her the due date of December 21, and Jordan had cried like a baby. When she'd started the new year, she'd never imagined she'd be a mother before the year was out.

"Aw . . ." Tears filled Stacyee's eyes and her chin trembled.

"Please don't." Jordan pointed at her friend, bringing her index finger close to her friend's nose. "You're not seriously about to cry, Stace. If you drop one tear, I'm kicking you out."

Stacyee pursed her mouth together and looked to the ceiling. When she glanced at Jordan again, her face was void of the emotion that had been there a few seconds ago. Sighing, Stacyee said, "You can't drop something like that on me and then expect me to be my normally stoic self."

"I need you to be the Stacyee I've always known. Believe me, I've cried enough to last me several years since I found out."

"When did you find out? And . . ." Stacyee gasped. "We had wine. A lot of wine."

Jordan had already talked to her doctor about their wine-down days at the salon, and was assured she should be fine. "I know. I already disclosed that to the doctor."

"I'm going to assume it's Bryson's baby."

"It is."

"So, have you told him?"

Jordan shook her head. "I saw him, but I just couldn't say anything. His father died, for heaven's sake. What was I supposed to do? Blurt it out over the casket?" She didn't bother telling her friend about the private moment on the deck last night. Jordan was a firm believer in only sharing need-to-know information.

"What are you going to do?"

"He's supposed to be coming here today. I do know they had a private burial this morning." Jordan glanced at her watch. "He should be here soon."

Stacyee leaned back in her chair. "Wow, J. This is deep. If anyone got pregnant, I thought it would be Maddie."

"Right." Jordan agreed.

"How are you feeling?"

"I'm happy I haven't thrown up today. So, that's something."

Over the last few days, Jordan had vomited each morning around the same time. It didn't even seem to take much to get her to expel whatever was on her stomach. It could be the smell of mustard on a sandwich she was serving, or the taste of the salt on a cracker. There was no rhyme or reason to her sickness at that point.

"And look at these things." Jordan pulled the bottle of prenatal vitamins out of her apron pocket and set them on the table. "They're huge. I can barely get them down."

"Any other symptoms?" Stacyee asked, studying the bottle.

"My boobs are on fire," Jordan replied. "And I've been having the weirdest, craziest dreams."

"Ooo. Do tell."

Jordan's cheeks burned. "You don't want to know."

She'd dreamed of her night with Bryson for the past few nights. It would always start out the same way, with them walking along the Santa Monica Pier, but each night she'd have a different food in her hand. The first night it was a pretzel covered in nacho cheese. The second night it was a bowl of vanilla ice cream with hot fudge, nuts, and pickles. And last night it was a large vat of Juicy Juice and beets.

"I think I have an idea," Stacyee said, waggling her eyebrows. "You're sprung."

"I am not," Jordan argued. "It's probably because he was the last guy I was with."

"Or because you still want him?"

Jordan rolled her eyes. "Whatever. You haven't seen him yet. He's not like the Bryson you remember."

The bell above the door chimed, and as if they'd talked him up, Bryson stepped into the diner. *Shit.* He was glorious, every single inch of him. She wanted to touch him; with her finger she wanted to trace the muscles she knew were underneath his clothes. He was dressed in a pair of charcoal gray slacks and a black shirt, unbuttoned at the collar like he'd just removed his tie.

"Damn," Stacyee murmured. "You weren't lying. That man is fine as hell."

Bryson spotted her and smiled, his dimple on full display. Jordan clenched the dish towel in her hand. *That is an understatement.*

"He even smiles good. Your baby is going to be so adorable." Jordan pinched Stacyee. "Ouch." She swatted Jordan's hand away.

He stepped closer, his eyes locked on hers. Soon, Bryson was standing in front of them, the wide grin still on his face. "Hey," he said, tugging Jordan into a warm but quick hug. "Stacyee Lewis." He hugged her friend. "It's good to see you again."

Stacyee pulled back, her lips parted. "Wow, Bryson." She shrugged. "You look . . ." Jordan never thought she'd see the day Stacyee was at a loss for words. Her friend had always been able to articulate, even in the most stressful of situations, even when she was going through divorce at age twenty-two because her no-good ex-husband was caught smuggling drugs. "Great."

"You do, too," he told Stacyee.

Jordan eyed her friend, who was now blushing, in disbelief. "Do you want coffee, Bryson?" Jordan asked.

He nodded and took a seat at the breakfast bar. "Sounds good."

Stacyee finally snapped out of her Bryson haze and sat back down in the seat next to his. "I'm sorry about your father," Stacyee told Bryson.

Jordan had been so caught off guard by Bryson once again that she'd forgotten the bottle of prenatal vitamins on the counter. She rushed over to the counter to grab it but Stacyee swiped the bottle up first and tossed it into the bag hanging on her chair.

Jordan thanked Stacyee in her head and with her eyes, and her friend smiled, signaling she'd received the message. With shaky hands, Jordan filled Bryson's mug with coffee. "Cream or sugar?"

"Black," he said.

Jordan set the coffeepot on the counter. "I'm glad you came."

He eyed her over the rim of his mug. "Me, too."

Smiling, she busied herself checking out a few customers while Bryson and Stacyee caught up. When the afternoon hostess arrived for her shift, Jordan took her apron off and told Hailey she was taking a break.

"My first appointment of the day is in an hour," Stacyee said. "I better get going. It was good to see you again, Bryson."

Bryson stood and gave Stacyee a quick hug. "Good to see you, too."

When he turned back to face Jordan, she looked

behind him at Stacyee, who mouthed "Call me" before she dashed out of the diner.

"Want to have a seat?" Jordan asked, motioning to a corner booth.

"Lead the way," he said, grabbing his mug.

Once they were settled in, she took a deep breath. The entire speech she'd planned had evaporated from her mind just like that and she found herself struggling with how to tell him the big news. Somehow telling him he'd knocked her up didn't feel right. And telling him she was with child felt old.

He placed a hand over hers. "Are you okay? You look a little pale."

Jordan zoomed in on his hand on top of hers. Even his hands were sexy. Her mind flashed back to the dream she'd had last night, the one with the vat of juice and beets. They were bathing in the juice, and she was loving the attention he paid to her body. So much that she'd stop eating the beets to let him do her over and over again.

"Jordan?" he called, jerking her back to the present. "Talk to me."

Jordan clasped her knees together, and placed a hand over her rolling stomach. "Bryson," she said. "There's something I need to tell you."

He leaned forward. "You can just say it, ya know? You can tell me anything."

"I'm pregnant."

Pregnant.

Pregnant? Bryson met Jordan's gaze. "What?"

Blood rushed to his ears, and he sucked in a deep breath. He sat back, floored by her quiet admission. Bryson heard what she'd said, but he needed her to repeat it. He needed to hear it again to know that it was true.

"I know what you're probably thinking," she said, a desperate tone in her voice. "Believe me, I thought the same thing. Especially since I did take the morning-after pill. I did. I promise."

Of that, Bryson had no doubt. He knew that Jordan took the pill. It wasn't in her nature to be dishonest or manipulative. Perhaps, if it was someone else telling him she was pregnant with his child, he might feel another way. "Jordan, don't. You don't have to do that. How long have you known?"

"I found out the day they rushed Granddad to the hospital, the same day . . ."

"Senior died," he finished. "You didn't tell me."

"I couldn't bring myself to tell you. You were going through so much, and I didn't think it was the best time to drop this on you." She chewed on her bottom lip and rocked slightly in her seat. "I'm sorry. I know this is probably not something you wanted to hear, especially now. I don't expect you to drop everything and move here for this baby. I'm willing to do whatever it takes to keep you involved in the baby's life, if you want to."

Instantly, countless images flashed through his mind. He should be terrified. He should be angry. They did use protection and when that failed, she'd taken the morning-after pill. But no . . . all he could think about was her stomach full with his child, seeing his son or daughter for the first time, teaching him or her how to ride a bike, or helping his child with a kick-ass science fair project. Bryson thought about first words, first steps, and first dates.

Jordan called to him softly. "Bryson?"

He blinked. "Huh?"

"Are you going to say anything?" She twisted a piece of her hair around her finger before releasing it. "What do you want to do?"

"Do?"

"Yes, about the baby."

"You're not thinking of getting rid of the baby, are you?"

"No." She shook her head rapidly. "I would never do that. I'm keeping the baby."

He nodded. "Okay."

"Okay," she repeated. "I hate to put you on the spot, especially when you haven't had any time to think about this. But can you tell me what you think you want to do as far as custody or parenting time?"

"Jordan, yes, the timing is off. We haven't seen each other in a long time, but I can't help but think this is a sign. I want this baby," he told her. "With everything in me."

She sagged against the back of the booth and let out a shaky breath. "Good. Because I don't particularly want to do this alone."

For a moment, he considered proposing. But that was only a shotgun reaction to the circumstances, and she wouldn't go for it. That much he was sure of. Yet, last night on Parker's deck, she'd been there for him. She'd given him understanding, comfort. Even though she was going through her own shit, dealing with Granddad's illness and finding out she was pregnant, she'd pushed herself to the side to be there for him.

After she'd left, he'd made a decision to talk to her about trying. He hadn't fooled himself into thinking they were going to fall in love or even last past the first few weekend visits he'd planned on proposing to her. But he couldn't stop thinking about her. He couldn't stop dreaming of her smell, her laugh. And that was all before he knew she was carrying his child.

"Jordie, I don't want this baby to grow up like I did."

"I know. I feel the same way. Not about how you grew up, but just in general. I want our baby to have a good life with two parents who love her."

"Her?"

A whisper of a smile tugged at her lips and he found himself wanting to pull her onto his lap so he could kiss her. "I don't know. When I think about the baby, I keep imagining a little girl."

Bryson let himself dream of a little girl with golden brown skin, doe eyes, and big curls. Just like her mama. "She would be beautiful."

Jordan blessed him with a full grin then, and his chest seemed to crack open. "I think so, too."

"I agree with you," he said. "I want our baby to feel love from both parents and the only way we can do this is by working together."

"Yes." She nodded rapidly. "I completely agree. We get along, and we respect each other. That is a good start for any baby entering the world."

Bryson was sure that his next words would put a halt to the understanding they'd just had. Clearing his throat, he forced himself to focus. He needed to get this out. "I'm glad you agree because I would really like to do this under one roof, Jordan."

Jordan blinked. "Excuse me?"

"Yeah. I think we should move in together."

Her mouth fell open. "Wait, what?"

"Just hear me out," he told her. "The baby is going

to come before we know it. I want to be there for all the firsts. I want her to know me."

"But you live in California. And I can't leave my grandparents."

"We'll figure it out. We have always worked well together."

"Yeah, in high school. It's been years since we've spent any real time together."

"But we just kind of slipped back into Jordan and Bryson mode."

She sighed. "Bryson, this is not going to work. I understand that you want to be a part of the baby's life, and I appreciate that. But moving in together? That's crazy."

"You're having my baby."

"Yeah, I am. But this isn't the fifties. We don't have to live under the same roof to co-parent a child."

"What about us?"

"What about us?" she tossed back. "We shared one amazing night, and it resulted in this baby." Jordan pressed her hand against her stomach. "I can't regret that, just like I don't regret the night we shared. But we're not a couple. Not even close. We're friends and that alone will give this baby everything she needs to thrive in life."

"What if I can't do the friend thing? What if I want more?" he asked softly.

"Did you want more before you found out I was carrying your baby?"

"I did kiss you last night, Jordie."

"A kiss is not a relationship. Sex is not a relationship. For all we know, we're not compatible."

"I don't want to not explore this," he said.

"I can't do more. It's just too much for me right

now. I'm barely getting through the day, I'm so worried about Granddad. And now I'm pregnant. This"—she motioned back and forth between them—"is too complicated. Can't we just focus on the baby right now? Baby steps, Bryson."

He laughed. As much as he hated to admit it, she was right. But that didn't stop the twinge of hurt that he felt at her rejection. "Fine. When is your next appointment?"

"Four weeks. When are you going back to California?"

"I was supposed to leave Thursday." And Bryson would leave, all right. He needed to pack his shit and make arrangements to move back to Wellspring. Because . . . *this baby changes everything.*

Chapter 11

"You did what?" Brooklyn shouted.

Bryson and his sisters were seated in Parker's dining room awaiting the arrival of the attorney. The will reading would take place that afternoon. He scanned the shocked faces of his brother and sisters. It had been a day since Jordan had spilled the beans that he was going to be a father. He'd just shared the happy news with Brooklyn and Veronica.

"I asked her to move in with me," he repeated.

"Who does that?" Brooklyn said. "That is so stupid."

"Who's stupid?" Parker stepped into the room at that moment, carrying a tray of hors d'oeuvres. His brother set the tray in the middle of the table. "Bryson? Are you the stupid one?"

Bryson glared at his brother. "I'm not stupid. I just reacted."

Veronica giggled. "I know we don't know each other that well, but I agree with Brooklyn. That was seriously the wrong thing to do."

"What happened?" Parker asked.

"Bryson, you tell him. Because I can't." Brooklyn threw her hands up in the air in frustration.

Bryson scratched his neck. "Jordan's pregnant."

Parker's eyes widened. "With your baby?"

"Yes."

Brooklyn held her palm out to Parker and his brother pulled a bill out of his wallet and smacked it into her hand. "I told you," Brooklyn told Parker.

"You're betting on me now?" Bryson said incredulously.

"Yep," Brooklyn admitted. "And me and Kennedi won. I'll be sure to tell my dear sister-in-law to collect her winnings."

"Y'all make me sick," Bryson muttered. "Anyway, Jordan is pregnant and I'm okay with it."

"What did you do?" Parker asked.

"I asked her to move in with me."

Parker groaned and pinched the bridge of his nose. "What the hell? Who does that?"

"Me," Bryson said, jumping up and pacing the small room. "I did that shit, okay. I was caught up in the moment."

"So caught up that you forgot you lived in California?" Veronica asked.

Bryson shrugged. "Yes. No. I never forgot where I lived."

"How was that supposed to work exactly?" Parker asked.

"We didn't get to the logistics because she shut me down."

"Duh," Brooklyn said with a hard roll of her eyes. "You fucked that one up, brother."

Veronica placed a hand on top of his. "What was your thought pattern?"

The answer to that question was easy. The only thing he could think of when he'd heard the words was being with his baby, being with Jordan. He could admit he'd pushed her too hard and too fast, but he had meant it when he asked her to move in with him.

"I want to be in my baby's life," he explained. "And I want my child to know me. I want my child to trust me. And I want my child to love me because she knows that I'm always going to be there for her and support her through everything in her life."

Brooklyn turned to him then, tears in her eyes. "Bryson," she whispered. "I know you do. I get it. But asking Jordan to move in with you is not how you should have gone about this."

"She's right," Veronica said. "I don't know Jordan, but I know what I would do in her situation. A woman's worst fear is someone wanting to be with her out of obligation. And you asking her to move in with her is basically saying that now that she is having your baby, you want her close."

"I'm glad you didn't ask her to marry you," Parker said.

"God, that would have been a nightmare." Brooklyn shifted in her seat and turned to him. "I know Jordan. And while Veronica is right to a certain extent, I would be more concerned with asking Jordan to move in with you knowing her personal history with her mother."

Bryson sighed. *I fucked up.* "I didn't even think. I was just reacting to the news."

Jordan's mother left her at a very young age, and she'd once shared with Bryson that she suspected it had a lot to do with the fact that her mom and dad married *because* her mom had been pregnant with her. And the relationship went up in a blaze of glory because her mom wasn't ready to be a wife or a mother.

While it wasn't exactly the same situation, he could see why Jordan would feel apprehensive about it now. Jordan had made good points. They weren't a couple. And he'd been too tongue-tied and overwhelmed with the baby news to actually tell her what he'd been thinking when he'd arrived at the diner that morning. He'd wanted to explore them—*before* he even found out about their child.

"Yes, you have all these dreams for your kid," Brooklyn said. "Yes, you want to be better than Senior ever was, because he sucked as a father. He did irreparable and unforgiveable damage to all of us. And you want to be different than him. But, Bryson, you're already a hundred times better than him.

"I know it's going to be hard for you," Brooklyn added. "But you're going to have to give her some time. You just found out you're going to be a daddy. Let that soak in, get to know her again. Let things happen organically. Okay?"

Bryson nodded. "I can do that."

"What are you going to do?" Parker asked.

"I'm going back to L.A. Thursday, like I planned."

"And the baby?" Veronica asked.

"I'm going to make arrangements to move here," Bryson told them. "There is no way I'm going to be on the other side of the country and miss my baby growing up. No way. It's the last thing I wanted, but I have to believe that things happen for a reason."

The chime of the doorbell sounded and Parker rushed out to get the door.

Bryson looked at his sisters. "Go ahead and be happy, Brooklyn. Your attempt to look solemn doesn't fool me."

Brooklyn jumped out of her seat. "Oh my God! Yes!" She hugged him. "That's the best news ever. I'm so glad you're moving back."

Bryson chuckled. "Whatever."

Veronica squeezed his hand. "I think that's the stand-up thing to do. It already puts you miles ahead of our father."

The attorney, James York, entered the room with Parker. "Good afternoon," James said, taking a seat at the table.

Bryson didn't understand why they had to go through the formality of a will reading. He was wise enough to know that shit like that was only done in the movies for dramatic purposes. But Senior had specified that his children were to be present for a formal reading of the will, with no other people present. Brooklyn had argued against it, but Parker, ever the level-headed older brother, had stated that there was no harm in doing it Senior's way for the last time.

"If you don't mind, we can just get right to it," James said. "It shouldn't take long."

James glanced up at all of them before he started to read. The will started out normal enough, with the statutory language required, but it didn't take long to veer off in a direction only Senior had ordained.

"'I devise and bequeath my property, both real and personal and wherever situated, as follows,'" James read. "'To my son, Parker Wells Jr., I leave your grandfather's watch. It was his wish for you to have it.'"

James continued his reading of the will, outlining Senior's gifts for Parker, which surprisingly did not include shares of Wellspring Water Corp. Bryson figured that had a lot to do with the fact that Parker and Jordan already held controlling interest in the company because of their mother, Marie.

When Marie died, she'd owned the largest number of shares for the corporation, which was the reason Senior had forged her will. Over the last year, Parker and Brooklyn had been fighting to get the forged will overturned and had recently won the case.

Next was Veronica. In a surprise twist, Senior had left Veronica all of his shares of Wellspring Water Corp., which amounted to twenty percent ownership of the company.

"'For my daughter, Brooklyn,'" James continued.

"I don't understand," Veronica interrupted. "What about Bryson? Shouldn't he get the shares of the company?"

James glanced at Bryson before turning to Veronica. "I can't speak to Parker Wells Sr.'s motivations. But I'll ask that you let me finish before you ask any more questions."

Bryson didn't need him to finish to know what was coming next. The weight in his stomach seemed to get heavier as James read that Brooklyn was to get their grandmother's wedding ring and a large endowment for the foundation of her choice.

"'For my son, Bryson Wells,'" James read. "'Since you've spent your life trying to get as far away from me and my name as you could, I hesitated on leaving you anything. However, I hereby leave you the sum of one million dollars, to be paid upon one condition.'" The attorney shifted uncomfortably in his seat before continuing. "'You must reside in my home for one year. If you meet this condition, you will receive the sum of one million dollars and the home.'"

Parker sighed. "James, that's ridiculous. Why would Senior do that? Bryson, you can object. Don't worry about it."

Bryson's pulse sped up and his heart pounded in his chest. Closing his eyes, he said, "No." Then, he met his brother's concerned gaze. "You can't fight this battle for me." Bryson turned to James. "What happens if I don't take this offer?"

Taking the offer wasn't even an option for Bryson. Even with Senior dead, Bryson could not imagine ever stepping foot into that house and calling it a home. Because it was never *his* home. No amount of money would change that. Bryson had been content in his life, happy with his accomplishments. And he would continue living his life the way *he* saw fit.

James swallowed visibly. "If you choose not to meet this condition, you will receive nothing."

The loud gasps and curses from his sisters and brother filled the room. For a moment, he wasn't sure why the provision had surprised anyone in the room. They'd all been victims of Senior's sadistic ways.

Bryson flexed his fingers and rolled up his sleeves as anger washed over him—anger at Senior for playing God over his life and anger at himself for letting that man get to him. Even from the grave, Senior was still trying to pull their strings, dictate their choices. He barked out a bitter laugh. "Figures." He stood up abruptly, tipping his chair on its back. "I'm out of here. I don't want or need anything from Senior. That house can burn to the ground and join Senior in hell."

Without another word, Bryson stormed out of the house.

Hours later, he found himself knocking on Jordan's door. When she opened the door, she had a wide smile on her face. Bryson half expected her smile to fade when she saw him, considering their last interaction. But her grin was still there and she was radiant, beaming.

"Come in," she said.

"I'm sorry to just drop by. I was hoping we could talk."

Her smile wilted. "Is everything okay?"

"It's fine."

Jordan clasped her hand to her chest. "My grand-dad came home today," she told him. "We were just getting ready to sit down for dinner."

He retreated back a step. "Never mind then. I don't want to intrude."

She tugged him forward. "No. Stay."

That word on her lips . . . *damn*. She wanted him to be there, she wanted him to share in their welcome home dinner. He found himself nodding his response and following her deeper into the house.

The Clarks lived in a small, Craftsman-style home on five acres of land. The family owned several buildings in town and had amassed a small fortune leasing to businesses in town. Granddad had told Bryson a long time ago that living simply is a surefire way to keep money in the bank. Bryson had remembered that lesson throughout his life, rarely splurging on frivolous things.

Learning that Senior had made living in the house of horrors a provision for receiving money had infuriated Bryson. But that was the way his father had lived. Senior believed that money could solve anything or buy anyone. And Bryson just didn't agree.

Bryson's grandpa had left them all a sizable trust that would become fully accessible when each grandchild turned thirty. His father had often held that fact above his head because Bryson could have received a monthly allotment if he'd stayed and lived life on Senior's terms. When Bryson made the choice to leave, he'd walked away from guaranteed easy living. And he didn't regret a single struggle, because it had made him stronger. Bryson wasn't destitute. He really didn't need Senior's money. He'd made a few savvy investments at his young age that allowed him to live comfortably.

But the will had been Senior's final act of control, his final rejection of him. He'd essentially thrown down the gauntlet, and Bryson would either have to bend to his will or walk away—again—with nothing.

"Bryson! My main man!" Granddad limped over to him and pulled him into a strong embrace.

"Granddad!"

The older man gripped Bryson's shoulders when he pulled back and gave him the once-over. "You're all grown up now. Good to see you, son."

"I'm glad to see you're walking around and

smiling. We were worried when we heard about your illness."

"No pneumonia or cancer can keep me down."

Will Clark had always been strong, a force to be reckoned with. Bryson spent a lot of time with Granddad at the Bees Knees back in the day, after school. The man had taught him how to budget and change a tire.

Seeing the man who'd treated him so well walk with a limp was jarring. Bryson knew Granddad was sick, but he didn't expect him to look so small and frail. Granddad had lost a lot of weight, and he looked tired.

"I never thought it could," Bryson told him. "You're a fighter."

"That's right," Granddad said.

Dinner was a special treat—fried catfish, greens, pinto beans, and cornbread. Bryson hadn't eaten a good home-cooked meal like this since the last time he'd visited Remy's mother for Thanksgiving. But nobody could cook like Grams. Bryson felt like he was at home.

Grams kept the conversation moving, telling stories about crazy customer names and kitchen mishaps. After the afternoon he'd had, he didn't expect to laugh so hard. Sitting there with them had lifted a weight off of his shoulders. For a few hours at least.

"I'm going to clean up the kitchen," Grams said, pushing away from the table.

"I'll get the dishes, Grams." Bryson picked up her empty plate and set it on top of his. "You go ahead and relax."

Grams gave him a warm smile. "Thanks, Bryson. I appreciate that."

Grams walked over to Granddad. "Want to lie down, hun?"

"Don't mind if I do," Granddad said. It took Granddad a few minutes to stand but when he did, he waved at Bryson. "Bye, son. Don't be a stranger."

"I won't," Bryson assured him. "I'll definitely drop by to check on you."

"You don't have to wash the dishes, Bryson," Jordan said, when her grandparents disappeared around the corner. "I can take care of it."

"I want to. It's the least I can do for this slammin' dinner." Bryson gathered the rest of the dishes and got to work. Jordan joined him a few minutes later.

"You rinse, I'll load," Jordan said. "Grams is very particular about how her dishwasher is loaded. If it's not right, I'll hear about it."

He chuckled. "I would hate to get you in trouble."

They washed in silence, making quick work of the task. Once the dishwasher was loaded, Jordan cleaned off the table and counters while Bryson swept the floor.

Minutes later, they were outside, sitting on the cement patio off the kitchen. The Clarks had some of the most beautiful land in the county, full of lush trees, green grass, and plenty of planted flowers.

"Are you going to tell me what happened?" Jordan asked.

Bryson glanced at Jordan. The lights on the patio combined with the moonlight bathed her in a warm glow. "Today was the reading of the will."

"Really?" She tucked her legs under her bottom. "What happened?"

"Exactly what I expected."

Bryson gave Jordan the quick version of the events of the day. When he was done, Jordan was staring at him with wide eyes. "That's awful."

"It's Senior. No reason to expect anything different."

"What are you going to do?"

"I don't need the money. The house can be torn down or turned into a shelter. Anything."

"That's a lot of money to leave on the table, Bryson. Even if you don't need it, someone else does. A million dollars can do a lot of good in the community."

Bryson observed her. Was it too much to hope that she wanted him to stay? Up to this point, he hadn't told her of his intention to move to Wellspring. They hadn't gotten that far yesterday. The only thing they'd decided was that he would be a part of the baby's life.

He grinned her way. "Are you telling me that because you want me to stay?"

A pretty blush crept up her cheeks and she averted her gaze. "I'm saying money like that is nothing to balk at."

"I just don't think I can live in that house, Jordie. Too much has happened there."

She picked up his hand and squeezed. "Let's go."

Bryson stood. "Where are we going?"

"For a ride. I'll drive."

Bryson let Jordan lead him out of the house, suddenly realizing that he would go with her anywhere and everywhere, any time and every time.

Chapter 12

Jordan pulled up in front of Bryson's childhood home, and glanced at her passenger out of the corner of her eye. Set on a hill, the mansion was hard to miss. It was the biggest home in Wellspring. "You ready?" she asked.

"What are we doing here?"

"You trust me?"

He nodded. "Yes. But, Jordie, I haven't been to this house in almost a decade. I don't want to go in there."

She shifted in her seat, and turned to him. "Bryson, I know today was hard for you. But I want you to see the positive in this situation. That's why I brought you here."

Jordan wouldn't pretend to know how Bryson felt in that very moment, but she hoped she could get him to see that he could turn things around for good. She slowly pulled into the driveway and parked the truck.

She'd chosen Granddad's pickup truck to drive, because she knew the tools she needed were in it.

When Bryson hopped out, she rushed to the back and pulled out a big bag.

Bryson hurried over to her and took the bag from her. "I got this."

"I'm pregnant, not an invalid," she muttered.

He shot her a skeptical look. "What are you up to? If you wanted to be alone with me, all you had to do was ask."

Jordan laughed. "Please, you wish."

They stared at the massive estate for a few minutes. "I don't know if this is a good idea, Jordie."

"It will be okay. I promise. Come on." She grabbed his hand and pulled him toward the door.

Jordan had listened as Bryson told her about the reading of the will, and it broke her heart. The hurt in his voice had done something to her, made her ache with him. She wanted to give him a purpose, something to look forward to, even in the midst of the pain.

After their conversation yesterday at the diner, she hadn't known what to do. He'd scared the shit out of her when he'd asked her to move in with him. But after they'd parted ways, she soon realized that what terrified her the most was not that he'd asked her, but that she'd actually considered it—for a moment.

On the porch, Bryson pulled the set of keys they'd picked up from Parker on their way to the house. He unlocked the door, and they stepped in. A light was on in the hallway, and she trekked through the house, peeking in the rooms. When she realized Bryson was not behind her, she turned. He was still standing at the door.

Approaching him, she said, "This won't work if you just stand there like a log."

The bag in his hand hit the floor with a loud thud. "Jordie, I appreciate what you're trying to do, but it's not necessary. I'm not going to move in here just because Senior put a stupid provision in his will."

Jordan searched his eyes. "Bryson, look at this house." She gestured to the opulence around them. Senior's decorators had made the place look like a showroom. A domed ceiling and a double staircase made the entrance grand. The elegant chandelier and the marble floor completed the classic look. There were expensive pieces of art on the walls, priceless vases and antique pieces displayed throughout the area, and top-of-the-line furniture. It was worth way more than the one million dollars. "How many bedrooms?"

"Eight," he answered, no emotion in his voice.

"Wow! That's a lot of rooms."

Jordan had only been to the house once. Bryson had brought her there one time when he'd thought Senior was out of town. They were studying for a project when Senior arrived home early and proceeded to berate Bryson for daring to bring "that girl" into the house.

It was common knowledge in town that there was no love lost between her grandparents and Senior. But she'd been taken aback by his behavior and immediately called her grandfather to pick her up. When Granddad had arrived, he and Senior had words before he escorted her off the property. It was a tense ride home, but when they'd pulled up at their house, Granddad had turned to her and warned her to stay away from Senior, that he was not to be trusted under any circumstance.

"Where's Senior's office?" she asked.

Bryson let out a humorless chuckle. "I'm not going in there."

"You said you trusted me, right?"

He picked up the heavy bag. "Fine. Come on."

Jordan couldn't help but be amazed at the house. It was a work of art. Residential architecture and real estate was a hobby of Jordan's. She loved looking online at various homes. It was something she did to wind down, to escape from life. When she lived in Detroit, she would often visit the huge brick homes in the city during open houses just to get a look inside. She'd imagine coming in and gutting the homes and restoring them to their glory.

Although she'd planned to go to law school, Jordan had purposefully chosen to get her undergraduate degree in business administration as well as a real estate license. She'd hoped to gain experience as an agent, while working toward her Juris Doctor. In her mind, it was the best of both worlds. She could study law and work on a passion of hers. Before Granddad got sick, she'd already contacted an agency to do part-time work. And looking around the massive home she was standing in, her mind was racing with all types of ideas on how to turn the place around and brighten it up.

The office was a direct contrast to the rest of the house. It was dark, cold. Jordan hugged herself as she walked around the space. It was bigger than her last apartment, with wood paneling on the walls and a huge desk in the middle of the room.

Bryson set the bag down on a sofa, and Jordan

unzipped it and pulled out the sledgehammer that Granddad always kept in his magic bag, as he called it.

"We have a lot to discuss, you and me," she said. "But one thing that you told me yesterday stuck with me. I thought about it all day. You said that you wanted to be there for our kid. You don't want our child to grow up like you did."

"Right, but I meant that I—"

She placed her hand over his mouth. "Let me finish." When she was satisfied that he wouldn't interrupt her again, she removed her hand from his mouth. "I suspect that your desire to be there for our child has a lot to do with Senior. You want to be better than him."

"He sucked," Bryson admitted on a sigh. "I don't want to be that type of father."

"You won't be. I know that."

"How do you know that?"

"Because, even though we haven't seen each other in years, I don't think I've misjudged your character. The Bryson I knew was already ten times better than Senior. If you're worried about being like him, don't."

With a tight set of his jaw, Bryson growled, "That still doesn't mean I want to live in the house where I felt unloved and unwanted for the entire time I was here."

Jordan surveyed him. In the few minutes since they'd arrived at the house, there was a visible change in Bryson's demeanor. Anger had replaced the elation he'd displayed earlier over their baby. Instead of the dimpled smile that she'd grown to love, he wore a scowl that seemed to take over every inch of his face.

She squeezed his arm, noting the way his muscles jumped under his skin. He was tense, filled with anguish, dread, and hatred for the man that had made his life miserable. And Jordan hated to see him that way. She didn't want Bryson to give Senior a minute more of his life.

"Bryson, look at me." When his eyes met hers, she said, "The house is just a shell. The building doesn't make this a home. The people inside do." She placed a hand over his heart. "Just like your heart makes you nothing like your father."

He leaned his forehead against hers, and she pulled him into a hug. They stood like that for a while, holding each other. Finally, rearing back, she gripped his chin in her hand. "I know you don't want to live here, Bryson. But I would hate to see you walk away because that's what Senior expected you to do. Don't let him win. Make this house what it should have been all along. A house of love, understanding."

Jordan gave Bryson the sledgehammer and stepped back.

He held it up. "What's this for?"

She motioned to the room. "What do you think? Tear this shit up."

"What day is your next appointment?" Bryson asked Jordan, taking a handful of the microwave popcorn she was munching on. They were lying on the floor in the television room, after destroying Senior's office.

Bryson had never felt so close to a person who was not his sibling or Remy. She'd actually handed him the sledgehammer and cheered when he'd pounded the wall, crashing the metal head into the oversized picture of Senior on the wall. She'd even made up a little song while he was demolishing the room, and did a little dance every time he flipped over a piece of furniture. It was therapeutic, pulling the wood panels off the walls and crushing the huge oak desk in the middle of the room.

"I have a twelve-week appointment on June 8."

"I want to be there." He turned to her. "You don't mind, do you?"

She glanced at him before turning her attention back to the ceiling. "I wouldn't expect anything different from you, Mr. Move-In-With-Me Wells."

He laughed. "It wasn't my best moment, but it wasn't my worst either."

"Jury is still out on that."

"Have you told anyone about the baby yet?"

"My grams and Stacyee. You?"

Bryson told her that he'd shared the news with his siblings, and he also told her what Brooklyn's response was. After Jordan stopped laughing, he said, "Jordie, I hope you know that when I came to the diner I was going to ask you if you wanted to . . . see each other."

She leveled him with an incredulous stare. "What?"

Shrugging, he said, "That kiss on the deck . . . It was good."

"Oh God, Bryson," she said. "You can't say things like that."

"Why?"

"Because it just makes this more complicated."

"It's the truth."

Turning on her side, she asked, "How were you going to propose we did that?"

"Weekend visits, something. I just knew I wanted to see you again." He reached out and rubbed her cheek, loving that her eyes fluttered closed. "You're so beautiful."

"Stop," she giggled, burying her head into the pillow he'd tossed on the floor for her to use.

"It's true."

"You're just saying that because I rocked your world that night in Santa Monica."

Bryson chuckled. "That's true, too." They'd had the best sex of his life that night. And Bryson wanted a repeat. *Or two. Or three.*

"Seriously, Bryson. We connected well in the bedroom, but we don't really know each other anymore."

"We do know each other."

"We *knew* each other," she argued. "There's a big difference. You don't know simple things about me. Why do I hate beans?"

"You hate beans because Granddad made you eat them for lunch all the time. Pork 'n beans and hot dogs. And now you don't eat any type of bean."

Jordan averted her gaze as a blush worked its way up her neck. "Except green beans. I love those," she grumbled.

"See, I do know you."

"Okay, so I told you that story. But you don't know what my new dreams are, why I want to be a lawyer. My experiences in the military, in college, in relationships . . . they've shaped me into the woman I am now. I'm not the same person I was when you left."

"Jordie, life shapes you, yes. But you're still you.

That hasn't changed. You're competitive, you laugh with your entire body, you tug on your ear when you're nervous, you're one hell of a friend, and you're still the smartest woman I know. You love with everything in you, even though you haven't always received it in return, even when you've been hurt. The years apart haven't changed the fact that you're one of the most important people in my life. Yes, there are little things that I probably don't know. But my point is, I *want* to know them."

Jordan glanced up at him. "What if I'm not the woman you've built me up to be?"

"Somehow I doubt that. But that's the entire point of dating. To spend time together, to get to know each other on a different level."

Jordan smirked and pushed at his shoulder. "You're bringing this conversation down, Bryson. I thought this night was supposed to be about you. Not us."

"Okay, okay. I'm done." He lifted his arms in surrender. "I won't push you."

"Can I ask you something?"

"What is it?" he asked.

"Why did you leave the way you did? Why didn't you call me or write me?"

Bryson knew that leaving town hurt his siblings, but he hadn't stopped to think about what it had done to his friends. Jordan had been a true friend to him, and he'd walked away from her, too.

"I honestly thought I would die if I stayed," he told her. "Senior was a monster. I didn't understand how one person could be so damn evil. The ruthless businessman was a ruthless father, a terrorizer. It wasn't just verbal or emotional. It was physical."

She gasped. "You never told me."

"It wasn't the easiest thing to admit. None of us said anything. Parker protected me as much as he could. But when Parker wasn't there, I didn't have that same protection. It wasn't until Parker fought back that Senior chilled out a little."

"I'm sorry." She cradled his cheek in her hand. "I would have told Granddad had I known. Maybe he could have intervened."

"It would have only made it worse."

"When you left, it hurt me. I thought we were better friends than that. I hate feeling abandoned. My mother left me with no word, and it just . . . It sucks."

"Have you ever thought about trying to find her?"

"All the time," she said with a shrug. "But I've never actually hired the private investigator."

"Why?"

"Because. Why should I spend money and time searching for someone who didn't think I was worth more than a three-line note? I'm her daughter. The least she could do is try to find me, which isn't hard, by the way. Grams and Granddad have lived in the same house for years. There is really no excuse."

Bryson let her words sink in. They really did have a lot in common. He guessed some of her fears mirrored his own. Both of them had suffered rejection from their parents that had lasting effects on their lives and relationships.

"I'm sorry, Jordie. I should have kept in touch with you. But I'm here now."

"For how long?" she asked.

Forever. He laced his fingers through hers, pleased when she curled her fingers around his. The hurt she felt was written on her face, in her beautiful green eyes. The armor she usually wore was crumbling. She'd let him in with her admission and he knew that was hard for her to do. Today was the first day she'd really let her guard down and he loved it.

"Jordie, I had already planned to move back, even before the will reading."

"You were?"

"I told you, I'm going to be here for you and the baby."

"I just don't want our child to get used to seeing you, then you decide to leave again."

"I would never leave our baby." *I'll never leave you.* Bryson wanted to lay all his cards on the table, but Jordan wasn't ready to hear it. That much was clear. She'd opened up to him, and that would have to be good enough for now.

"What do you want to do with the house?"

He sighed. Jordan had effectively changed his mind about Wellspring *and* Senior's house. Righting some of Senior's wrongs might be just what he needed. The house was massive, with eight bedrooms, twelve full bathrooms, and three half baths. It made more sense to live there than buy another house in Wellspring. Bryson knew it wouldn't be easy, but he'd give it a try. And if he made it the year, he'd donate the money to charity.

"You're right," he told her. "I can turn this thing around. I'm going to hire a crew to come in and take all this shit out. Hire painters, buy new furniture, make this place more modern. I don't want anything left of Senior in this house. As for the office, I'm going to have that entire wing turned into a game room."

Senior's office was located in the back of the house, with stunning views of Wellspring and the Grand River. When they were kids, they'd begged Senior to build a pool in the backyard, but he'd told them a pool was a waste in Michigan. So Bryson would hire a company to design and install an in-ground pool in the backyard.

"Maybe I'll even put a few bowling lanes in that area," Bryson said.

She laughed. "That's overkill, don't you think?"

"I've always wanted my own personal alley."

"I didn't know you still bowled."

"Every week," he admitted, tucking a strand of her hair behind her ear. "I'm on a league with Remy."

"Oh, that's cool. Maybe we can go bowling one night. That'll be fun."

"Can you bowl?"

She shoved him playfully. "I can bowl. I can kick your ass in bowling."

"You can try," he teased. "But you don't stand a chance."

"Well, once I have this baby, I'll see you on the softball field."

"You still play?" he asked.

Jordan had been active in the community softball league and had been the star player for Wellspring High. Bryson had gone to every single home game to support her.

"I played on the military league my entire career, but I just kind of stopped when I came out. I do still go to the batting cages every so often to get a few hits in, but that's pretty much it."

"Brooklyn told me there's a place on the south side of town that had batting cages."

"Sport-o-Rama," she told him. "It's nice. I went there a few times on visits back to see Grams and Granddad."

"We can go there. I'd like to see it. Is Spring Bowl still here?"

Bryson had fond memories of the bowling alley. The owner had taught him a lot and even paid for him to enter several tournaments back in high school. Bryson's love of the game had propelled him to create a bowling team at the school.

She nodded. "It's been newly renovated, too. They turned that entire area into the fun zone."

Unable to help himself, Bryson reached out and traced her bottom lip with his fingers. "I'd really like to kiss you again." He leaned forward, bumping noses with her. "Say yes."

In a breathy whisper, she said the magic word and he brushed his lips over hers. She sighed against his mouth and he pulled her closer so she could feel just how much he needed her, how much he wanted her. *Shit.* She felt good. Everything about her made him want to do whatever it took to get a taste of her. He'd thought about being with her again every day. He'd dreamed of being with her again every night. He was drowning in her, but he couldn't bring himself to come up for air.

He trailed kisses over her collarbone, her neck, her cheek, before meeting her lips again in a hungry kiss. His hand slipped beneath her shirt, traced the waistband of her pants before unbuttoning them.

"Bryson," Jordan said, pulling away. "We can't do this."

Sighing, Bryson dropped his head to her shoulder. "Okay."

It took everything in him not to beg her to let him in. The need to be inside her made him feel crazed. But he'd take his time, give her some space. He fell onto his back, stared up at the light fixture above them, and focused on the brass and design. Anything to get his body under control.

"Bryson?" she called.

He looked at her. "Yes."

"I don't think it's a good idea to sleep together."

"Forever?"

Jordan giggled. "I can't say forever. But . . . while I'm pregnant, I feel like we should just concentrate on the baby. Adding sex to the equation might make things worse."

Bryson closed his eyes, and counted to ten. "If that's what you want," he grumbled.

Her fingers brushed his skin when she gripped his sleeve. "I think it's for the best."

"Jordan, I'll do whatever it takes to make this better for you."

"Thank you," she whispered. "You said you were leaving Thursday?"

He nodded. "I'll be back before the appointment, though. I have to give my job a sufficient notice, and pack up my condo."

"Are you going to sell it?"

Bryson hadn't thought about it, but he didn't see a reason to sell it. It wouldn't hurt to have a piece of property in California for when he visited. Or even to use as extra income. "I'll probably keep it."

She shot him a strange look. "Okay." Jordan stood up and brushed off her clothes. "I better get back home. I'm tired."

"Do you need anything before I go?" he asked.

Shaking her head, she said, "No. I'm fine."

"Can I ask you for a favor?"

Her eyes lit up. "What?"

"While I'm gone, I'm hoping a lot of the easy work will be done here. I'll ask Brooklyn and Parker to oversee the removal of Senior's stuff, but I could use your help with the decor. It will take years to collect enough furniture and stuff to fill up the house, but I'd like to at least have two bedrooms and a nursery identified."

"Don't you want to be here to figure this stuff out?"

He waved a hand in dismissal. "I don't need to be here. I trust you."

"If you're sure . . ."

"I'm sure." He brushed his lips over her brow.

The drive back to the Clarks' home was quiet. Bryson wanted to break the silence but he couldn't find the words. Jordan had made herself clear that she wanted to keep things friendly between them. He didn't agree, but he would respect her wishes. And wait. Because the woman next to him, focused on the road in front of them, did want him. It was in the way she looked at him, the way she responded to him. The only thing he could do was wait for her to come to him. And she would. Then there would be nothing that would stop him from making her his. *For good.*

Chapter 13

"Pregnant? What the hell, son?"

Ten minutes, five frames, and a pitcher of beer later, and those were the first words Remy had said to him since Bryson had delivered the happy news. He'd been back in California for two weeks, but had yet to talk to Remy, who'd been out of town on business.

"Thanks for the support, Remy," Bryson grumbled.

Remy sighed. "You know I got your back, son. I'm just shocked. You dropped a few bombs on me." Remy ticked off everything Bryson had told him that afternoon. "The will, the house, and a baby. That's a lot."

Bryson agreed with Remy. So much had happened in such a short time. "Things are definitely moving fast."

"You're moving back to Michigan after you vowed to never do that. To make matters even more complicated, you're going to be living in a house that you fought like hell to get away from. Are you sure this is what you want to do?"

"What else can I do, man? She's already pregnant. I'm not going to live on the other side of the country and miss out on my kid's life."

"I get it. Believe me, I do. I wouldn't suggest you leave your kid, son. You know that. I just . . . I'm . . . I don't know. In all the years I've known you, you've always been so obsessive about your fifteen-year plan and staying focused on your goals. And you went and got someone pregnant? Did you leave your brain *and* your condoms at home?"

Remy was absolutely correct. Bryson wasn't impulsive by a long shot. He'd planned out his entire twenties. To the letter. Undergraduate degree in environmental engineering. *Check.* Graduate degree in planning. *Check.* Home ownership. *Check.* The remaining years of his plan consisted of working, meaningless hook-ups, and traveling. Settling down with one woman and getting married were earmarked for his mid-thirties. And babies were the start of his midlife plan, and definitely not on the agenda prior to marriage.

"I didn't leave my brain or my condoms at home."

"Why aren't you more upset about this?"

Bryson wasn't upset at all. Shocked, maybe. Wary, definitely. But upset wasn't an emotion he'd felt regarding the baby. "Is there a reason I should be mad? Because I'm not upset. I'm actually okay with this. And like I told you before, I'm not going to abandon my child."

Remy studied him. "Or its mother. Son, I'm not sure who you think you're fooling. Because if this was any other woman telling you she was having your baby, you'd be falling-down drunk somewhere or breaking every piece of glass in your house. The only reason you're not is because it's Jordan. The pink dress syndrome."

Bryson laughed. "Whatever, man. You act like I've been pining over Jordan to the exclusion of every other female."

"Maybe not pining. But I watched you at the funeral. She's got you wrapped around her fingers, her toes . . . everything."

Throwing his towel at Remy, Bryson stood and picked up his bowling ball. "Fuck that. Don't play me like I'm some lovesick fool over her. I'm not whipped."

"Sheeiiiit."

"What the hell is that supposed to mean?" Bryson took his turn, grumbling a curse when he knocked all the pins down except one.

"I didn't stutter. One night with her, and you lost your damn mind. I wouldn't have believed it if I didn't see it with my own eyes. Every move she made, you followed."

"Have you seen her?" Bryson asked. "She's fine as hell."

Remy shrugged. "Good point. Actually, every woman I met in Wellspring was lovely. Did your daddy add something special to the water or something?"

Before Bryson could tell Remy he was crazy as hell, his phone vibrated. Frowning, he glanced at the screen. A smile tugged at his lips when he saw that Jordan had sent him a message. He quickly tapped the Messenger app.

Jordan: "I think I remember that you preferred black and white. No color. But gray is in. Okay?"

Bryson: "I like gray. Is that your choice for the walls?"

Jordan: "Pretty much. Even though, I'm tempted to paint one of the walls red."

Bryson: "Go for it."

Jordan: "Seriously?"

Bryson: "I told you . . . Do your thing. I trust you."

Bryson chuckled at the rainbow-colored GIF that Jordan sent in reply. Another text came shortly after. It was of her holding a variety of color swatches. He squinted at the screen. Who the hell invented emerald green paint?

Bryson: "Although I would prefer to not feel like I'm going to see the wizard when I walk into my house."

My house? When did Senior's house become his house? The thought sobered him, and made him want to break something. Just thinking about how his father had played him infuriated him. It had taken every ounce of restraint and willpower for him not to rip that damn will up and take a bulldozer to the house. The money didn't mean anything to him. But Jordan had made valid points. He would try to make it work, at least for the year. After that, all bets were off. It would help if Jordan moved in with him, if they could raise their child there together. Although she'd told him no, he wasn't giving up. Telling her to decorate two bedrooms and a nursery was his way of making sure she had a place to stay in the house when she changed her mind.

   Jordan: "Are you busy?"
   Bryson: "Bowling."

If he could call it that. Since they'd arrived at the alley, Bryson had yet to roll one strike, which was unlike him. He averaged 230 points per game, and he'd yet to hit 100 in the sixth frame.

   Jordan: "I want to show you something."
   Bryson: "Give me a sec."

Standing, Bryson tilted his chin toward the door, letting a smirking Remy know he was going out. His phone vibrated, signaling that Jordan was trying to video chat with him. Tapping the button, he waited for her face to appear. Bryson felt his chest tighten when Jordan waved at him, a goofy smile on her face.

"Hi," she said.

"Hey, Jordie."

Jordan's curls were swept up in a high, but messy bun. Other than the streak of paint on her cheek, her face was bare. She wore no heavy eye makeup or lipstick. Yet she was still the most beautiful woman he'd ever seen. "Bryson, I wanted you to see the wall."

And I want to see you.

He could hear people in the background. "Who's there with you?"

"I hired painters. Parker recommended a local company. They're very efficient. But I'm torn on the color scheme. And before you say anything, I know you told me to make the decision, but I thought it would be good to get your input. By the way, I would have never picked that emerald green color. Ew."

"Good." Bryson laughed. "I wasn't sure if you'd lost your love of neutral tones."

Jordan's mouth fell open. "Hey, I've evolved. I like a little color now."

And I like you.

"So, there are a lot of different grays and I want to be sure we're on the same page." She winked. "Okay?"

"Where are you going?" he asked when he noticed she was moving.

"Right here." She switched the view on her phone and soon he was staring at five big lines on a white wall. All were different shades of gray. "Damn, Jordan. That's a lot of gray."

"I know, right?" she said. "It's so hard to narrow it down. I've stared at this wall for an hour."

Even though he could no longer see her face, he envisioned her biting her lip in concentration. "I think I like the darker gray, the one on the far right."

"Me, too!"

Now turn the camera back around so I can see you. "So, it's settled?"

"No!" A few seconds later, Jordan's face was back on his screen. "I think you need an accent wall."

"What the hell is an accent wall?"

"Something to break up the gray, so that it doesn't look washed out in here. Something that shows your personality."

Bryson blinked. "I don't think I care about that stuff."

"You're such a man."

"I would hope so." Bryson smirked when a pretty blush spread over her cheeks. "Jordie, I told you, do what you want. I'm easy."

"You say that now, but when you come home, you might feel totally different."

"As long as it's not green, I don't care. Red, blue, brown . . . whatever you want."

Jordan looked skeptical. "Bryson . . ."

"I promise you I won't be upset."

She seemed to accept that, because she told him, "Fine. I'll keep going. Oh, I picked a buttercup yellow for the nursery."

"What about the other bedrooms?"

Jordan tapped her chin as if in deep thought. "How about I surprise you? Now that I know which gray you prefer, I think I can do this. Everything will flow."

"Is Brooklyn helping you?"

"Yes, she is. Actually, all of your siblings have been extremely helpful. I'm glad they're around."

"And you? How are you feeling?"

Jordan sighed. "I wish I could say it's been a piece of cake. My body is going through some serious changes. Things ache that I didn't know could ache. Like my elbow. Out of the blue my elbow started hurting the other day."

Bryson barked out a laugh. "You're silly. Maybe your elbow hurt because you slept on it wrong?"

"Well, how do you explain the aversion to eggs that ruined breakfast the other day? Grams made me an omelet and I couldn't eat it. Mind you, all day I had been thinking about it. But when she set it in front of me, I lost it. Barely made it to the bathroom."

"Wow. It's a sad day when you can't eat one of Grams's omelets. I've never had better."

"Tell me about it. But today is actually a good day. No vomit, no heartburn. I'm winning. How are you? You good?"

"I'm good." He smiled.

"It's probably hard to pack up and leave your life behind."

Surprisingly, it hadn't been hard for Bryson. It didn't feel like he was leaving anything behind. When he'd arrived back in California, he'd promptly given his notice to his employer and contracted a property management company for his condo. No hard feelings, no regrets. Bryson knew he was doing the right thing.

"It's not that hard."

Her eyes widened. "I don't know if I could do it."

"You did. You're back in Wellspring now."

"To help Grams and Granddad. It was never going to be permanent."

Bryson frowned. They'd never really talked about her plans to stay in Wellspring. "And now?"

"And now . . . I really can't imagine living anywhere else. Not in the immediate future. Besides, I would think wherever I go, you would have a say in that. Or at least, you would be vested in my decision."

Bryson let out a slow breath. "I definitely would, Jordie."

Jordan grinned. "Good. Well, I better let you go. I'm sure you're anxious to get back to your game. Bye, Bryson."

He wanted nothing more in that moment than to be with her, discussing paint swatches and bonding over the baby. Bryson wanted to go to sleep knowing that they were in the same house, and eventually the same bed. He wanted to make love to her through the night and kiss her awake in the morning. Every morning.

"Okay. Bye, Jordie."

Hanging up the phone, Bryson thought about the conversation he'd had with Remy before Jordan called. Bryson wouldn't give Remy the satisfaction, but his friend had been right. He wouldn't abandon his baby or his baby's mother. The more he talked to her, the more time he spent with her, he realized that his feelings for her hadn't dulled in the years they'd been apart. They'd been lying dormant, waiting for a chance to consume him again. Because she was all he could think about. His mind was tuned to the Jordan Channel. All day, every day. And he didn't want to change a thing.

Jordan had spent the better part of ten minutes trying to find pants that actually fit. It seemed her gut was expanding rapidly. *And so is my butt.* Everything she'd tried on made her feel like a cucumber. No curves, no shape. And her boobs? The things were busting out of her bra, spilling over the cup and straining the seams.

"Are you ready to go?" Maddie asked from her spot on Jordan's bed.

Her friend had come to take her shopping for new undies and bras. "I can't find anything to wear," Jordan whined. "I'm not even out of my first trimester and I'm blowing up like a house. Maybe I should call the doctor? I might be carrying an alien or something."

Jordan had researched every step of the pregnancy journey. She knew that at eleven weeks, her baby was the size of a fig and had human characteristics, like hands and feet. Fingernail beds were beginning to develop. Her little darling was already kicking and some of the little bones were starting to harden.

Now Jordan was hungry. For the past few weeks, she'd been nauseous and could barely keep good food down. Now she was ravenous and emotional. That morning, she'd cried over a stupid Cheerios commercial. And not just a lone tear, but full-on bawling like a baby, complete with tattered tissues and huge gulps of air because she felt like she couldn't breathe.

True to his word, Bryson had left town so that he could pack up his California life and move back to Wellspring. Jordan couldn't deny the warmth that spread in her gut when she thought of him moving closer to her.

They'd talked several times on the phone and sent texts throughout the day. Mostly, he was checking on her, making sure she had everything she needed. And she was texting him pics of the house and the changes going on inside. It was amazing what a little money would do. In less than three weeks, the house had been cleared out and repainted. She'd picked out several pieces of furniture for the living areas, including a new kitchen table and a huge sectional for the den. She'd also purchased a huge big-screen television.

Jordan had hired Angelia Hunt to help with the color scheme. Angelia had recently sold her shares of Hunt Nursery to Parker, and opened her own interior design company. When Jordan had met with her, she found that she'd liked her ideas. The plan was to brighten up the house, paint the walls in warm colors, and tear down the outdated wood walls that Senior seemed to have a proclivity for.

Jordan growled as she combed her closet looking for a pair of loose-fitting shorts and a tank top. "Maddie, I'm not going."

Maddie nudged her out of the way. "Sit down. Yes, you are. Then we're going to the salon so you can get your hair done. You look a mess, girlfriend."

Jordan frowned, and picked up a strand of her hair and gulped down the urge to cry yet again for her friend's bluntness. "I don't look crazy. I look fine."

"In whose world? Stacyee is so going to kill you for that matted mess on top of your head."

Okay, so doing her hair hadn't been a priority. There was too much going on for her to focus on herself. The doctor had increased Granddad's treatments, and she'd helped Grams at the restaurant every day. And since Grams was running herself ragged taking care of Granddad, Jordan was taking care of Grams, making sure she ate and had clean clothes.

"What am I supposed to do?" Jordan said. "I'm doing the best I can."

Maddie's eyes softened, and she stepped closer to her. Rubbing her cheek, she said, "J, baby, you're pregnant. Not dead." Her bestie shoved an outfit against her chest. "Get dressed. It's time to go."

"Oh, that feels good," Jordan groaned as the pedicure bowl filled with hot, soapy water. "I'm so glad you talked me into this, Stacyee."

After a quick trip to the Woodland Mall in Grand Rapids, Maddie had driven Jordan to the salon for a little pampering. It was a slow day at StacyeeLynn Salon. With one look at her, Stacyee had promptly ordered her to the chair. While her feet soaked, the jets swooshing around her toes, Stacyee finished her client.

"Thanks for bringing me here, Maddie."

Her friend was in the chair next to her, texting on her phone, and taking advantage of the massaging action of the chair. "Now, you know there's no need to thank me. It's what we do for each other."

Jordan bit into the Triple Chocolate Chunk cookie she'd stashed in her purse. She'd driven to Jimmie John's and picked up ten, just to keep with her. They were addictive. "I wish we could have realized our dream of being mothers together."

When they were kids, Jordan and Maddie had vowed to get pregnant at the same time and do baby yoga together. Stacyee had told them both that she was not the mothering type but would be the fly godmother who'd swoop in and spoil the kids before she rushed off to a party or something fun.

"Babies are a long way off. Have to have a boyfriend or a husband for that." Maddie cringed.

"Sorry, J. Or a hot one-night stand," her friend added with a shrug.

Rolling her eyes, Jordan grumbled a curt thanks. Even back then, they'd had lofty expectations of any man they would be with. Maddie had always been attracted to blue-collar types, while Jordan had always been partial to nerds. Stacyee, on the other hand, wanted a thug genius. Oddly enough, they'd all sort of ended up with what they'd envisioned for themselves.

Trent was a mechanic, but he was also a businessman, and Stacyee had married—and divorced—a straight-up thug right out of college. As for Jordan, even though she and Bryson weren't a couple, he was as nerdy as they came in high school. But now he was going to be her fine, nerdy baby daddy.

A while later, Stacyee shook Jordan awake. "What?" Jordan said, wiping her eyes.

"You're done," Stacyee told her, pointing to her freshly painted toes. "Get your ass in my chair."

Jordan couldn't believe she'd fallen asleep in the chair. That was so unlike her. "Where's Maddie?"

"She left. I'm going to take you home when I get off."

Jordan shuffled over to Stacyee's chair and sat down. "What are you going to do to my hair?"

"Anything is better than what it is. First, I'm going brighten your color up. Just because you're pregnant doesn't mean you have to walk about here looking washed out."

Frowning, Jordan said, "Y'all are going to stop with the 'Jordan is busted' shit. I don't look that bad."

Stacyee gave her a sad smile. "You don't look bad. But you don't look like my friend."

As Stacyee colored and styled Jordan's hair, she yapped about the opportunity she had to create a hair care line. If Stacyee decided to move forward, she would have to go to Los Angeles for several months to work with the corporation. The multimillion-dollar company was looking to increase sales to African-American women and had been interviewing stylists around the country who had an interest in making their own product. Stacyee was a finalist.

Jordan couldn't be happier for her friend. Stacyee had worked hard, and was finally seeing a payoff.

"So, what's been up with you, J?" Stacyee asked, meeting her gaze in the mirror. "How's the big house coming along?"

"It's going," Jordan answered. "Bryson kissed me before he left."

Stacyee's eyes widened. "J, that was a long time ago. And you're just telling me this?"

"I know. I just couldn't say it out loud."

But she'd been thinking about it. Every day, every night. It was the kind of kiss that people waxed poetic about at open mic nights or composed lyrics about in songs. It wasn't a simple touch of his lips to hers. The heat of him, the connection between the two of them, seemed to scorch her, it was so hot. And Jordan didn't want to get burned.

"Why?" Stacyee wrapped a strand of her hair around the curling iron rod. "He's going to be the father of your child. You're obviously attracted to him, and I would even venture to say that you're more." Jordan opened her mouth to argue with her friend, but Stacyee shushed her. "Girl, stop. Listen, we never talked about this in high school, but I always thought you two would make a cute couple."

Shocked, Jordan frowned. "What? You never thought that."

Stacyee nodded rapidly, picking up another strand of hair and curling it. "I did. Because there was an understanding between the two of you that was so sincere."

"Probably because it was innocent."

"Innocent on your part, maybe," Stacyee muttered. "How did you not see the crush he had on you? Or maybe you did see it, and pretended like you didn't because it was easier?"

"No," Jordan said. "We were friends. Real friends. I want to get back there, I do. But part of me is worried that he's only here because of the baby."

"But he wanted you before he even knew about the baby, J."

Brooklyn walked into the salon. "Hey, Stace!"

Stacyee greeted Brooklyn with a hug before she turned her attention back to Jordan's hair. "I'll be done in a few minutes, Brooklyn."

"No rush. Hey, Jordan."

Jordan smiled. "What's up, Brooklyn? How are you?"

A flash of sadness passed over Brooklyn's face before she offered a wobbly grin. "I'm okay. It's good to see you. Heard from Bryson?"

Jordan and Brooklyn had been working together at the house. They'd spent hours making sure every last piece of Senior's had been removed before Bryson returned. "He texted me and told me his flight would arrive tomorrow evening. My plan is to meet him at the diner so we can go over to the house and check out the progress."

Brooklyn smirked. "That's so cute."

"Oh Lord," Jordan groaned. Brooklyn had been firmly on Bryson's team and had tried to wear Jordan down to give him a chance at more. "Brooklyn, I told you it's not like that."

Stacyee snorted, then in a stage whisper told Brooklyn, "She's in denial."

Brooklyn giggled. "Girl, don't I know it. She reminds me of Kennedi's ass."

While they were at the house, Brooklyn had shared Parker and Kennedi's story with Jordan. Jordan also learned about how Carter won Brooklyn's heart. Admittedly, Jordan had swooned. She loved love.

"Hey, stop. Bryson is grieving. He shouldn't be making decisions during this difficult time. I'm just looking out for him." *And for me.*

Brooklyn walked over to her and gave her a hug, glancing at her in the mirror. "I just want you and my brother happy. But that won't happen unless you let him in, Jordan."

Stacyee pointed her curling iron in her direction. "See. That's real."

Jordan stuffed the rest of her cookie in her mouth. Even if she could admit that part of her wanted to see where things could go between them, she knew that actually letting Bryson in would probably be the hardest thing she would ever do.

* * *

Bryson's flight landed on time, and he couldn't wait to see Jordan. The time away from her had only cemented his desire to be with her. He'd missed her. He'd itched to taste her, to slip into her warm heat, had dreamed of it. The only thing standing in his way was her. *And their past.*

While he was gone, she'd sent him pictures of the many changes she'd made to the house. Bryson had never looked forward to going back to Senior's home—*my home*—before. But he found himself excited because she'd been excited. He could tell by the selfies she'd taken and the multiple exclamation points and hearts in her texts.

In front of the Bees Knees now, Bryson put the car in park and hopped out. He noticed Jordan through the window and smiled. She was beautiful. Her hair was straightened, with sweeping waves hanging down her back. He wanted to rake his fingers through her hair, feel the strands against his skin.

Jordan threw her head back, laughing at something. No, someone. A surge of jealousy coursed through Bryson, blinding him momentarily at the sight of *his* Jordan talking to that asshole Jamari Coleman.

It was like Bryson had been transported back to that damn Valentine's dance, standing in the hallway watching as Jamari lured his date away with some Mike and Ikes. As far as he was concerned, even fourteen years later, Jamari Coleman was the enemy. Bryson imagined the airy sound of Jordan's laughter mixed with the stupid chuckle of that punk, and it made him want to pull the door off the hinges.

Grumbling a dark curse, he clenched his fist, warred with himself about whether he should go inside and insert himself into the conversation. Either way, he'd probably end up looking like the crazy one. And any caveman-like actions would undoubtedly piss her off, which was the last thing he wanted to do. He was trying to play the nice, understanding friend, not the deranged, jealous baby-daddy. *Fuck.* It was time for him to go. Shooting one last glance at the two of them, he walked away.

"You look like shit," Parker said, holding his door open.

"Thanks," Bryson muttered, pushing past his brother and heading straight to the wet bar in Parker's living room. He poured a healthy shot of cognac and gulped it down.

"Whoa, what's going on?" Parker asked. "Didn't you just get back? Was the flight that bad?"

Bryson shook his head. "The flight was fine."

Parker approached him. "Are we drinking tonight?"

"No. I just needed something to take the edge off." Bryson didn't have to look at his brother to know Parker was studying him. "I'm trying hard to be cool, to be the understanding father-to-be, but I'm not that good. She's driving me crazy."

"Ah," Parker said, realization dawning on him. "Jordan."

One name, one woman had the power to bring Bryson to his knees. He didn't like how it felt to be *that* guy again. Over the years, despite his rocky start in the woman department, he'd managed to flip things around. He'd become the player, not the played. It had been a long time since he'd chased after a woman, and that same woman was now going to be the mother to his unborn child.

"What happened?" Parker asked.

"Nothing." Because nothing happened. Bryson was just being a jealous prick. "I flipped out because I saw her talking to Jamari Coleman at the Bees Knees. And instead of going in and talking to her, I left."

"Welp, I'd say you're on your second strike. First, you ask her to move in with you and now you're acting like a punk."

Bryson glared at his cackling brother. "Shut the hell up."

"Trust me." Parker placed a hand on Bryson's shoulder and squeezed. "I've been there. Kennedi gave me the flux, man. Had me acting like a damn lovesick puppy."

Bryson couldn't help the laugh that escaped. The thought of his older brother letting Kennedi lead him around by the leash was hilarious. "How did you do it? How did you get her to give you a chance?"

"Persistence. She had to trust that I wasn't going to leave her, that I was in it for the long haul."

"So, there's no quick fix. That's what you're saying, right?"

"Unfortunately, not, bruh. But you have time. What, about six months?"

In six months, they'd be parents, and he hoped he wouldn't still be trying to convince Jordan that he wanted to be with her. Bryson knew what he had to do. Pulling out his phone, he typed out a quick text asking Jordan to meet him at the house.

"Thanks, bruh," Bryson said. "I'll handle this."

Parker raised his fist in the air. "Make me proud."

At the house, Bryson was sitting in the den staring at the new big-screen television. It seemed Jordan had thought of everything, because he'd forgotten to ask her to purchase a TV. When he'd arrived a few minutes earlier, he'd been pleasantly surprised.

The monotone voice of the alarm system indicated that the front door was opened and he waited. Jordan poked her head into the room moments later and smiled. "You're here."

No, Bryson wasn't quite the lovesick puppy yet, chasing after Jordan. But the sight of her looking at home in his house made him want to lace up his running shoes so he could catch her and convince her that *this* could work.

"Why didn't you pick me up at the diner like we'd planned?"

Bryson eyed her, standing there looking so innocent and sexy at the same time. "I did come to the diner."

Her mouth fell open. "What? I didn't see you."

"That's because you were talking to that clown Jamari Coleman."

Her eyes sparkled with amusement. "You saw him? Today?"

"Yes, I did. And I saw you laughing with him."

"Bryson, he comes in all the time for lunch. Besides,

I don't have anything against him. He's happily married with one kid and another on the way."

"I didn't like it," he admitted. "I'll just leave it at that." Because if he told her that the thought of seeing her with another man made him want to lose his shit and fight like his life depended on it, she would run. And he wanted her to stay. "Come here."

Her eyes widened in surprise, probably at his tone, but she walked over to him and plopped down on the sofa next to him. "What's up?"

Bryson leaned against her. "Thanks for the TV."

"You didn't have it on the list, but I felt like you needed one. If only so you can watch the PBA Tour."

Laughing, Bryson wrapped an arm around her. "Don't do me like that. Bowling is interesting to watch."

"Yeah, like golf." Bryson didn't miss the sarcasm in her voice.

"I like what you've done with this area." The fresh paint on the walls made the place feel like a home, not a museum. The sofas were comfortable, not stiff. Gone was the oversized, drab painting of some country setting. In its place were several smaller African paintings that combined to make one stunning piece of art. The ugly antique vases had been replaced as well with Afrocentric sculptures. How she knew what he liked astounded him.

"I remembered your love of African art. Figured I'd incorporate a few pieces in this area. Brooklyn's friend, Ryleigh, is a lover of sculptures and recommended M. Scott Johnson. I've already contacted him to see about getting a piece commissioned."

If it was even possible, Bryson wanted her more.

She'd put thought into decorating, and he appreci-ated her. He stood. "Take me on a tour."

Once he'd looked at all the redecorated rooms, they ended up back on the sofa in the den. Bryson had made it clear that Senior's master bedroom would not be used, so Jordan had chosen one of the other master bedrooms and the two rooms next to it to redecorate.

"Why didn't you buy furniture for the nursery?" he asked.

She shrugged, picking at imaginary lint on her shirt. "I just . . ." Her gaze locked on his. "I thought you might want to do that together."

Her soft admission made him want to pull her on his lap and kiss her until she begged him to move her in that night. But he would keep his distance for the time being. "Hungry?" he asked.

"Not really. I ate six big cookies."

He chuckled. "Six? Jordan, that's a lot."

"I know. I throw up when I eat anything healthy. And I figured the cookie could be considered a grain. And I heard that chocolate is actually good for you."

Bryson barked out a laugh. "Wow. I've never thought about it like that. What about protein?"

"Each cookie had five grams!" she said with a cheeky smile. "See."

"You're funny. How are you feeling?"

"Fat and tired."

This woman would be the death of him. He'd al-ready had a hard time not staring at her breasts. They seemed to have grown two cup sizes since he'd last seen her, and he wanted to bury his head in them. "Stop."

"It's true. I had to get new clothes. Already. That's crazy."

"You'll be all right. You could use a few more pounds."

She nudged him, and he fell back in a fit of laughter. When he sat up again, he said, "I've been thinking a lot about our conversation before I left."

"Which one?"

"I will admit that I pushed too hard and too fast on moving in together. But I still think it's the right move. The least we can do for our child is to give her a home with parents who love her."

"Bryson, I can't."

"The house is big, Jordan. What am I going to do here all by myself? You can have your own room. Hell, you can have your own wing."

"And what would we be? We're not a couple."

"Yet," he corrected.

She averted her gaze. "Bryson, you know where I stand. I can't move in with you. It's too close. It will confuse things for us down the line."

"I think you're overthinking this."

"And I don't think you're thinking about it enough. Yes, we have to be in each other's lives. We have to co-parent this child. But we can be really good friends who work together to make this child feel loved and wanted. Please . . ." She squeezed his knee. "Please, don't ask me again. It just makes me anxious that we're not on the same page."

He clenched his teeth together. He wanted to

argue with her, but he just couldn't put himself out there to be rejected again. So he nodded. "Okay."

She stood, and set the spare key to the house on the table. "I better get going. I haven't checked on Granddad all day."

"How is he doing?"

"He's getting stronger. They started him back on his treatment. And it seems to be taking well. He's more tired than usual, but the doctors are still optimistic."

"Good. I'm glad to hear it."

"Well, I'll call you tomorrow." A few moments later she was gone.

Chapter 14

Jordan stepped onto the porch. Granddad was sitting in his rocking chair. "Hi," she said. "Are you okay?"

"I'm fine, Punchkin. Where are you coming from?"

"I stopped by Bryson's house." She sat on the bench across from him. "How are you feeling?"

"Oh, I'm hanging in." Granddad met her gaze. "That Bryson is a good man. He sent over a crew to mow my lawn and cut my hedges today."

Jordan frowned. "He did?"

"Sure did. I appreciate the help."

Bryson hadn't mentioned anything to her in the time that she was over there. But the fact that he'd done that for her granddad, even while away, warmed her heart. It was important that any person she was involved with loved her grandparents and treated them with respect. And Bryson had always passed with flying colors. Even when they were friends, he'd spent time cultivating his own personal relationships with them. That meant the world to her. "I'll let him know."

"How's that baby doing?"

Jordan smiled. She'd told her Granddad about the baby weeks ago, and every time he saw her, he asked about it. "As far as I know, everything is good. We have a doctor's appointment next week."

"You taking care of yourself?"

"I am."

"What is Bryson going to do? Is he going to do the right thing?"

"I don't know."

Jordan wondered what the "right thing" was at that point. She thought she was doing the right thing by cultivating the relationship between her and Bryson, but she wasn't so sure. It seemed she was split in two. Part of her wanted to run toward him, while the other part wanted to run away from him. He almost seemed too good to be true. Bryson was everything she thought she wanted in a man. Yet, she wasn't sure if she could trust herself—or him—to make it work.

With every day, every hour, her feelings for him grew by leaps and bounds. If he left her again, it would wreck her. And it wasn't just her anymore; she had a baby to consider. Her child needed a strong, capable mother. Their baby needed an advocate, someone he or she could count on to be there. Jordan couldn't afford to let her guard down, and if that meant keeping her distance from Bryson for the time being, so be it.

She knew her Granddad was old school, though. In fact, he'd been the one to encourage her father to marry her mother, even though neither of them was ready for the commitment. Jordan hoped Granddad wasn't holding out for another shotgun wedding.

"I think it's good that you two got back in touch."

Granddad's smile gleamed in the moonlight and she couldn't help but feel blessed that she could still see his smile, take in his scent, and hear his voice. Moments like this were priceless and she wouldn't take them for granted.

"You always had a special friendship, even at a young age," Granddad continued. "That boy has grit. He's a tough one. All of those Wells children were, to deal with Senior. And I have no doubt he'll do right by you and your baby."

"He thinks we should move in together, so we can take care of the baby together," Jordan confessed.

"What do you think?" he asked.

She lifted her shoulder in a half shrug. "I don't think it will work. I just . . . I don't even know if we're compatible and I won't let this baby push me into a loveless relationship where both of us will be miserable and one of us ends up getting hurt."

"You two are good friends. That will bode well for the baby."

"We *were* good friends a long time ago, Granddad. He left, disappeared with no contact for almost ten years. Even if I could forget that, it doesn't mean that we can make a relationship work. We don't know each other anymore."

"Well, you knew enough about each other to"— he motioned to her belly—"you know."

Jordan covered her grin at her grandfather's exaggerated hand gestures toward her stomach. "I'm just saying . . . Look at Mom and Dad. They got together because of me, and it ended badly."

"Punchkin, I've watched you use your parents' failures to keep you from committing to anyone. Like that one cabbage head you brought over here.

He was ready to marry you, but you turned him down in front of everyone."

Jordan bowed her head. Phillip Harris had dropped down on one knee during the Fourth of July fireworks, in front of his entire family, and proposed. She'd turned him down, and told herself at the time that he was too . . . She couldn't even remember what he was. She just knew it would never work.

"And then that teacher guy, Albert. Brought him here and made a show of introducing him to all of us, and soon as he gave you a ring, you dumped him."

"His name was Arnold, Granddad. And he wanted me to forget about law school to have his babies."

Jordan was glad he didn't know about Tom. That botched proposal was the worst of them all. He was the first man to propose to her. They were stationed together on the same base. He'd popped the question at a basketball game, on the big screen. That "no" she said was captured on tape and seen by viewers around the world. In her defense, though, Tom had only proposed because he was being deployed to Afghanistan and was afraid he was going to die and not leave behind a legacy. They'd only been dating for four months when it happened.

"Well, you're not in law school now," Granddad said. "And you're having a baby."

"That's different, Granddad. This wasn't planned." And Bryson would never tell her to drop out of school to mother his children. That much she was sure of. Although, Jordan would be lying if she said she hadn't thought about school and how the long hours would affect the baby. Her desire to go to law school seemed so far away from her now. She wasn't sure what her plans were long-term, but she knew she wanted to actually enjoy her baby in its first year or two of life. That meant delaying admission for at least another year.

"I think you're just afraid." Granddad pinned her with his eyes. "Jordan Mila Clark, listen here." Jordan zeroed in on her grandfather. He'd called her by her full name, so he was about to drop some wisdom. "The mistakes your parents made are theirs, not yours. Your mother had a whole set of problems that had nothing to do with you or your father. We've raised you to be kind, giving, competent, dependable, and responsible. You are already a better mother to your child than your mother was to you."

Tears welled up in Jordan's eyes. "What if it doesn't work out?"

"If it doesn't work out, then you'll deal with it then. But you can't remain stagnant, afraid to walk through the door, because of what *might* happen. Your grandmother took a chance on a stranger. And here we are, forty plus years of marriage and I love her more today than I ever have."

Jordan had been blessed with two loving grandparents who'd given her the best example of real, lasting love. And she wanted to feel that type of love. But was Bryson the man she should feel it with?

Granddad stood, and held out his hand. She put her hand in his and stood. Gripping her shoulders, he said, "Bryson is a good man. Let him off the hook." He kissed her brow, and a lone tear streaked down her cheek.

"I love you, Granddad." She hugged his waist.

"I love you, too, Punchkin." He took his seat again. "If you need an extra suitcase, I have one in the shed."

"I didn't say I was going to move in with him, Granddad. I came to town to help you. And you're trying to push me out."

"You act like the Wells's house is not ten minutes away on a good day. You're still close enough to try and boss me around."

Jordan kissed Granddad's cheek. "Thank you."

"You're welcome."

At Brook's Pub, Bryson and Veronica clinked beer bottles. "Here's to us," Bryson toasted. "Siblings unite."

Veronica grinned. "Hear, hear."

He took a long pull from his bottle before setting it back on the bar. "That's good."

"It was. Thanks for inviting me out."

Bryson scanned the busy bar. Brook's Pub was a popular night spot in Wellspring and Thursdays were the biggest nights. The owner, Juke, was a friend of Bryson's and Brooklyn's. They'd all gone to school together.

"Thanks for coming."

After Jordan had left, Bryson had left the house. He couldn't bring himself to sleep there alone. He'd texted his siblings to meet him for drinks, but Brooklyn had complained about it being one of her "stank" days and Parker had essentially told him that he was trying to get lucky with his wife. But Veronica had responded with a yes and had met him at the bar on time. They were on their second beer and third bowl of peanuts.

"Are you planning on going back to Indiana?" Bryson asked Veronica.

"There's nothing really to go back to. I mean, my mom is there, but she just remarried and they're still in the honeymoon phase. Besides, she deserves to be happy."

Bryson thought about his own mother. They weren't as close as he'd like, but he did wish happiness for her. Unfortunately, her relationship with Senior had left her a little damaged and mistrustful of men. So she'd remained single. He'd often told his mom to start dating, but she told him she'd found God and was happy with her church ministry and her dog.

"That's good. What about you? No man to go back home to, huh?"

She scrunched up her nose. "Not anymore."

Veronica explained that her last boyfriend had recently broken things off because he wanted a woman who wasn't so damaged. Bryson wanted to pummel that fool to the ground. Despite the fact that he'd only met Veronica a few weeks ago, she was still his sister. And he didn't like to hear of anyone hurting her.

"He's an asshole," Bryson told her. "You deserve better than him."

"That's what I said," she agreed. "It was for the best, though."

"Why do you say that?"

"We had different goals in life. Always have, really. We'd just spent so many years together that it kind of became a habit. It was actually a relief when he broke it off, because I'm not sure I would have done it. I was comfortable."

Bryson sighed. "It sucks because that's time wasted."

"Yeah, but why keep yourself locked in a relationship that's not working? There has to be something better out there."

Juke walked over to them. "Bryson, long time no see."

Bryson shook Juke's hand. "Juke, man, what the hell have you been up to?"

Juke had been the second person Bryson met when he moved to Wellspring. They'd met on the playground, during afternoon recess on his first day of school. Bryson had once again been alone when a chubby Juke approached him and asked for a dollar to buy a candy bar. Juke had explained that his mother had put him on a diet and wouldn't let him eat chocolate.

That day, Bryson had just so happened to have a bite-sized Snickers bar in his pocket and gave it to Juke. Juke would later beat a boy to a pulp for destroying Bryson's science fair project. Bryson returned the favor by helping Juke pass his math exam. And to think, all of that stemmed from a leftover piece of Halloween candy.

Juke motioned to the bar around them. "Brook's Pub. That's what I've been up to."

"Man, you really hooked this place up. I just had to come see it for myself."

Growing up, Juke had always told Bryson of his dream to own a bar. Bryson was proud to see that his friend had made it happen.

"I'm glad to see you finally came home," Juke told him. "Brooklyn must have been giddy with excitement."

"You know she was, man." Bryson pointed at Veronica. "You met my sister Veronica, right?"

To a stranger, Juke probably looked downright scary with his tattooed arms and mean mug. But Veronica just grinned. "Hi." She shook his hand. "Good to meet you."

Juke kissed her palm. "Welcome to Wellspring." Then he winked at her.

Bryson frowned. "You just winked at my sister, man."

Ignoring him, Juke asked Veronica what she was drinking. When she replied, he told her he'd bring her another. On the house.

"He seems nice." Veronica stared at Juke's retreating back.

"You like him?" Bryson said.

She shrugged. "He's cute."

"Yeah, I'm not that type of brother. Don't tell me that." Brooklyn used to try to talk to him about her potential suitors. He didn't like it then, from her. And he didn't like it now, from Veronica. "You should talk to Brooklyn about that. She'll probably try to hook you up."

Laughing, Veronica popped a peanut in her mouth. "You know, I'm glad I'm here. I was an only child, didn't have any siblings or anything. It feels good to be one of the crew."

"I told you, you're one of us now. Get used to the craziness."

Juke came back over to them and set Veronica's new beer on the bar top. "Here you go, sweetheart. Let me know if you need anything else."

"I will," Veronica told Juke. "Thank you."

She smirked as she took a sip out of her new

bottle. "What?" she asked, after Bryson had stared at her for a long while.

"That's against God's plan, you know?"

Veronica swatted him playfully. "You're crazy. Anyway, tell me about Jordan. I'm assuming you wanted a night out because of her."

"For someone who just came into my life, you seem to have things figured out."

"Hey, I'm a woman. And I know women."

Bryson thought about Jordan for the millionth time that day. She'd rejected him once again, and even though he wasn't too keen on trying again with her, he couldn't *not* try. "I'm not sure but something is holding her back."

"I'm going to say this and you can tell me to shut up if you want."

"No, go ahead. I won't tell you to shut up until I've known you for at least two months. Right now, we're in the nice phase of our newfound sibling relationship."

She laughed again. "Okay. You're there. Jordan isn't. You have to stop rushing her. She'll come to you when she's ready. Be patient."

Because if I don't, I'll lose her. Bryson could read between the lines. Veronica hadn't said it, but it was implied. "I'm going to try it your way. I'll keep it cool."

Patting his shoulder, she nodded hard. "Good. Now, I heard you bowl."

"Don't tell me you know how to bowl?" Bryson asked.

"I do. I was in a league back home."

"Then we have to hit the lanes."

Bryson was excited. Not only because he'd found he had something in common with Veronica but because he genuinely liked her. Yet another reason why he couldn't regret moving back to Wellspring and proof that what Senior had meant for bad had turned out to be good.

An hour later, Bryson was back home, in the empty house. Sighing, he kicked off his shoes and unbuttoned his shirt. It was still early, and he figured he'd watch a movie before bed. When the doorbell sounded, he frowned and walked to the door. Pulling it open, he was surprised to find Jordan standing on the other side, a rolling suitcase sitting next to her.

"Jordan? What are you doing here?"

She let out a deep breath. "You asked me to come live with you, right?"

He nodded, unable to form a coherent, verbal response.

Gripping the handle of her suitcase, she said, "I'm here. I'm home."

Chapter 15

Bryson slipped the handle of her suitcase from her hand and ushered her inside without a word. He was afraid that if he said anything, the spell would be broken, and she'd disappear like a vapor.

Jordan stood in the foyer, nibbling on her bottom lip.

They stood there, staring at each for what seemed like forever. Eventually, he couldn't take the silence any longer. "Jordie, what does this mean?" he asked finally.

"I thought about what you said earlier. We do owe it to our baby to give her the best of both of us." She shifted on her feet and twirled the handle of her purse around her finger. "So, I'm willing to try. Living together," she added.

"Are you sure?" he asked. "I don't want this to be something you're only doing because I suggested or asked. This won't work if you don't really want this."

"I'm sure. So, which room is mine?"

Bryson wanted to tell her she could have the moon. At this point, she could have all the rooms and he'd sleep on the floor. He was just happy she was there, standing in front of him looking too freakin' adorable and vulnerable.

He stepped closer to her, needed to be closer to her, to touch her. But when he reached out, she reared back so fast she nearly fell back. He steadied her with his hands around her waist, and *damn it*, just that simple contact made his heart beat so hard and so loud, he was sure she could hear it.

"Bryson," she said, retreating back, out of his grasp. "We need to talk."

"Okay, we—"

"I mean, really talk," she interrupted.

There was a bench in the foyer area. He pointed to it. "There, or do you want to go in the den?"

"Over there is fine." She walked over to the bench and sat down, crossing her legs at the feet. "Come sit with me."

He joined her. "What's going on?"

"I'm agreeing to move in, but I want to make some things clear." He urged her to go ahead with a nod. "You're attracted to me."

Duh. He'd been semi-hard since she breezed past him a few minutes ago. She hadn't even touched him yet, and he was imagining pulling her shirt off and laving attention on her tight nipples and slipping his hands under the waistband of her capri pants. He was sure she'd be wet for him, wanting. He wanted to feel her come on his hands, in his mouth, on his . . .

"Bryson?"

He blinked. "Huh?"

"I'm going to need you to stop looking at me like that. I can't concentrate."

Pictures of him burying his face in her sweetness assaulted him and he stood abruptly and stepped back, away from her and away from the light scent of her. Because if he stayed there, she'd be sitting on his face in a matter of minutes.

"I think it's better that I stand."

Her gaze dropped to his erection, poking out through his pants, and she shifted on the bench, closing her knees together. A flush crept up her cheeks, and Bryson couldn't help the smirk that tugged at his lips. Apparently, he wasn't the only one affected by their nearness.

She swallowed visibly. "Um. Like I was saying, I know that you're attracted to me."

"I want you, yes," he admitted.

She sucked in a shaky breath. "And I'm attracted to you, too. Which is why living together, in the same house, is so complicated."

"It doesn't have to be, Jordie."

"Bryson, I would prefer we take this slow." She raised her chin. "I'm not ready for intimacy between us again."

His shoulders fell, and he tilted his head up to peer at the ceiling. *Why me?* His chest tightened, and he rubbed the back of his neck to release some of the tension building there. Then, he remembered what Veronica had just reminded him that evening. *Be patient.* And with the willpower and strength of a damn monk, he nodded and concentrated on making his tone even. "If that's what you want."

Jordan's head snapped up. "Really?"

"Yes," he said, tapping his fingers against his legs. "We're a team. I'll do whatever it takes to make you feel comfortable here." *Even if it is gutting me, slowly.*

With a palm pressed to her heart, she murmured a thanks before standing to her feet and stretching. He turned away, choosing to not focus on the hardened peaks of her nipples, visible through her light T-shirt. He picked up her suitcase. "I'm sure you're probably tired. I'll carry this up to your room."

They headed to the bedroom he thought would be perfect for her. Once inside, he flicked the light on. Jordan had this room painted in a soft gray with red accents. The big king-sized bed in the middle of the room would be perfect for nights when she'd have to bring the baby to bed with her to breastfeed.

Frowning, he thought about all the things they hadn't talked about yet. Like was she even planning to breastfeed, or did she want to formula-feed? Did she want to use disposable or cloth diapers? Or did she believe in vaccinations?

But it was late, and he was horny. That would be a conversation for another day. He observed her as she walked around the room, brushing her fingers over the dressers.

"This is actually my favorite room."

Bryson had figured that, which was why he'd brought her there. It was his first night in the house, so he hadn't yet decided which room he wanted to sleep in before she'd arrived on his doorstep. "I thought you would say that."

She tilted her head and peered at him. "You told me to decorate two bedrooms and a nursery. Did you know that I would change my mind?"

He chuckled. "I had hoped that you would. In any case, I figured you would need a room. Even if it was for privacy while you were here visiting."

"Thank you, Bryson."

Walking to the door, he said, "I'm going to let you rest. I'll be in the other bedroom." *More than likely relieving my tension with my hand.*

"Good night, Bryson," she said.

He turned to her and smiled. "Night, Jordie."

Later, Bryson was so frustrated he wanted to kick something. He was lying in his bed, staring at the ceiling. There was no television in his bedroom, and it was too quiet. He'd already taken matters into his own hands, bringing himself to orgasm two times that night.

Having her so close, yet so far, was driving him crazy. Grumbling a curse, he shifted in the bed, turning on his side. *Fuck.* He kicked the thin sheet off, and shuffled downstairs to the den.

The soft light on in the kitchen made him change directions and head that way. *I thought I turned that off.* As he neared the kitchen, he heard a whispered voice. Jordan. Who was she talking to? *It better not be Jamari Coleman.*

When he rounded the corner, he stopped at the sight of Jordan, pacing back and forth, her hands flailing in the air. She was wearing one of those not sexy pink fluffy robes, but underneath . . . she only wore a thin tank top and pink panties.

Bryson bit back a low groan at the sight of her. She seemed to be talking herself out of something, or berating herself for something. "Jordan?"

She yelped, whirling around to face him. "Bryson! You're like a stealthy assassin, sneaking up on me like that. I told you to stop doing that."

He grinned and stepped farther into the kitchen. "Is everything okay?"

"Everything is fine. I couldn't sleep. New house,

new bed, new baby . . . Figured I'd make tea." The whistle of the teapot sounded and she reached to pull a mug out of the cabinet. As she stood on the tips of her toes to reach the cup, her shirt lifted, giving him a glimpse of her smooth brown skin. She turned to him. "Join me?"

He nodded. "Sure."

Jordan tucked her feet under her bottom as she settled in on the sofa. It had been a long, stressful, emotional whirlwind of a day. But she hoped things would start to even out, now that she'd finally made the decision to move in with Bryson.

After her talk with Granddad, she'd gone in and started packing. It had only taken her a few hours to get everything she'd needed. She'd ask Bryson to grab the rest of her luggage out of the trunk in the morning.

He joined her on the sofa, mug in hand, and picked up the television remote control. "Want to watch anything in particular?"

She scratched her chin. "My shows are off for the summer."

"Do you still watch that crime show about the behavioral analysis unit?"

Scrunching her nose, she shook her head. "Too gross. Plus, my favorite character was written off the show and it's not the same."

"They wrote off the nerd?"

"No, he's still on there. My other favorite character."

Bryson flicked through several channels before settling on the Home & Garden Channel. They sat in comfortable silence, watching a couple choose between three expensive-ass houses in Burbank, California.

"I wonder how these people can afford these extravagant houses," she mused aloud.

"It's TV. Even reality television is scripted. There is no way he can afford that house working as a schoolteacher. Not in Burbank."

"Right. And she doesn't even work. Maybe they have some sort of inheritance."

"Maybe." He sipped his tea, and winced.

She laughed. "You don't like the tea."

"Nah." He set the mug on the table. "I tried, but I'd rather have coffee."

She groaned. "I miss coffee."

"I read that you can still enjoy a cup every now and then."

Jordan couldn't pretend that him reading about her pregnancy didn't make her stomach flutter. After their little talk earlier, she knew that living in the same house was going to be hard on her libido. Lying in that bed, alone, with him in the next room was torture. And she'd forgotten to bring her vibrator in, so she'd used her hand to get a much-needed release. She suspected that would be a regular occurrence being so near Bryson.

"I plan to allow myself one cup a week," she told him.

"Good. Have you had any cravings? Besides chocolate chip cookies."

"Not really. Yesterday I wanted French toast, but that's normal when Grams is in the restaurant. She makes the best around."

He groaned. "I've been meaning to get a Denver

omelet. I've visited many diners over the years, and no one can make an omelet like Grams."

The Bees Knees was known for its Denver omelet. It was a recipe Grams had brought from Colorado. Just talking about it made her mouth water. "You're so right. I may get one of those tomorrow."

"Maybe I'll join you. That sounds good."

"Sure. How was everything in L.A.?" They chatted every day, but he hadn't talked much about his job. "Was your boss upset you turned in your notice?"

Bryson shook his head. "No. He was happy for me. Assured me that he would give a glowing recommendation for my new job."

"Have you thought about where you want to work?"

Jordan didn't want to assume he'd go to work for Wellspring Water Corp., especially given the history. Senior had wanted all of his children to work in the company. But only Parker had taken on the mantle. The eldest Wells served as chief executive officer of the company. From what Jordan could tell, Parker had done a good job with the company over the past year.

"I don't know," Bryson answered. "Parker wants me to work for him, in research and development."

Jordan knew that Bryson worked as an environmental engineer from their time in California. He'd mentioned that he was interested in switching gears and working as a city planner eventually, but he loved the work he was doing.

"Is that something you're considering?" she asked, eyeing him over the rim of her mug.

"Not really. I'm not in a rush. I have money saved. I just want to be sure I'm making the right career decisions. As much as I'm trying to move past Senior and everything, I don't think I'll be happy at Wellspring Water. It's too much."

"Well, I think you should do what feels good to you."

"I agree. What about you? Are you still planning to enroll in law school?"

Jordan had decided to put law school on hold. At least, until the baby was old enough to walk. "No. Law school is going to have to wait for now."

"Do you want to stay home with the baby?"

"That and I kind of like helping my grandparents out at the diner. They're getting older and Grams really wants to be with Granddad more during the day. And I have my real estate license. I was thinking of doing that for a while, until I can go back to school."

He reared back. "Really? I didn't know you had a license."

"Yeah, I got it a few months ago actually."

"Wow. That's what's up. I can see you showing houses and making deals."

She smiled. Bryson had always been supportive, and she was glad to see that hadn't changed. In fact, there wasn't much that had changed about him. He was still giving, encouraging, and funny.

Rubbing her belly, she said, "I really need to be sure I'm doing the right thing by this baby."

"You are," he said, clasping her hand in his. "I can tell you're already in love."

It was still early, but Bryson was right. She loved their baby, and that love grew stronger every day.

Just knowing there was a life inside her, depending on her to make wise decisions with food and environment, made her feel protective.

"I am, Bryson. It's weird because I've never felt this way before. This is kind of a chance of a lifetime, to have a baby, to bring another person into the world, to mold that person, to teach her everything I know."

A slow grin formed over his face. "Yeah. I can't wait to show her how to bowl."

Jordan laughed. "You're so funny."

"Do you really think it's a girl?"

"I do. I don't know why. I just do."

"Have you thought about names?"

"If we do have a girl, I want to name her Willow, after my granddad."

"Willow?" Bryson shifted closer to her. "What about a boy? Will?"

Jordan felt warmth spread through her body. Bryson understood her need to honor her grandfather. "I picked the girl's name, so I wouldn't care if you picked the boy's name."

"I'm okay with Will. I'd be proud to name our son after your grandfather. He's important to me, too."

"What are you most excited about?" Jordan knew her answer, but she wanted to hear his.

"I just want to love her. I want to hold her in my arms and tell her that I'm her daddy. I want to lay eyes on her and know that she loves me." He reached out and brushed his palm over her stomach.

Jordan didn't know what Bryson was doing to her,

but she liked the feeling he evoked in her. And, Lord help her, she wanted more.

Bryson jumped up, taking his warmth with him. "I have something that you are going to love."

Jordan immediately missed the contact, but tried to focus. "What?"

He walked over to the television and opened the entertainment center underneath. "I brought this back with me." He pulled out two remote controls and held up a game.

Squinting, Jordan leaned forward. "Is that . . . ? Mario Kart!" She hopped to her feet and snatched the game away from him, running her finger over the picture on the front. They'd spent hours playing that game back in the day. Just hearing the cheesy music used to put a smile on her face. Shoving the game into his chest, she said, "Get ready to get your ass beat."

She fell back on the couch and he loaded the game system before plopping down next to her. "In your dreams."

Chapter 16

Jordan couldn't calm the flutters in her stomach. They were on their way to the doctor's appointment, the twelve-week check-up, after stopping for a light breakfast of toast and scrambled eggs. She knew she probably shouldn't be, but she was nervous. She didn't know what to expect. Sure, she'd read all the blogs and baby tracker sites, but nothing about this pregnancy was what she'd expected.

The past week flew by as she and Bryson navigated the waters of co-habitation. They'd fallen asleep on the couch that first night, after playing Mario Kart for hours. The following morning, he'd made her breakfast and they'd chatted about the baby again. He'd asked all kinds of questions, like whether she was planning to breastfeed or if she'd thought about a college fund.

And Bryson had doted on her, making sure she ate balanced meals and checking in on her throughout the day while she was working at the Bees Knees. He'd even dropped by to sit with Granddad during the day. The two men had spent time fishing on the river and had even gone to watch a superhero movie at the theater. He'd also driven Granddad to treatment when Grams had her own doctor's appointment. To thank him, Grams had cooked a big meal last night and they'd all sat down to enjoy dinner together.

Jordan had heard from her father. He and Rebecca were doing well, and he sounded happy. Her concerns about her new stepmother were alleviated when her father had let it slip that they'd signed a prenuptial agreement prior to the wedding. It was a decision both of them hadn't entered into lightly, but in the end, it was best for them.

"Supposedly, we'll be able to hear the heartbeat clearly now with the Doppler machine," she announced in the quiet car. Jordan had seen the heartbeat on the tiny ultrasound machine, but she looked forward to actually hearing it.

Bryson placed a hand on her knee and squeezed. "Don't be nervous, Jordie. Everything will be just fine."

She planted her hands on top of his, drawing strength from him. "I know, but this is important. I just want everything to be perfect."

"It probably won't be. But that's okay. Your body is going through a lot of changes. We can't expect all of those changes to be welcome. But we know the end result will make this all worth it."

Jordan laced her fingers through his and he turned his palm upward. "Right. You're right. It will all be worth it in the end when we can see our baby's face."

"Did you want to find out the sex?" he asked.

"I don't know. Do you?"

"I kind of want to be surprised."

Jordan had spent a lot of time thinking about it, but she was leaning toward finding out the sex. It would be better for planning purposes. Stacyee and Maddie had been going over the pros and cons with her all week. Either way, it was too early to determine with great accuracy, so she'd tried to put it out of her mind.

"We still have a while to decide," she told him. "I have a lot of questions for the doctor, though."

He glanced at her out of the corner of his eye. "Like what?"

Jordan felt huge, like she was gaining twice the weight she should. And it was uncomfortable. The morning sickness had sort of died down, which was normal according to her baby tracker, but she still couldn't be around ketchup without gagging. It made for a harrowing day at work sometimes. Grams was back to working most days, and would often step in when a customer ordered meat loaf. The smell of the ketchup-based glaze made Jordan sick immediately.

Then there was the constant need to pee. Jordan felt like she was constantly in the bathroom. It didn't matter what time of the day or night.

"I just wonder why I'm gaining so much weight, so soon."

Yes, she'd been on a cookie rampage, but Bryson had talked her off the ledge and had started packing her fruit or celery sticks to carry with her. Jordan learned that Bryson was a health nut, which *was* different from when they were young.

Sometimes, he'd eat sweets, but it wasn't often.

And he worked out every single morning. The house already had a gym, but he'd purchased new equipment in the past week.

"Don't you think that's normal?" he asked. "I mean, you're eating for two and the baby is growing."

"Yeah, but I want to make sure I'm not gaining too much weight. I don't want to end up with gestational diabetes or preeclampsia."

"That's understandable. Did you write down all of your questions, so you won't forget them?"

She nodded. "I have them on my phone."

"Good girl."

When they arrived at the doctor's office, he let her out at the front and parked the car. Inside, she checked in and took her seat against a far wall. Bryson entered the office later and scanned the area for her. But before he spotted her, a nurse stepped out of the back and greeted him. "Hello, can I help you?"

Jordan frowned. That same woman had seen her and pointedly ignored her. Now, the lady was standing in front of Bryson with a goofy grin on her face, poking her chest in his direction. Bryson said something Jordan couldn't make out and the woman laughed.

When he finally saw Jordan, he grinned and pointed in her direction. The brazen woman watched him strut over to her, before she walked to the back, and Jordan fought the urge to get up and tell the dumb nurse to keep her eyes to herself.

Jordan was jealous. And she was never jealous, had never even felt a twinge of jealousy—until today, until Bryson. She silently fumed when he sat down

next to her. She wasn't angry with him. Not really.
She was pissed at herself for wanting to drop-kick
that damn nurse.

"It's nice in here," Bryson said, pulling out his
phone.

"Hmm," she grumbled.

He looked at her then, his brow knitting together
in a frown. "What's up?"

Jordan shifted away from him. "Nothing."

"Sure?"

"Yep," she said.

"You picked a good office. That nurse was sweet."

She glared at him over her shoulder. "What?"

"She offered me coffee or juice."

The lady didn't offer Jordan coffee or juice. She
didn't even offer her a cracker. Jordan pulled out a
pack of saltines from her purse, opened the wrapper, and bit down on one. Hard.

"And she asked me out," he said.

"You've got to be kidding me," she blurted out.
"That is so disrespectful. Obviously, you're here because you're someone's baby's father. And she asked
you out?"

Bryson glanced over at her, amusement on his
face. "Just kidding."

Jordan swatted him. "You get on my nerves."

He grinned. "Jealous?"

Elbowing him, she turned away from him.
"Hell, no."

He barked out a laugh.

The perky medical assistant called them to the
back. Bryson waited outside the bathroom while
she gave a urine sample. He smiled at her while the

medical assistant took her vitals, squeezed her hand when the nurse arrived in the room later with requisitions for blood work and the ultrasound they'd chosen to have.

Jordan and Bryson had decided beforehand not to do all of the genetic-type screenings available, but had agreed on doing the blood tests and an NT scan, which is a noninvasive ultrasound that helps assess the risk of the baby having complications such as Down syndrome.

Next, they headed to the lab, where Jordan got her blood drawn. After which they were escorted to a private ultrasound room located within the doctor's office, which was convenient. Jordan was anxious.

Several minutes later, a technician arrived with a wide grin on her face and a pink set of scrubs. Jordan considered asking her where she got her scrubs because they looked comfortable, but she refrained from doing so.

The tech made quick work of getting the machine ready while chatting about the weather. Jordan squeezed her eyes shut and counted to ten. She needed to breathe. *Everything is going to be fine.*

"Jordie, you're all right. Everything is going to be okay," Bryson whispered in her ear. He clasped her hand in his and brushed his lips over her temple.

Jordan nodded. "I know. I'm just . . ."

"I know, but we got this. The baby is going to be fine."

Jordan had read a lot of horror stories about the twelve-week ultrasound and genetic testing. She figured it was because she didn't know much about her mother's genetic history. Her father hadn't really been present for many of the prenatal appointments because of his military job, so he didn't know much either.

"Okay, I'm going to apply this warm gel to your abdomen, so we can get started," the tech announced.

Bryson helped Jordan push her shirt up, baring her stomach to the tech, who then squirted the gel on her skin. Jordan squeezed Bryson's hand when she felt the wand press against her.

"Okay, Ms. Clark," the tech said. "Oh."

Jordan's face snapped up. "What?"

The tech frowned. "This is . . . oh my."

"What is it?" Bryson asked, leaning forward to peer at the screen.

It took a minute for Jordan to make out what she was seeing on the monitor. "Is that . . . ?"

"Two babies?" Bryson finished.

On the screen, instead of one baby, there were two tiny specks swimming and kicking. If Jordan weren't so shocked, she'd be gushing over the movements. The babies were obviously alive and seemed to have already bonded with each other and almost appeared to be waving at her. A small smile tugged on her lips at the sight. But she was still in disbelief.

With a sigh, the tech said, "Yes, it is. The records that were sent from your original doctor didn't note the presence of the second baby in the initial ultrasound."

"That's because it wasn't there," Jordan said, perching herself up on her elbows. "I saw it myself. There was only one baby."

"Sometimes one baby hides behind the other," the tech explained. "It doesn't happen often, but it can get missed in an eight-week ultrasound."

Bryson grinned. "We're having twins."

Jordan glared at Bryson, who was now talking to the babies in her belly. For the life of her, she couldn't understand why Bryson wasn't terrified just like she was. *Two babies?* The rest of the ultrasound went by in a blur. The tech measured the babies, announced that they were identical twins with one placenta and growing as expected.

A little later, they were in the exam room.

"You don't have to change into one of those gowns?" he asked, tugging at her sleeve.

"We're having twins, Bryson," she said. "Two babies."

"I know." He smirked. "Exciting, huh? Did you see them in there? They were moving around."

Jordan shook her head. "No. I'm not prepared for this."

He squeezed her knee to halt the shaking she'd been doing since she'd sat down. "Neither am I, but what can we do? We're going to have to just deal with it. Like I told you earlier, we got this. Together."

A few minutes later, the doctor knocked on the door and entered the room. "Good morning," Dr. Jones said. Jordan had picked the doctor based on a recommendation from Brooklyn, who had been coming to the doctor for a few years.

"Hi, Dr. Jones," Jordan said on a sigh.

"And who is this?" Dr. Jones asked, gesturing at Bryson while she attached her laptop to the dock.

Bryson stood. "Bryson," he said, reaching out to shake the doctor's hand. "I'm the father."

"Good to meet you," Dr. Jones said. She scooted the chair closer to Jordan. "How are you feeling, Jordan?"

Jordan swallowed past a lump in her throat. "I'm feeling okay."

"I just viewed the ultrasound CD. Congratulations. You're having twins."

Jordan blinked, and clenched her teeth together. Of course, she was having twins. She didn't need another announcement. "It appears so. Does this change anything?"

"A little," Dr. Jones admitted. "The second baby was missed on your first ultrasound."

It was a good thing Jordan had decided to discontinue care at her first doctor to come to Dr. Jones. The older woman had missed an integral piece of the picture. "The tech said that it's rare, but not uncommon."

"True."

Dr. Jones asked if Jordan had any questions about the ultrasound and Jordan shook her head. "But I guess it answered the question I had about my rapid weight gain."

The doctor explained that everything might be more intense with twins. She was now at a higher risk for gestational diabetes and preeclampsia. And she'd have to be seen more often than she would be with just one baby.

They also learned that the vast majority of twin pregnancies would not last until the due date, so the doctor told her to prepare for possibly having the baby a little after Thanksgiving. Dr. Jones also suggested she try to stay off her feet for long periods of time as she progresses, which presented a problem since she'd been helping her grandparents at the Bees Knees.

Bryson's attention was glued to the doctor. He

asked about Jordan's comfort level, and whether she would be in more pain or if there was something he could do to ease some of the symptoms.

"I'd say, just be there," Dr. Jones told him. "She'll need your support."

Bryson glanced over at her and winked. "That's not a problem."

"So how are you feeling, Jordan?" Dr. Jones asked, while she typed notes into her laptop.

"I think the morning sickness is dying down," Jordan replied. "Although I am having a few issues with certain smells."

"That's normal," the doctor replied. "That may last for quite a while. Try to keep a bag of crackers with you, and please stay hydrated. It's extremely important to push the fluids."

Jordan swallowed. Hard. "Okay."

"Are you feeling any pain?"

"No," Jordan answered.

"Good. Don't be alarmed if you start to feel some minor pains. You're housing two little ones in there."

This is my life.

"It's perfectly fine to feel surprised at this news." The doctor patted Jordan's knee. "And I don't want you to feel hesitant to call my office if you have any concerns. If I'm not available, there is always a doctor on call to assist. Now, I know you've seen the babies, but are you ready to hear the heartbeats?"

Bryson helped Jordan up onto the exam table, and Dr. Jones instructed her to pull her pants down and her shirt up. More jelly on her abdomen, and a few minutes later, she heard the whooshing sounds of her babies' heartbeats.

Tears pricked Jordan's eyes. "Oh my God," she whispered. "I hear that."

Bryson brushed her hair back, before he kissed her brow. "It's beautiful."

Jordan looked at Bryson, who'd held her hand the entire time. He really was going to be a good father. He'd been so tender with her, so caring. "It is," she agreed, staring at him, thinking he was beautiful, too. "It is."

Back at home later, Jordan kicked off her shoes and headed to the kitchen. She was hungry. Opening the refrigerator, she groaned at the absence of any food she wanted to eat. There were plenty of vegetables and fruit, but she wanted cheese. Preferably on a big burger.

Bryson strolled into the kitchen. "Want to order some lunch?"

He stepped closer, placing his hands on her shoulders and massaging the knots there. She hummed with approval, and leaned forward. "That feels good," she moaned.

She felt his lips on the back of her neck and purred. Suddenly realizing what was happening, or what she wanted to happen, she tensed, and slipped out of his embrace.

She tugged down on her shirt. "Um, I guess I could eat."

He smirked, but opened the junk drawer and pulled out the take-out menus. Bryson was talking but Jordan didn't hear anything. Just the sound of his voice made her heart soar, and she willed that traitorous thing down. She bit down on her lip. Hard. *Don't move. Don't go to him no matter what.*

But she found herself stepping forward, inching closer bit by bit. When he looked at her she stopped. "You okay?" he asked with a frown.

She nodded. "Yes, I'm fine."

Then his gaze raked over her body once before he turned his attention back to the menus. The heat in his eyes, for just that tiny moment, must have held some sort of power because she'd set the rules and now *she* was the one who wanted to break them. She knew she needed to stay away from him. She shouldn't be imagining his strong hands on her body, or his tongue on her core.

Damn, I can't stop wanting him to touch me. She fanned herself with her hand. For some reason, she was hot. "No." She felt hot. Burning, actually.

No, Jordan. No.

His eyes snapped to her. "What?"

Jordan blinked. "Huh?"

"You said no."

"No, I . . ." Jordan couldn't tell him what she'd been thinking, because he'd take it and run with it and she'd be helpless to stop him. "I said no, I don't want Chinese," she lied.

"I didn't ask if you wanted Chinese."

"Oh." She bit down on her fingernail. "I was just thinking to myself. At first, I thought I wanted some Orange Chicken. Then I was thinking no, I don't want Chinese."

Her explanation sounded like straight bullshit, but she'd run with it.

"What about pasta?" he asked.

Jordan's gaze dropped to his lips as he talked. She

wanted to go to him, and climb him like a tree to get to that mouth.

"Jordan?"

"Huh?" she asked.

"Did you hear me?" he asked, a concerned look in his eyes.

"What did you say?"

"I said maybe you should take a bath, soak a little. Wash that gel off?"

"Oh." Jordan wondered if a bath right then was the best idea. But when he stepped closer to her and wrapped her into a hug, she realized it was the perfect time to get away. Or she would not be liable for her actions.

Chapter 17

Bryson jogged up the stairs to check on Jordan. She'd been acting strangely since they'd come home from the doctor's. And the way she'd been looking at him . . . It made him want to bend her over and pound into her with abandon.

Outside of her room, he knocked. "Jordan?" When he didn't hear an answer, he opened the door. It had been an hour since she'd bolted up the stairs to take a bath. He hoped she hadn't fallen asleep in the tub.

The bathroom door was ajar, so he poked his head in. *Oh shit.* He jerked back, pacing the bedroom in long strides.

Bryson was teetering on the edge of a nervous breakdown and it was all Jordan's fault. What the hell had he been thinking when he asked her to move in? Sure, he thought he had a plan. But she'd turned all of his best-laid plans upside down with her smell, her laugh, and her body. A body full with his children.

The image of Jordan in the huge tub, filled with

bubbles, her nipples poking out of the water was seared on his brain. It tormented him, made him want to kick things and then charge in there and jump in with her. He took a few deep breaths and fought the urge to go into his room and once again take matters into his own hands. He'd been hard for an hour now, because his mind was playing the same thing over and over. Jordan all day, every day. He clenched his hands at his sides. This wasn't going to work. He wasn't strong enough to be in the same house with her and not touch her. His fantasies, no matter how hot and vivid, would only take him so far. *My dick is going to explode.* He ached with a need he'd only felt for her, with her.

"Bryson?" Jordan called, jerking him back to reality.

When did she get out of the tub?

"I'm glad you're here," she said. "Do you mind rubbing lotion on my back?"

And now she was standing in front of him begging him to touch her. Albeit only to rub lotion on her back.

He stared at her, trying to form a response to her innocent question. All he would have to do is tug lightly and the belt of that damn pink robe would give and he'd be treated to her naked body. Because his *roommate* was naked under that robe. And just the knowledge of that made all his blood travel south.

Pictures of him burying his face in her sweetness assaulted him and he stepped back. Away from her and away from the light scent of her.

Swallowing, he lowered his eyes to the mound of flesh peeking out of the opening of the robe, the drops of water on her golden skin. He let out a shaky breath before he forced his eyes back to hers. "You're . . . What are you doing?" he asked.

"The question would be what are *you* doing?"

"I was checking on you. I didn't know you were still in the bathtub. I'm sorry."

She shrugged. "It's not like you haven't seen it before. Can you put lotion on my back?" she repeated.

Fuck it. He couldn't resist her anymore. He didn't want to fight it. He just wanted her. He stalked toward her and tugged her to him, taking her mouth in a kiss and deepening it. The feel of her lips, the taste of the mint of her toothpaste, the warmth of her skin against his made him crazy. She made him crazy. The moan that escaped her mouth made him want to rip that damn robe off and kiss every part of her body. It wasn't just any kiss, it was deep, possessive hot.

Pulling away from her, he told her, "Jordan, this isn't going to work. You're driving me insane."

"What? I'm sorry."

"Don't apologize." He stepped away from her. "One minute, it feels like you want more from me, but the next minute you're pushing me away. I've made it very clear what I want. I just want you. And it feels like you want this, too. But what I don't understand is why we can't act on it. Am I crazy here? You tell me."

Jordan's eyes widened, and she pulled her robe closed. Her gaze dropped to the floor and she mumbled something to herself. Frowning, he watched as she seemed to be warring with herself.

"Jordan," he called.

Finally, she looked at him and he held his breath.

Her green eyes were dark, bear black. Then the robe was in a puddle on the floor. He let his gaze travel up her legs to the apex of her thighs, to her belly, then her breasts, then her face.

Stepping into him, she peered up at him. "You're not crazy," she said before she pulled his mouth to hers. He lifted her up and carried her to the bed.

He was lost in her, consumed by her scent, her taste, and the feel of her body against his. He gently lowered her to the bed and climbed over her. His blood pounded in his ear, his heart raced.

"Bryson?" Her voice was husky, soft.

"Please don't tell me to stop," he told her, searching her face. "Not now."

There were so many reasons to push him away, to jump up and put on her clothes. His taste, his smell gripped her like a tight fist. She wouldn't be able to pull away. She knew she shouldn't want this, shouldn't give in. But she couldn't stop him because she loved every minute.

Jordan felt wild, crazed. In her entire life, no one had looked at her the way Bryson did. It was intense, hungry, like he could see everything she didn't want anyone to see. Her pulse was beating rapidly, and she felt heat creep up her neck and her cheeks.

With his lips only a whisper away, he said, "I need you." Then, his mouth was on hers, and Jordan was lost. The kiss was gentle at first. His tongue swept out, teasing and coaxing until she moaned. She wanted more.

"More," she managed to say, when he pulled away to tug his shirt off.

Bryson kissed his way down her body, and when he lowered his head and brushed his mouth over her belly, she melted. It was so tender, so sweet, tears pricked her eyes. He kissed lower still, finally brushing his lips over her inner thigh and rubbing his face against her skin.

Her back arched off the bed when she felt his tongue on her, feasting on her, lapping up her arousal before he sucked on her bundle of nerves. While focused on her throbbing clit with his mouth, he slipped his fingers inside her heat. Jordan didn't need to wait long. In a few moments she was coming on a hoarse cry.

Jordan struggled for breath as the pleasure pulled her under the rolling waves. She hadn't done anything. She'd only been lying there, letting him pleasure her, but she felt like she'd just run a marathon. When her heartbeat slowed, she relaxed into the mattress.

Slowly, Bryson kissed his way back up her body and planted his mouth over hers. "I need you," he repeated.

There was something about him needing her the way he did that made her feel powerful. She wrapped her legs around him.

"Condom," he grumbled.

Jordan bit down on his lip. She was so ready for him, so open, so wet. "Too late for that."

Her eyes fluttered closed and he sank deep inside of her. Bryson's head fell to her shoulder and he stayed like that for a moment. "Shit, you feel so good."

"Bryson, please." She lifted her hips, pulling him in deeper.

He captured her bottom lip in his teeth and tugged.

"Open your eyes, Jordie." Her eyes popped open, and he smirked. "I want to watch you."

Bryson never took his eyes from her as he began to move in and out, in and out. It started out slowly, but soon their need to release took over and they picked up the pace. He pounded into her hard, a sheen of sweat on his brow and his face desperate with need. They moved together in unison, meeting each other with equal force. She was crazy with need for him, so crazy she felt like she would burst open if he wasn't touching her or kissing her or making love to her. Jordan cried out as they both exploded, each of them climaxing long and hard.

Bryson rolled over on his back, and pulled her with him. "That was . . . damn."

Jordan grinned, sweeping a hand over his stomach. "It was. What took you so long?" She felt the tremble of laughter in his gut, and thought it was the best sound she'd ever heard.

"I was waiting for permission," he said.

"Stop."

Silence descended over the room, briefly. Jordan wondered if Bryson had fallen asleep. "Bryson?" she called.

"Marry me."

Jordan giggled. "Boy, I know it was good, but don't go getting all crazy on me."

"I'm serious."

Perching herself up on her elbow, she met his gaze. "What?"

"Jordie, this feels right to me. Let's make it official. Marry me."

Jordan sat up, raking her fingers through her hair. "Bryson, I can't marry you." His face fell, and she felt bad. She didn't want to keep hurting him, but there was no way they were ready for marriage. She picked up his hand and kissed his palm. "I think it's easy to get caught up in the emotion of our situation. You're reeling from the death of your father and the pregnancy. Then, we just found out we were having twins. It's been an emotional day. You're just reacting."

He tipped her head to face him. "No, I want you. I'm ready to take this to the next level."

Jordan averted her gaze. "I don't know if I'm ready. In fact, I know I'm not. I thought we agreed to focus on the babies."

"Why can't we do both?"

"But marriage? That's moving way too fast."

"Don't you think it's a sign that we're having these babies? After everything? It has to mean something." Bryson surveyed her. "I can't go back to life yesterday, or even a few hours ago, when I couldn't touch you or kiss you."

"I'm not asking you to do that."

Jordan couldn't live without his kisses and touches if someone offered her good health for the rest of her life. She wanted him and she knew she was falling in love with him. But she couldn't promise to marry him. Not now.

Bryson cupped her face. "This." He kissed her eyelids. "Means." He kissed her nose. "Something." He pulled her into a heated kiss, stealing her breath and her common sense because she wanted to say yes. Because she got lost in his heartbeat every single time he was near.

"Bryson," she moaned when he pulled away. "You're relentless."

"I just know what I want, what I've always wanted."

"Always?"

He traced her lips with his finger. "Always. But I won't push you, Jordie. I'm a patient man. I've waited this long, and I can wait a little longer."

"Why?"

"Because it's going to happen."

Bryson's cocky attitude should have been a turnoff, but it had the opposite effect on Jordan. "But—"

"No buts. Now, get over here and sit on my face."

Jordan awoke with a start. She glanced over at the empty spot in the bed, picking up the piece of paper that had been left on the pillow. In his distinctive handwriting, it said, "Come here. In the kitchen." She fell back on the pillow. After Bryson had made her come so much she couldn't see straight, he'd held her in his arms until she'd drifted off.

Jordan had never felt so good. It wasn't their physical connection. It wasn't the fact that he seemed to know her body almost better than she knew it. It was their shared history, the way he handled her, the way he loved her.

They'd turned a corner, and she welcomed the change. She looked forward to getting to know him, to learn what he'd been doing all these years. And she was excited to share pieces of herself with him.

She picked up her phone and checked the time. It was still early, and she hadn't checked on Granddad and Grams yet. Dialing her grandmother, she smiled when she heard Grams's voice over the receiver. "Hi, Grams."

"Jordan? I've been waiting for you to call all day."

Jordan picked at a loose string on the bedspread. "I know. I meant to call you, but I got busy." *Busy doing Bryson.*

"How did the appointment go? I've been waiting with bated breath."

"You're going to love this. Or you might not."

"What is it, chile? Tell me. I'm too old to guess."

Jordan relayed the news that she was going to be great-grams to two babies, not one. Grams's shout of joy brought a smile to Jordan's lips. In the background, she heard Grams telling Granddad.

Then, he was on the line. "My punchkin is having two little punchkins."

"I am," Jordan said. "Are you ready to babysit?"

"You know I don't babysit. That's your grand-mother's thing. But I can't wait to tell them all the history of our family."

Jordan remembered sitting on her grandfather's lap and hearing about the Clark family and the history of Wellspring. Her great-great-grandfather was the town's first mayor. It was an impressive history and inspiring legacy that she couldn't wait to pass down to her children.

"I want us to start writing down this history, Granddad."

Jordan had been getting on her grandparents to start documenting things. Sometime last year, they'd sat down and told Jordan where she would be able to find all of their paperwork if something should happen to them. While the conversation was hard, Jordan knew it was necessary. But once they were done, she'd asked them to not only think about end of life, but to also think about leaving a legacy.

Her grandfather had a wealth of knowledge about many things. And Grams was notorious for cooking from memory and hadn't written down her recipes. It was high time they put something on paper.

She spent another few minutes catching up with her grandparents before she hung up and went off in search of Bryson. The blare of the speakers and the smell of bacon drew her attention to the kitchen.

When she rounded the corner, she paused at the sight of Bryson standing at the stove, spitting a rap and flipping pancakes. Leaning into the door frame, she watched as he expertly squeezed fresh orange juice and set the table. He moved with power, but there was a grace to his movements, a confidence that had developed in the years he'd been away. She liked it. No, she loved it.

"Are you going to stand there all night, or come in here and eat?" He hadn't even looked at her, but he'd known she was there.

Stepping into the kitchen, she said, "I was admiring the view."

With a wicked grin, he poured her a cup of tea and brought it to her, planting a sweet kiss to her lips. "I figured you would be hungry."

Her stomach chose that exact moment to growl. And for the first time since she'd found out she was pregnant, the smell of bacon didn't make her want to empty the contents of her stomach in the toilet. She sniffed the tea. It was her favorite. Passion fruit. Lifting the mug to her mouth, she took a sip. He'd remembered how she liked it, too.

Turning to her, he asked, "Is it good?"

Jordan eyed him. "How do you do that?"

He frowned, using the spatula to lift pancakes off

the griddle and transfer them onto an empty plate. "Do what?"

"Know exactly what I need."

"I watch you," he said with a shrug.

Jordan wanted to hear more, but she was too distracted with his physique. He was wearing a pair of low-riding sweats and nothing else. Her gaze drifted down to the thin line of hair that ran from his stomach into his pants. Fully clothed Bryson was hot, but shirtless—*or naked*—Bryson was insanely hot.

"If you don't stop looking at me like that, you'll find yourself bent over that breakfast bar in two seconds."

"Would that be so bad?" she teased.

"Not if you want to eat burnt bacon and black pancakes." He motioned to one of the empty chairs. "Have a seat."

She did as she was told, and he slid a plate in front of her. "I didn't know you cooked. You're always game to order out."

"I can do a few things. I have a weak spot for pancakes so I perfected them once I moved away from here. Not as good as Arlene's but they're pretty good, if I must say so myself."

Arlene was the housekeeper-slash-cook for the Wells family while Bryson was growing up. Jordan knew he'd been close to the woman. "What happened to Arlene?"

He shrugged. "Parker said she retired when Senior got sick. She still lives in town. I had planned to go see her soon."

"That would be good." She leaned back when Bryson pushed a couple pieces of bacon on her plate. Picking one of them up, she bit down and moaned. "Oh goodness. This is good."

"Don't moan like that."

"Why?" she asked, finishing her piece of pork.

"You make me want to do things to you so I can hear that moan in my ear."

Jordan threw her head back in laughter. "Bryson, you're insatiable." *And I don't mind.*

"Only because it's you." He joined her at the breakfast bar.

Biting into her pancake, Jordan groaned as the sweet cake practically melted in her mouth. She pointed to her plate with her fork. "This is good."

"Thanks."

They ate in silence for several minutes, before she asked, "Are we going to be okay?"

He took a sip from his tall glass of orange juice. "As far as . . . ?"

"We're having twins, Bryson."

"It's pretty awesome, huh? I want to frame the sonogram picture. Or put it on the refrigerator."

Jordan studied him. "You surprise me at every turn, Mr. Wells."

"Then, I'd say I'm ahead of the game." He leaned in and kissed her nose.

The man next to her was everything she remembered and more. He was wearing her down minute by minute. *If I'm not careful, I'll be in love before the twenty-week mark.*

Chapter 18

Bryson peeked in the large carry-out bag and smiled. "Thanks, Grams."

"No need to thank me. I have to make sure my great-grandbabies are eating well." She leaned over the counter. "How is everything?"

Sighing, he told her, "She's good. I guess."

The truth was Jordan was anything but good when he'd left her that morning. Now, at twenty weeks pregnant, she'd been having a hard time sleeping, and had been crying at the drop of a hat. Bryson was at a loss. A crying Jordan wasn't something he liked to see. He wanted to protect her, make sure she was happy. But it seemed that every day there was a new reason for her to be unhappy.

The day before, she'd cried for an hour during an episode of *Love It or List It*. When he'd asked why, she simply told him because she was upset the couple "loved" it instead of "listing" it. Then earlier in the week, she'd cried because she was hungry. And when he'd surprised her with dinner, she cried again because it wasn't what she'd had a taste for.

They no longer slept in separate beds, which was good. But every night, she'd spend the night tossing and turning, moaning and groaning. One minute, she was kicking the covers off and the next she was asking for an extra blanket. To help, Bryson had bought her a personal fan and a compact heater. Then she'd cried when he brought them into the house.

"She's wearing you out, huh?" Grams laughed. "Look at your eyes." She motioned to his eyes, which he was sure were dark with exhaustion.

Smiling, he told her, "I just do what I can. How's Granddad?"

Grams blessed him with her dimpled smile. "He's doing great."

The doctors had given him a clean bill of health. His last scans showed no sign of the cancer, and he'd recently completed his last treatment. They'd all celebrated with a hearty meal of homemade lasagna, green beans, and garlic bread. Oh, and pickles for Jordan.

"He's excited about tonight," Grams added.

Jordan had planned a bowling gender reveal party. She'd told him about her idea one night while they were sharing a bath. At first, he'd been skeptical, but she'd convinced him it was a perfect way to get out with their friends and family, enjoy each other, and eat. Bryson suspected it had more to do with the food at the bowling alley than the bowling itself.

She'd planned everything, and had even arranged for Remy to be there via videoconference since his best friend couldn't make it. Over the past several weeks, they'd shopped for baby stuff and repainted the nursery because the original color wouldn't work for both babies, according to Jordan.

"Tell Granddad I said get ready to lose," Bryson teased.

As soon as Jordan announced the venue for the gender reveal party, Granddad had insisted on pulling his bowling ball out of storage and cleaning it off because he wanted to "show y'all young people something." Bryson was glad to see the spark back in Granddad's eyes.

"Oh please." Grams waved a hand in dismissal. "He's just talking stuff. He hasn't bowled in years."

The bell above the door chimed and Bryson looked over at it, surprised when Samuel Lester stepped into the diner. Mr. Lester was the city planner of Wellspring, and had been a mentor for Bryson in high school.

"Mr. Lester?" Bryson walked over to the older man and shook his hand. "It's good to see you."

Samuel grinned. "Bryson, my boy. I had heard you were back in town. It's been a long time. I'm sorry about your father."

Unsure what to say, Bryson simply nodded. He'd grown accustomed to the condolences from many people in town, and appreciated the concern from the residents of Wellspring. But he was always lost on how to respond. When Remy's mother died, his friend's standard response to the people was "It's hard, but I'm making it through." And when people had asked Parker or Brooklyn how they were doing after Marie died, they'd always responded with "We're hanging in there" or "We really miss her."

None of those explanations applied to Bryson, though. It hadn't been hard at all. He wasn't simply "making it through." He was thriving, enjoying his life. He *was* definitely hanging in there, but he couldn't say he missed his father, though. Of course, he knew that had a lot to do with Jordan and his babies. She'd brought light to his life, just like she'd done when they were eleven years old in the lunchroom.

"How long do you plan on staying in town?" Mr. Lester asked, pulling Bryson back to the present.

"I moved here a few months ago."

"That's great news. Do you have a minute to chat with me?"

Bryson glanced at the bag of food waiting for him on the counter and weighed his options. Could he risk showing up with cold food and another crying fit?

As if she sensed his turmoil, Grams said, "Go ahead and sit down, Bryson. I'll make sure she has a fresh breakfast when you're ready to leave."

Grams slid a piping hot mug of coffee his way, and he mouthed, "Thank you," before joining Mr. Lester at his table.

A little later, Bryson entered his house, calling Jordan's name as he went to the kitchen and set the bag full of food down on the counter. When Jordan didn't meet him in the kitchen, he started to search the house.

He found her in the nursery, sitting cross-legged on the floor. *Damn.* She was crying again. Every time was like a fist to the gut. Most of the time, there was nothing he could do for her, but he always tried to help.

Without a word, he walked over to her and sat down in front of her. "Jordie, what's wrong?"

Jordan met his eyes and sniffed. "I'm hungry."

"I brought you something to eat, baby," he said, stroking her knees with his thumbs.

"Did you get me a Slurpee?"

Shit. He forgot the frozen drink in his haste to get back to her. "I forgot. But I'll make you a strawberry smoothie with whipped cream."

Her eyes lit up then and he sent a silent prayer of thanks up to God. "Sounds good."

"Is that why you're sitting in here crying?"

She shook her head. "It's not that, silly."

Bryson wanted to ask why he was silly because she had cried over lost food, bad food, and no food over the past few weeks. But instead, he repeated, "What's wrong?"

Jordan picked up his hand and placed it on her lower abdomen. Using her hand to push his harder against her skin, she asked, "Feel that?"

Bryson was just about to say he didn't feel anything when he felt a soft push against the palm of his hand. His eyes snapped to Jordan's. "A kick?"

She gave him a wobbly smile. "Finally."

Jordan had been worried that she hadn't felt the babies kicking yet. After a visit with the doctor, Dr. Jones had explained that the reason she hadn't felt the kicking was probably due to placental placement. That didn't stop Jordan from obsessing about it, though. She'd worried that something was wrong with the babies, and didn't calm down until Dr. Jones did an impromptu ultrasound in the office to show Jordan that their babies were, in fact, fine.

"I'm so happy," she cried. "They're moving."

Bryson swallowed past a huge lump that had formed in his throat. The urge to cry filled him. Leaning down, he lifted her shirt and brushed his lips over her growing baby bump. "I can't wait to meet you," he told the babies. "You're so strong. I love you both."

Jordan's hand smoothed over his head. "They love you, too. I can feel them moving as you're talking to them."

He cupped her cheeks and pulled her down to him for a kiss. "I love you, too."

Her eyes widened. "You do?"

"I do. And I have good news."

"What is it?"

"I ran into Mr. Lester today at the diner."

Jordan furrowed her brow. "Really? Do I know him?"

"You'll recognize him if you see him. He's the city planner for Wellspring. Anyway, he's retiring soon, and is looking for someone who can come in and learn the job under his tutelage."

Samuel Lester had asked Bryson what his career goals were, and Bryson answered him truthfully. He'd basically told him his entire school and employment history. Essentially, he'd interviewed for the position because Samuel then offered him the position of assistant planner for Wellspring.

"What?" Jordan screeched when Bryson had finished his story. "He offered you a job?"

Bryson grinned. "He did. He told me I would have to go through the screening process, and submit a formal application, but he assured me it was a formality. I have to go in and meet the town officials next week."

Jordan hugged his neck, squeezing tightly. "Oh my God, you're so kick-ass. Who gets a job while picking up breakfast at the diner? I'm so happy for you, baby!" Cupping his face in her hands, she kissed him hard. "You deserve this. Everything you have, you deserve."

God, I'm so in love with this woman. There was no one more supportive than Jordan. There was no one who made him feel like he could singlehandedly solve every problem in the world. She made him feel invincible and like he could do anything, be anything. His home was hers; his body was hers. If she'd let him, he'd spend every minute of every day with her for the rest of his life.

"You're so beautiful." He kissed her chin. "You're so mine." He kissed her neck, just below her ear. "I love you so much."

"Bryson, I—"

He shut her up with another kiss. "Shh. You don't have to say it, Jordan. I just want you to know how I feel." Standing up, he helped her to her feet. "Let's go get you something to eat."

"I'd like to propose a toast." Parker held up his bottle of beer in the air. "To my brother, Bryson. You have never let your situation keep you from being great. I'm proud of you. Congratulations to you and Jordan on your new family, and congrats on your new job."

The sound of clinking glasses and hearty cheers filled the party area at the bowling alley. Although Bryson would have preferred Parker not spill the beans about the job offer, he was ecstatic that his brother was so happy.

As people walked up to him with best wishes, he scanned the area, looking for Jordan. She'd disappeared with Stacyee and Maddie several minutes ago.

"Brother!" Brooklyn pulled him into a hug. "I'm so happy for you."

Bryson wrapped his arms around his sister. "Thanks, sis."

She peered up at him. "You have never looked happier than I've seen you tonight. It warms my heart."

Carter stepped over to them, and reached out to give him some dap. "You did good, man."

Bryson nodded. "Thanks, bruh."

Grams came over next. "Boy, you are full of surprises. We're so happy for you."

Hugging Grams, he asked, "Where's Jordan?"

She shrugged. "She walked off with her crew. You know how they are. They're probably somewhere yapping away."

"You're probably right."

Grams cupped his chin. "I couldn't be more proud of you if you were my own son."

"Thanks, Grams. I feel like I'm your own son. Thanks for accepting me into your family."

When her chin shook, she turned away. "Aw, hush. I can't be crying in public like this."

"My main man," Granddad said, clasping Bryson's hand. "Since you're celebrating so many big things tonight, I'll hold off on that butt whoopin' in bowling. It's your night."

Bryson barked out a laugh. "Okay, Granddad. I look forward to whoopin' *your* butt another day."

Out of the corner of his eye, he saw Jordan wobbling back toward them. Stacyee and Maddie were holding trays of food in their hands. They'd reserved half of the bowling alley for their party, so most of the people there belonged to their group. Jordan had insisted they let the bowling alley kitchen staff cater, instead of letting Grams cater. And now he knew why.

His girlfriend was greedy. Bryson watched as she sat down and did a little happy dance as she dipped a soft pretzel into a cup of processed cheese sauce, then bit into the pretzel. In her other hand, she had a chicken wing covered in ranch dressing.

Shaking his head, he made his way over to her. Bending low to her ear, he whispered, "This is why you really wanted to come to the bowling alley, isn't it?"

She froze, her chicken wing right at the entrance of her mouth. "No. I knew you liked to bowl and I thought it would be cute to do the gender reveal like this." She bit into the chicken and let out a low moan of delight. "This is so good. They have the best fried chicken wings in town. Don't tell Grams."

"The doctor said to watch the sodium, Jordan," he warned. "Take it easy."

She held an uneaten piece of chicken up to his mouth, and pushed it against his lips. "Taste it. You won't be sorry."

Bryson took a bite. Jordan wasn't lying. The chicken tasted like it was fried in someone's mama's house, not at all like he would expect in a bowling alley. He grabbed the rest of the wing from her and finished it off. "I guess these are okay. But dump that processed cheese, baby."

A little later, Jordan and Bryson stood in front of their guests. He was holding his bowling ball, readying himself for the reveal. During the last ultrasound, the doctor had given the information to them in a sealed envelope because Jordan thought it would be fun if they found out the sex of the babies at the same time everyone else did.

The alley manager was the only one in the building who knew what they were having. For the reveal, Bryson would roll his ball, and when the pins reset, they would either be pink or blue or both.

"Thank you all for coming," Jordan said, placing her hand on Bryson's shoulder. "We love you all. I don't know what we would do without you." She waved at the phone Stacyee was holding up. Remy's face was there. "Hi, Remy."

"Hey, Jordan," Remy said.

Bryson had briefly talked to Remy before handing his phone to Stacyee so she could hold it while he shot the ball. His friend had agreed to join them for Thanksgiving.

Jordan continued her speech, talking about community, love, and support, before turning it over to him. "Anything you want to say, baby?" she asked.

He shook his head. "Not really." Everybody laughed. He leaned down and kissed her softly. Everybody *aww*ed. "I think you covered everything."

She shoved him playfully. "Go ahead and bowl."

After he made his shot, Jordan rushed over to him and hooked her arm in his as they waited for the pins to drop. The sound of the ball hitting the pins and the pins crashing together echoed in the building. He'd rolled a strike, so he did his normal fist pump. A beat later, the new set of pins lowered, and the color was . . . pink. All pink. They were having two girls.

The crowd erupted into a loud chorus of cheers as everyone celebrated the big news. Bryson wrapped his arms around Jordan's waist and lifted her. "I told you," she murmured before planting her mouth over his.

After the party, Bryson and Jordan entered their home. She kicked off her shoes. "I need a bottle of water."

Bryson called after her, "I told you to stop eating that food."

She'd complained about a stomachache the entire ride home. "Shut up."

He laughed. "Drink the whole bottle, Jordan. I'm going to the office to work on this application."

They'd turned one of the living rooms into an office. When he entered the room, he turned on the light. Jordan had chosen the cherrywood desk and the furnishings for the space. It felt modern, nothing like Senior's old office, which was now being turned into a storage area.

He'd originally planned to turn it into a game room, but had decided against it because he just didn't want to have to be in there for any reason. He took a seat at the desk and powered up his laptop.

He worked for a few minutes, updating his resume, when he heard a soft knock on the door. Looking up, he smiled at Jordan. "Feeling better?"

A slow grin spread across her face. "Much."

His gaze swept over her. She was wearing a hot pink nightgown that looked more like a shirt, it was so short. And he loved it. "Come here," he ordered.

Jordan sauntered over to him and leaned against the desk. "You come here," she replied, with a wink.

He slid his chair over and planted his arms on either side of her body. "You're so sexy. I want to taste you." A blush crept up her cheek, and she lowered herself onto his lap, straddling his legs. Her belly pushed against his, and it felt freakin' amazing. He brushed his palms over her stomach. "Tonight was pretty awesome. Thank you."

She smiled, using her thumb to trace a line over his brow. "We have good family and friends."

"That we do."

"I told you it was a girl."

"I won't doubt you again." He kissed her neck, cupped her breasts in his hands.

"Bryson?"

"Yes, Jordie."

Jordan closed his laptop and set it on a small table adjacent to the desk. She leaned forward, pressing her lips against his. "I need you."

And that was all he needed to hear. Bryson shoved the rest of the stuff on the desk aside, sending everything to the floor. Gripping her waist, he perched her up on his desk, tugged her nightgown up and off, and tossed it behind him. He caught the tip of one breast between his teeth, then laved it with his tongue before he sucked it hard. She wrapped her legs around his hips and let her head fall back against the hard surface. With one motion he pulled her panties down and cupped her sex in his palm.

Jordan unbuckled his jeans and pushed them and his underwear down. She gripped his penis in her hands and stroked him, drawing a low moan from his throat. This was his life. *She is my life.* He stared at

her, taking in her flushed skin, her pert breasts, her
round stomach, and her . . .

"Stop playing around, Bryson. I need you inside
me. Now."

Spurred on from the whimper that escaped her
mouth, he plunged forward, pressing himself into
her. He closed his eyes as he filled her completely.
She fit him like a leather glove, snug and warm.

"So good," she moaned. "More."

He couldn't think, couldn't feel anything, smell
anything, but her. Her sweet scent and the way she
whispered dirty things in his ear made him snap.
Groaning, he gave in, pumping into her hard and
fast. Her loud moans told him that's exactly how she
wanted it.

"Shit," he said with a loud grunt. "You like that?"

Her eyes popped open. "I love it."

The truth in her eyes unraveled him at the seams.
He gripped her hips, thrusting into her with long,
deep, hard strokes. In and out. Over and over.

He slipped his hand between them and massaged
her clit. Then her mouth fell open and she broke,
screaming his name as she jerked against him. The
sensation of her climax triggered his own and he
buried his face in her neck as he came.

Chapter 19

Jordan was living in a daydream, one filled with Bryson. She heard him in her music, saw him in the clouds and the stars, felt him in the wind on her skin and the fabric of her clothes, smelled him in her tea. He was everywhere, all over her. And because of that she was in a state of arousal. Jordan had never had a problem concentrating until now. Until him.

It wasn't just physical longing either. Because let's face it, he knew how to make her come apart with just a touch. No, it was deeper than lust, more than anything she could have imagined. She didn't just want to be with him, she wanted to lose herself in him, burrow under him, bask in him. She loved him.

If she could just say it, she might feel better. But she couldn't bring herself to say the words. She couldn't bring herself to tell him that she loved him desperately and hopelessly. Instead, her throat closed up as she watched him pick out his outfit for Thanksgiving dinner at Brooklyn's house. His defined abs made her want to lick him, to kiss his entire body. She admired his corded, muscular back;

the way his pants always sat low on his waist; and the happy trail that disappeared under his pants.

"We're not having sex, Jordie. We're already late."

Her cheeks burned. "What?" she asked.

"You're looking at me like you want some." His gaze raked over her, the heat in his eyes unmistakable. He wanted her. All she needed to do was push him. Just a little.

She smirked. "You know the doctor told me that sex could kick-start labor?"

He blinked, and a slow smile spread across his face. "Did she really?"

Bryson had been working as the assistant city planner for a few months and had been gone for longer hours lately. As a result, Jordan had assured him she was fine to go to her thirty-six-week appointment without him. The doctor didn't expect her to go much longer, as twins typically arrived before the actual due date, and Jordan was way past ready to meet her baby girls.

"She did," Jordan told him, stepping into him and pulling him into an intense kiss. His low groan as she took control, sweeping her tongue into his mouth, was enough to drive her into a frenzy. There was nothing about this that didn't feel right to her. And she knew he deserved her words, her affirmation of love for him. But for some reason she couldn't just say the damn words. So she showed him.

She pushed his sweatpants down and gripped his erection in her hand. He was hard and thick, throbbing in her hand and soon . . . *in my mouth.*

Dropping to her knees she licked his penis from base to tip before taking him into her mouth.

"Jordie," he groaned, wrapped a hand in her hair. "No."

He pulled away, and helped her stand. She pouted. "Bryson, I—?"

"Turn around," he ordered. "And bend over. I'm going to give you what you really want."

Jordan did as she was told and turned around, bracing her hands on the wall. His hands on her body were like tiny little flames burning her skin. She felt his arousal against her ass and groaned in anticipation. "Bryson," she breathed, pushing back against him.

"Tell me how much you want me," he demanded, biting down on her shoulder.

"Oh God, I want you."

He rubbed his hard length over her slit. "Tell me how much you need me."

"I need you, Bryson," she cried. "I need you so much."

"Tell me you know that I'm the only one that can make you feel this way."

"You're the only one." She let out a desperate cry when he ripped her panties off, tearing them at the seams, and pushed one finger, then two inside her heat. "Shit, I'm coming."

"Not yet," he said, replacing his fingers with his dick. "Not without me."

"Bryson!" Brooklyn gasped. "It's beautiful."

Bryson watched as his sisters ogled the ring he'd purchased Jordan. He'd picked it out a few weeks earlier. The cushion-cut white diamond center stone was surrounded by a halo of pink and white bead-set diamonds. He knew it was perfect the moment he'd spotted it.

"I'm going to cry," Brooklyn said, fanning herself.

Veronica took the box from Brooklyn. "You did good, Bryson. When are you going to pop the question?"

Bryson knew he wanted to do it soon. But he wasn't sure if he wanted to do the public proposal thing, especially since Jordan had turned him down once. But so many things had changed since that first proposal.

"Did you tell Parker?" Brooklyn asked.

"I did. He actually went with me to the jeweler."

Bryson had dragged his brother around as he'd shopped for rings. And he'd had to listen to his big brother's advice on married life and fatherhood for the entire day. But he didn't mind. Parker and Kennedi were happy with their bundle of joy, his new-born nephew Anthony. Bryson hoped to one day be as happy as they were.

Brooklyn embraced Bryson. "I can see that you love her so much."

Bryson knew that he loved her, and had told her so numerous times. But Jordan had yet to say the words. Still, it hadn't given him pause because she'd shown him she loved him every day. It was in the way she took care of him when he came home from work, the way she listened to him, the way she made love to him. As his daughters grew bigger inside her, he couldn't help but love her more and more every day. She'd been there for him in ways no one had ever been.

"Are you nervous?" Veronica asked.

"A little. But not because I'm not sure. I know I want to be with her. But Jordan is . . . tough."

"You have to follow your heart, brother," Brooklyn said. "That's all you can do."

"You're right." Bryson stood. "Let me go find her. We need to talk."

"When is the wedding?" Stacyee asked, waggling her eyebrows.

"Right," Maddie agreed.

They were sitting in Brooklyn's office, taking a break from the festivities out in the main area of the house. Thanksgiving dinner was amazing, but Jordan had started to feel a little uncomfortable. It was probably because she'd eaten herself into a stupor. Too much ham, too much turkey, too much peach cobbler, too much potato salad. *Shit.* She rubbed her belly, wincing at the squeezing sensation that seemed to take her breath away.

She shifted in her seat. "What are you talking about? Whose wedding?"

Stacyee shook her head. "Yours, J. Yours and Bryson's."

Jordan held her breath as the babies rolled. Over the past few weeks, the distinctive kicks she'd once enjoyed feeling had turned into sweeping rolls inside her belly. The last few weeks had been quite the experience. She ached everywhere, couldn't sleep, had started peeing all day, every day again, and couldn't see her feet or anything else but her belly.

Bryson had been wonderful, and had massaged her feet and her swollen ankles. Because yes! She had cankles. Even still, he'd kissed her, made love to her, told her she was beautiful every single day. He'd been an angel. *Her* angel.

"Where are you getting this marriage thing from?"

Bryson hadn't brought it up again to Jordan, so she wondered why her friends were talking about it.

"Because you're in love. You're having his babies. He obviously loves you," Stacyee said. "Stop playing and let go."

"We're not thinking about getting married, Stacyee." Jordan looked at Stacyee, then Maddie. "Seriously."

"What's the holdup?" Maddie asked.

Jordan shrugged. *I don't feel good.* Frowning, she told her friend there was no holdup. "We're just trying to do what's right for the babies. And we don't have to be married to do that."

"Don't you love him?" Maddie asked.

"Yeah," Jordan admitted, for the first time to anyone. "I do love him. But sometimes love isn't enough. What if once the babies are born, he leaves? Or worse, he tries to take them away from me like Senior took him away from his mother."

Yet, even as Jordan said the words, she knew Bryson would never do that. *What is wrong with me?* Bryson had proven himself to be someone she could trust with her life. Why couldn't she just let go and be with him?

"Have you told him you love him?" Stacyee asked.

Jordan averted her gaze, effectively giving her answer. Her friends were hitting at an open wound.

She knew that it was time to tell Bryson how she felt. She knew that she was being a coward.

"Shit, J," Stacyee said. "What are you thinking?"

"Nothing. I just haven't said the words. But I show him daily."

Maddie kneeled in front of her, taking Jordan's hands in hers. "You know, as your friend, I have to tell you . . . you're on some bullshit."

Jordan gasped. "What?"

"Why can't you let yourself feel his love and stop overthinking everything?" Maddie asked.

Bryson had once told her she was overthinking things between them. And she'd denied it then. Now her best friend was telling her the same thing. Maybe there was really something to it.

Stacyee squeezed her shoulder. "Stop comparing your relationship to your parents' relationship. It's time to put up or shut up. Commit to that man. If you don't, you might lose him."

Jordan would hate to lose Bryson, but . . . "I just think he's moving too fast."

"That's just an excuse," Maddie said. "This isn't an average situation. You're having his babies any day now."

"Look, we're not talking marriage." Jordan blew out a deep breath. "And I'm not ready. I don't know if I'll ever be ready. So that's that. I don't want to talk about it anymore!"

Maddie's mouth fell open and Stacyee's eyes widened as they zeroed in on something behind Jordan. A feeling of dread settled in Jordan's stomach, and she shifted in her seat. Bryson was standing there, a deep frown on his perfect face.

"You know what?" Bryson lifted his hands up in surrender. "You win." He stormed out of the room.

"Bryson, wait!" Jordan shouted.

But Bryson needed to get the hell out of there before he did or said something he'd regret. He felt like an idiot, waxing poetic about her, envisioning a life with her and his babies. A permanent life. Not a temporary one. And she'd played him. Again.

"Son, where are you going?" Remy asked when he zoomed through the living area.

Bryson didn't want a scene, but he was in a house full of people, and it was unavoidable. "Out of here," he grumbled.

"Wait," Brooklyn called. "Bryson!"

"Please, Bryson!" Jordan shouted from behind him. "Don't go."

He heard the breathy tone of her voice behind him and stopped. He wouldn't make her chase him. He knew she'd been struggling with shortness of breath the farther along in her pregnancy she got.

Slowly, he turned to her. "Are you okay?" he asked. Even in his anger, he didn't want anything to happen to her, he didn't want her to feel any discomfort.

Jordan blinked. "Yes."

"Then let me go."

"Please, don't walk out. We need to talk about this."

Scanning the room, he met the faces of his friends and family. They were worried, watching the scene unfold before them. "What is there to talk about,

Jordan?" he asked. "You made yourself perfectly clear."

"It's not like that," she argued.

"Do you even love me?"

Her face softened. "Yes, I love you."

He'd waited months for her to say it, but the words seemed hollow to his ears. "I don't believe you." He heard a gasp from behind him. "Why?"

"Why?" Jordan was frustrated, frazzled. "Because I do."

"I know why I love you. I don't even have to think about it." He stepped closer to her, not thrilled that she retreated back a step. It was indicative of their relationship. For every step he moved forward, she moved back. And he wasn't going to live his life like that. "I love you because you took a chance on me. You were my first friend here, and you opened your life to me. You shared your grandparents with me. I love you because, even after fourteen years, I can't get the vision of you in that damn pink dress out of my head. I love you because you smell like heaven and your smile is like the sun."

A sob burst from Jordan's mouth. "Bryson."

"I love you because you see me, even though you fight against it. I love you because you take care of me when I've had a long day. You were there for me when my father died. You understood without me having to say anything how it affected me. I love you because you're you. And I can't imagine living life without you."

With his heart beating out of control, he waited for her to say anything. But there was nothing. Sighing, he said, "I wanted to build something with you. But I can't take another rejection from you, Jordan. And I won't. So I'm going to give you what you want. You wanted us to focus on the babies, to co-parent. That's what we'll do. That's all we'll do."

Chapter 20

I fucked up.

Bryson slammed the door on his way out and Jordan sunk to the couch. Then the tears came, blinding her. The fellas chased after Bryson, leaving her there with the women.

Stacyee gripped her hand. "J, are you okay?"

"I made a mistake," Jordan croaked, holding a hand against her chest. "I made a mistake, Stacyee." Frantic, she stood and rushed to the door. She had to get to Bryson, she had to tell him how she felt.

But the sharp pain shooting down her side made her cry out and stop in her tracks. Soon she was surrounded by her friends.

Maddie was in her ear, telling her to slow down, leading her over to the couch. "J, you have to sit down. Bryson just needs some time."

Jordan shook her head as panic welled up in her. "No. He needs to know."

"Maybe I can tell him," Brooklyn said. "I'll call him and tell him to come back."

The look on Brooklyn's face, her tone, told Jordan

that she looked like a crazy maniac and they would say anything to calm her down. "Brooklyn, I'm sorry."

"What are you apologizing for?" Brooklyn asked.

"I hurt your brother. You must hate me."

Brooklyn exchanged a glance with Maddie. "I don't hate you. I just think you need to calm down."

Another sharp pain had Jordan screaming aloud as she doubled over. "Shit, that hurts." She let out a ragged breath.

"I think she's in labor," she heard Kennedi say. "We should probably start timing the contractions."

Five minutes later, while her friends were running around gathering her coat and purse and making calls, Jordan shrieked a few choice curse words as she gasped for breath. "Somebody call Bryson. I need him."

"Hey, Bryson," Grams said, opening the front door, clad in a robe and a bonnet. "What brings you by this late?"

Bryson didn't know why he'd shown up at Grams's house. He'd just started driving and ended up there. "I don't think it's going to work out between me and Jordan."

Without a word, Grams stepped back, letting him into the house.

He followed her into the kitchen. Grams and Granddad had chosen to have a quiet Thanksgiving dinner at their home, just the two of them. He wondered if his first Thanksgiving with Jordan would have gone the way it had if they'd been there.

Grams made him a cup of coffee and sliced him a

piece of her sweet potato pie. Then she sat next to him at the table. "What happened?"

Bryson explained everything, not leaving out any details. He then pulled out the ring he'd bought. "I was trying to figure out when I was going to give this to her. But . . ." He sighed. "I don't know how I messed this up. How did I get it wrong?"

The older woman patted him on his hand. "Babe, you didn't do anything wrong. And neither did Jordan. You both have a history of abandonment and rejection. It's hard to move past that, it's hard to trust again."

"But I'm ready, Grams. I want the commitment. I want the family."

"You're there, she's not."

Veronica had basically told him the same thing months ago. Then, it made sense, but now . . . it pissed him off. "Am I supposed to wait forever for her to realize she wants me?"

"I'm not telling you to wait forever because I know you won't have to. I know my granddaughter. And she's as stubborn as the day is long. She'll fight everything tooth and nail. Always has been that way. I tell her to go one way, she turns and goes in the opposite direction. But she eventually comes around."

"Eventually."

"I see the love between you two."

"Tonight was the first time she's told me she loved me. I've been saying it for months."

"It probably took a lot for her to tell you that."

Bryson wanted to believe Grams; he wanted to believe that Jordan loved him, but his heart . . . "I can't do this anymore. Why should I keep going through this?"

"Do you love my granddaughter?"

"Of course, I do. I always have. But my father rejected me time and time again. And I opened myself up to Jordan and she does it, too? I can't keep putting myself out there like that."

"Sometimes a little empathy goes a long way, Bryson. You know, Jordan really struggled with her mother's abandonment. She rarely lets people in because of it. But I watched her with you. Then and now. And you brought out something in her that I've never seen. But you scare her. And it's not because she doesn't care. It's because she cares too much."

"I've been hurt, too."

"Isn't it something how God brings people together? Two very hurt people somehow found their way to friendship first, then love. How awesome is that? Let me share something with you, son." Grams sipped her coffee. "Jordan doesn't know this, but a long time ago, I left my husband and moved back to Colorado."

"Granddad?"

She nodded. "Yep. Jackson was a baby, and I took him and left. I had no plans to come back."

"Why did you leave?"

"Because I was scared. I was in a new town, with a new baby and husband. I had no support here, and Will worked all the time. I was terrified I was going to mess up being a wife and mother, so I removed myself from the situation. And I didn't just leave. I said some of the most awful things to Will. I hurt him terribly on my way out the door. And you know what?"

Bryson had a feeling he knew where this conversation would end. But he still asked, "What?"

"He let me go."

I didn't expect that. Frowning, he said, "I'm at a loss here, Grams. How did you end up back together?"

"I realized I was crazy to let that man go. I cried for days, sunk into a deep depression. Then, after a week in Colorado, I packed up my stuff and came home."

Bryson saw many parallels in that story and his. "How did Granddad react when you got back?"

"He opened the door and let me in. He told me later that he let me go so that I could come back. I had to learn the lesson myself. You see, he already knew. But I wasn't there yet."

Bryson bowed his head. The message was crystal clear. But could he receive it?

Grams squeezed his shoulder. "She'll get there, son. Sooner than you think. You did just let her go, after all."

His eyes flashed to her wise ones. "Thank you, Grams."

She gave him a kind smile. "You're always welcome, Bryson." The landline rang, and she frowned. "I wonder who that is. Hello?" she answered. Her eyes met Bryson's. "Okay. We'll be there as soon as we can."

When Grams hung up the phone, Bryson asked, "Is everything okay?"

"Yes. Jordan is in labor."

* * *

Bryson rushed into the hospital, after a quick stop at home to get Jordan's bag and the diaper bag, with Grams and Granddad a short distance behind him. Jordan had made him promise that no matter what, he would make sure she had her bag. They'd packed the diaper bag together, and she'd made it a point to explain why they needed everything in the bag.

Veronica rushed up to him. "I'm so glad you're here."

"Where's Jordan?" he asked. "Did she have the babies that fast?"

His sister shook her head. "Not exactly."

Bryson's heart dropped in his chest. He prayed there was nothing wrong with Jordan or the babies. "Are they okay?"

Veronica shifted on her feet. "After you left, she was hysterical, crying and winded. She tried to go after you, but she started contracting. That's when we realized she was in labor. We got her here in record time. Maddie and Stacyee are in the birthing room with her. When we got here, she was only at three centimeters dilated. The nurse explained she couldn't have the epidural until she was at least five centimeters dilated. That's when she went crazy. They're in there trying to calm her down."

"Take me to her," he said. They took off at a quick pace, with Bryson checking on Grams and Grand-dad behind them every so often.

Veronica pointed to a door to his right, and raised her hands in the air. "You got it from here, brother. I'm not going in there. The car ride was bad enough."

Bryson made a mental note to ask for details later.

He exchanged a look with Grams, then Granddad, then Veronica again. "Where's Brooklyn?"

His attempt to stall for time must have been obvious, because Grams said, "If you don't get your behind in that room . . . She needs to see you."

"Brooklyn stayed home to wait on the fellas. They'd run off in search of you. They should be here soon."

"Grams, what if I can't do this?"

"Son, you have no choice," Granddad interjected. On the thirty-minute drive to the hospital, he'd talked with both Granddad and Grams some more about what had happened. The older, wiser man had basically told him the same thing Grams did, and added that Bryson shouldn't give up on Jordan.

Bryson knew they needed to have a serious, *private* conversation. One where they could lay their feelings on the line and try to work through them.

On the other side of the door, he heard Jordan yell, "This is some bullshit!" Then the door swung open and Stacyee poked her head out.

When she saw him, her eyes narrowed. "Get your ass in here. Your girlfriend is a freaking lunatic. I have to go find a doctor or something."

Bryson felt a push from behind, and he tripped forward into the room. "Be great, son," Granddad said.

Bryson steadied himself and glanced toward the bed, and straight into the eyes of Jordan.

"Bryson?" she said. "You're here."

He approached the bed. "I told you I wouldn't miss it. I brought the bags."

She gave him a watery smile. Jordan was lying in

bed, two big circle things strapped to her belly and a blood pressure cuff on her arm. Her hair was in two big French braids, like she used to wear in middle school sometimes.

"It hurts," Jordan said, her voice soft. "I can't . . ." A tear fell down her cheek. "It hurts."

He leaned in, touching his forehead to hers. "We got this."

She clasped the collar of his shirt. "Promise?"

He nodded, before pulling back. "I promise."

Jordan swallowed. "This is some bullshit," she grumbled, repeating what he'd heard her yell only a few minutes earlier. "I just wanted you to know that."

He laughed and reached out to brush the back of his hand over her cheek. "Veronica said you're in a lot of pain?"

"Yes, she's in a lot of pain," Maddie interrupted, snatching her hand from Jordan's grasp and showing it to Bryson. "See this?" She held her hand up and waved it in the air. "I don't have any feeling in it. Your turn."

Bryson held out his hand and Jordan took it, lacing her fingers with his. It was fine for a minute, then Jordan let out a low growl before she squeezed his hand so hard, he wondered if he'd impregnated Wonder Woman or something. He gritted his teeth together and tried to focus on the endgame and not the shooting pain in his hand.

Maddie raised her brow, giving him a knowing smirk. "See."

"Where is Stacyee?" Jordan asked, fire in her eyes. "She was supposed to get the doctor. I need something."

A few minutes later, Dr. Jones appeared and gave

him a sympathetic smile before talking to Jordan. "I'm going to break your water now, Jordan."

Bryson wasn't a twitchy guy. He'd never had an aversion to blood and gore. In fact, he loved horror movies and crime shows. He'd never flinched during alien birth scenes where the little baby alien busted through the unsuspecting female—or male— abdomen. He'd never balked at blood spraying from eyes, ears, noses, or beds. But when Dr. Jones inserted the long needle into Jordan's happy place and the water gushed out of Jordan onto the floor, he felt like he would lose his dinner.

"No," Jordan cried. "My socks are getting wet. Take them off. Ew."

He hurried over to her and snatched her socks off, replaced them with a new pair of the good hospital socks, while Dr. Jones checked her cervix. Still only three centimeters.

A while later, Jordan was in the throes of another contraction when she shouted, "Bryson, I can't have this baby if you're mad at me, so we have to talk!"

He was walking with her around the room, because she'd told him she could no longer lie down in the bed. They were the only two people in the room. Maddie had escaped hours ago.

"There's nothing to talk about, Jordan. We need to focus on this right now."

"But I don't want to bring the babies into a world where their daddy hates their mama."

He gave her a side glance. "Really? I don't hate you, Jordan. I love you."

"But you're mad at me."

"I'm not mad," he argued, fanning her neck with a piece of paper. He'd figured Jordan's labor out.

When she was getting ready to have a contraction, she got really hot. So he made sure he had something in his hands at all times to fan her or wipe her brow.

"Liar."

"Okay, I'm still a little upset. But it's my own fault. You told me you weren't ready, and I stupidly believed I could change your mind."

One thing he'd learned from his conversations with Grams and Granddad was that Jordan would have to "get there" at her own pace, in her own time. And while they seemed to think she would realize he was the one for her sooner than later, Bryson couldn't deny he had his doubts. Either way, now wasn't the time to discuss it. In a few hours, they'd be parents to two little girls who needed both of them.

"Bryson, I—"

Jordan let out a loud, low scream and her legs buckled. Luckily, he was quick on the reflex because he caught her and scooped her up into his arms and carried her over to the bed. "I. Need. Drugs." Her voice had changed from soft to possessed in seconds.

Bryson pushed the call button, but when medical staff didn't come, he hurried out to the waiting area. "Grams," he pleaded, meeting her gaze. "Please help."

The older woman had already been in to see Jordan, but had told him she was going to wait outside until it was time to push. But he needed her now. The crew had arrived and were patiently waiting on the news with their cameras and balloons, but he needed Grams.

But it wasn't Grams who stood up. It was Granddad

who pushed past Bryson and stepped into the birthing room. When he entered the room, Granddad was sitting on the edge of the bed, rubbing Jordan's back and singing Louis Armstrong's version of "When the Red, Red Robin Comes Bob, Bob Bobbin' Along" in a low, soothing voice. For the first time in hours, she looked at peace, calm.

A smile tugged at his lips because he'd remembered Jordan telling him that Granddad used to sing that song to her every morning and it had always made her feel safe and warm . . . happy. He'd often wondered why it was that song that could soothe her, but in that moment, he was grateful that Granddad was well enough to sing it.

When Granddad was done singing, she sat up and smiled. "I love you, Granddad."

Granddad pinched her chin. "Love you, too, Punchkin."

Peace washed over the room as Jordan settled back against the pillows. She met his waiting gaze. "Did you find the doctor?"

He shook his head. "I pushed the call button. Someone should be coming any minute."

Jordan blew out a gush of air and muttered another curse. And just like that, all the work Granddad had done just evaporated into the air. And instead of singing again, Granddad just got up and walked to the door, patting Bryson on his shoulder before he stepped out. *Damn.*

Frustrated, Bryson walked out of the room and headed straight for the nurse's station. "Can you please get someone in there to check her? She hasn't been checked in hours." His patience was dangling on a tiny string and he had to fight to keep his voice even. Because if he had to walk back in that room again with no nurse, she was going to kill him, and he was going to let her.

Luckily, he didn't have to die because Jordan's nurse chose that exact moment to breeze past him. "I'm so sorry," she said. "We're swamped here today. I'll check her now."

Bryson followed her in the room, and waited while the nurse checked Jordan's cervix again.

"Oh," the nurse said. "You're already at eight centimeters."

"Eight?" Jordan and Bryson said simultaneously.

"Yes, I'll page the doctor. Shouldn't be much longer."

Bryson interrupted her retreat. "Wait, can she get her epidural now?"

"Did you still want it? We usually don't like to give it this late in the game."

"But you told her she could get it at five centimeters," he hissed. "It's not her fault you all took so long to examine her. She's in pain. Do something."

The nurse swallowed, and looked to Jordan, who was moaning "bullshit" over and over again. "Jordan, did you still want the epidural?"

Jordan's eyes snapped to the nurse. "Hell yeah, I want that shit. Now."

The epidural was the miracle of modern medicine. Bryson sighed when Jordan finally relaxed back into the mattress. And now, as if by magic, their disappearing family members piled into the room. Soon, people were laughing while Veronica told the story of the car ride to the hospital.

Chapter 21

At 3:19 in the morning, on Black Friday, Jordan gave birth to two beautiful girls, Addison Lynn and Willow Diana. It wasn't hard to choose the names. Bryson and Jordan wanted to honor Granddad and Grams, hence the name Willow Diana. And they thought it would be cute to salute both Brooklyn and Stacyee with the middle name "Lynn" and Maddie with the similar "Addison."

They were perfect, little cutie-pies with full heads of hair. And Jordan was tired. Exhausted, really. She still didn't quite understand how two babies came out of her, but she wouldn't trade them for the world.

The crew had taken turns cuddling and meeting the twins while Jordan watched the scene, her heart in her chest. It had been a long journey, and she wouldn't have been able to do it without Bryson.

Right before it was time to push, Jordan had squeezed Bryson's hand and jerked him to her, telling him that they needed to talk. Because she wanted to tell him everything that she'd been too afraid to say, before the babies were born. Unfortunately, her stubborn daughters didn't want to wait and the urge to push had bared down on her. Three pushes later, Willow was born. Three minutes after her, Addison burst into the world.

But the entire time she was pushing, Bryson had been in her ear, telling her she was doing good, that he loved her so much, that he loved their babies, and that they would work everything out. Despite everything that had happened, he'd still been there for her. He'd still taken the time to make sure she was okay, that she was comfortable. He'd walked with her, rubbed her belly and her back, he'd wiped sweat from her brow, and he'd let her crush his hand. And he'd done all of that without a single complaint. And Jordan needed to talk to him. She needed to tell him what he meant to her, what she'd realized even before she went into labor.

Grams and Granddad were the last to leave, kissing their great-grands good-bye before telling Jordan they'd be back tomorrow to visit. She'd just hung up from her father, who'd stated he was planning a Christmas visit to meet his grandkids for the first time. Bryson had also called his mother, who'd told them she'd get on the road to head that way in the morning.

When they were alone, Bryson smirked at her and her heart opened up. He was holding both babies, one in each arm. And it looked so natural, so right. God, she loved that man with everything in her.

"Bryson?" Jordan called. "Can you come here?"

He walked over to her, rocking his daughters in his arms. "Hey, baby. You feeling okay?"

She nodded. "I have something to say."

With his eyes locked on hers, he inclined his head, signaling her to go ahead and talk.

"I'm sorry," she breathed. "I'm so sorry. I never wanted to hurt you."

"Jordan—"

"No, let me talk."

"Baby, you just gave birth. We can talk in the morning."

"It can't wait until the morning. Don't you think it's waited long enough?"

He sat on the bed next to her. "Okay. Let's talk."

"In the words of my best friend, I was on some serious bullshit." He chuckled but she plowed ahead. "But when you walked out, I just couldn't imagine it being forever. I couldn't imagine my life without you. Yes, I was scared, but I'd much rather be scared with you than without you. I love you."

He searched her face. "Why?"

"You taught me how to play Mario Kart and you let me win the spelling bee, even though you knew how to spell *hieroglyphics*." His gaze dropped to the bed as the corner of his mouth lifted. "You are the only one who liked me in that damn pink dress and you listened to all of my problems without interrupting. You took my grandfather to treatments, and you hired someone to mow his lawn when he couldn't, and you make my grams laugh. You know without me even asking when I need to eat, to sleep, or to even get off. You make me feel safe, you make me feel beautiful, and you make me feel loved." She cupped his cheek. "You've shown me what real love can be. I love you so much. I love the home we've built, the life we've created, even in the midst of pain and hurt. And I—"

Bryson shut her up with a kiss, and her heart swelled in her chest, pounding in her ears wildly. She cupped his face and opened for him, letting him take control. The soft sound of a baby mewling broke the haze and she reluctantly pulled away.

He shifted Willow in his arms, and her daughter settled down. Leaning forward he captured her bottom lip with his teeth and tugged. *I love when he does that.* Pressing his forehead to hers, he whispered, "I love you, too."

A wave of relief washed over her. "I'm so in love with you, Bryson."

"If feels so good to hear you say that."

"I don't want to waste any more time, baby." She sat up straighter, traced his jaw with the tips of her fingers. "So ask me again."

Jordan and her family entered their home together for the first time, after three days in the hospital. And although she'd read the books, got help from the lactation specialist at the hospital, the first few nights alone with the babies and no nursing staff had proved to be harder than they thought.

Jordan had given up on getting any sort of restful sleep. When one baby was asleep, the other was up. When one baby was dry, the other was wet. By the time one baby was fed, burped, and changed, the other one was hungry. Then the cycle would start again. And again.

Her only saving grace was Bryson, who'd been patient even when Jordan was crying her eyes out because one of the twins wouldn't stop crying or her nipples were sore from all the breastfeeding. He'd given her foot massages, sponge baths, and woke up with her when she got up to feed their baby girls. She didn't know what she'd do without him, and she hoped she'd never find out.

At the hospital, she'd asked Bryson to ask her again. She wanted to make things right, she needed to convince him that she was there with him. But instead of proposing again, he told her that he needed some time.

Jordan didn't particularly like it, but she had no choice but to give him his time. Because he'd always been patient with her, she figured she could do the same with him. But he did tell her that he wanted their life together, which was good. *I guess.*

Everybody told her not to worry and assured her that Bryson was in it for the long haul. But she couldn't help but think she'd really messed up that Thanksgiving. It was Remy who gave her the most perspective when he'd visited them at the hospital before he left to return to California.

While Bryson was out in the waiting area talking to his mother, Remy had confessed that he knew about her long before they'd met up in Santa Monica. Jordan had been shocked by Remy's admission. But before she could ask more questions, Remy said, "Bryson couldn't leave you in the past, so there is no way you won't be his future."

So Jordan had to wait.

Addison's soft cry reached her ear, and she looked down at her baby girl, squirming in her arms. "Wake up, wake up, you sleepyhead," she sang. "Cheer up, cheer up, the sun is new. Live, love, laugh, and be happy."

Granddad had always sung that to her when she was little. Jordan used to think he'd made up the song just for her. It wasn't until she was an adult that she realized he got it from Louis Armstrong, his favorite recording artist. Granddad had changed one word and left out a whole lot of other ones.

In the original song, the words called the sun red. In Granddad's version, he called the sun new. When she'd asked him why, he told her that every day, we get a chance to do better, to be better. He'd wanted her to know that every day was new, so that's why he'd changed the word. When she'd asked him why he only ever sung three lines of the song, he'd told her that those three lines were all she needed.

Granddad's wish for her every day was that she woke up grateful because she had another chance to walk in her destiny. And his wish for her life was that she lived life to the fullest, loved with everything in her, and chose to be happy with what she had.

Jordan hoped she could impart wisdom like that to her daughters. She'd carried those lessons with her always. They were priceless, more valuable than all the money in the world. They offered a perspective on life that couldn't be taught in schools or read about in books. The lessons Granddad taught were based on his experience, his life.

"She still fussy?" Bryson asked from the doorway. He had Willow in his arms, rocking and burping her to a beat all his own.

Jordan grinned at him. "A little. She's mostly quiet now."

"What are you thinking about?" He joined her in the room, taking a seat in the matching rocking chair next to hers.

"Granddad."

"Is he okay?"

She nodded. "He's just fine. Probably ready to come see these little ones again."

Her grandparents had stopped by every morning to visit, bright and early. Grams helped with the dishes and the cooking, while Granddad monopolized the television remote and talked to the "girls," as he called them.

Jordan ran her index finger over Addison's cheek. "We're pretty blessed, you know?"

"We sure are."

"Last year, this time I was getting excited about law school and not even thinking about dating. And now, I'm a mother and I have a permanent date."

He laughed. "Damn right, I'm your permanent date. Just the thought of you with anyone else makes me feel unhinged."

"Well, I wouldn't want you to unravel and go looking for Jamari Coleman because he dared to smile my way."

His chuckle was low, sexy, and utterly adorable. "You just tell that punk that smiling is not allowed and to take those big-ass teeth somewhere else."

Jordan giggled, shushing quickly when Addison stirred. "You're crazy." She stood and set Addison in the crib. Turning, she held out her arms and waited until Bryson placed Willow in her arms. She brushed her lips over Willow's brow before she placed her next to Addison.

They stared down at the babies, sleeping peacefully for once. And hopefully for at least an hour. With one last sweep of her fingers over each of their bellies she turned and left the room. Soon Bryson was next to her, walking with her toward the kitchen.

"Tea?" he asked.

She slid into her favorite seat at the breakfast bar. "Sure. You know what else?"

He put the teakettle on and turned to her. "What's that?"

"One year ago, I would have never imagined living in this house."

"Tell me about it. But"—he paused, lifting her hand to his lips before placing a soft kiss there—"I wouldn't change anything."

A smile tugged at her lips. "Really?"

He shook his head. "Nothing. Because everything had to happen to get us to this point. I'm happy. For the first time, I'm hopeful about my life, about my future. And that has everything to do with you." He leaned in and brushed his lips over hers.

She laced their fingers together, and pressed his palm to her mouth. "I feel the same way, baby."

"Jordie," he said, walking around the breakfast bar to her. He dropped down on one knee and pulled out a small Tiffany box.

Jordan held her breath as he opened the box, revealing a stunning ring with pink and white diamonds. "Oh my," she whispered. "Oh, Bryson." Then she frowned. "Wait. Is this why you had Stacyee come over to give me a manicure today?"

Stacyee had shown up earlier, talking about how she felt like seeing her goddaughters and pampering her best friend. Now, Jordan knew why her friend had insisted on doing her nails.

He laughed. "You once told me that you hoped someone would warn you if you were going to get proposed to, so you could make sure your nails weren't busted."

Jordan threw her head back in laughter. "God, you do remember everything."

"I do. Now be quiet and let me do this."

Swallowing, Jordan nodded, biting down on her bottom lip.

Bryson cleared his throat. "I fell in love with you that day in the lunchroom all those years ago. You ruined me for everyone else, my sweet Jordie. And when I left, I thought I could get past it, I thought I could move on. But when you walked back into my life, and we spent that night together, I knew then that one night would never be enough for me. I love you, Jordan Mila Clark. And if I could add on more time to every day so that I can spend it with you, loving you, I would. Will you put me out of my misery and finally say yes?"

"Yes," she breathed, through her tears.

He picked up her hand and slid the ring onto her finger. It was perfect. Just like he was. Just like they were together. He kissed her ring finger one time before he planted his mouth over hers, drawing a low moan from her lips.

Jordan thought she would burst open from the love she felt for Bryson in that moment. There was no one that had meant more to her than he did. "I love you so much," she murmured against his lips. "I can't wait to marry you."

He pulled back, searched her face. "That's music to my ears, baby. I love you, too."

Epilogue

Eight months later

"Mama."

"Yes," Jordan said, throwing up a fist bump. "Willow said Mama first. You owe me." Jordan did a little two-step and a twerk before turning her attention back to Bryson, who was staring at her as if she'd grown another head. Clearing her throat, she said, "I'm sorry."

"As I was saying," Granddad said. "Jordan, do you take Bryson to be your lawfully wedded husband, to have and to hold, in sickness and in health, to love and honor, in good times and woe, for richer or poorer, keeping yourself solely unto him for as long as you both shall live?"

"I do." Jordan smiled when Bryson winked at her.

After they exchanged rings, did the cute little sand ceremony where Willow flung a bit of sand in Jordan's updo and Addison drooled on Bryson's tie,

Granddad pronounced Bryson and Jordan man and wife.

"You may now salute your bride," Granddad instructed.

Bryson leaned down, pressing his forehead to hers. "I love you, my sweet Jordie."

Jordan beamed up at him. "Love you, too, baby."

Bryson tugged Jordan flush against him and kissed her, long and hard, in front of everybody and their mama. And their babies. When he finally pulled away, Jordan was dazed. And her grandfather was blushing.

"Um," Granddad said, "I present to you Mr. and Mrs. Bryson Wells."

Bryson and Jordan turned to the cheering audience, filled with their closest friends and family, and jumped the broom before they raced away.

They'd married in Santa Monica at the Casa Del Mar on the private beach. Jordan wore a sheath dress with bling for days while Bryson wore a khaki-colored suit. And, of course, her bridesmaids wore pink. Jordan had asked her granddad to marry her, because she'd wanted him to be a part of the ceremony. It wasn't a shock to him, as he'd married Brooklyn and Carter a couple years ago, so he'd happily accepted. When she'd asked Grams to be her matron of honor, though, her grandmother told her, "You're not going to have me up there looking a fool in that pink. Not everybody is pretty in pink." So instead, Grams was in charge of twin duty.

Everybody they cared about had attended, including her father and Rebecca, whom Jordan had come

to care for. All in all, it was the best day of her life,
aside from the birth of her girls.

Bryson stepped into her, gripping her hips in his
hands, and bent down to kiss the back of her neck.
They'd run off for a quick change in their room,
having both decided on comfort for the party. Although they weren't staying in the exact room they
were in that fateful night, she still felt a little nostal-
gic. It was at that hotel that she'd found him again.
And everything had changed for them.

They'd settled into a peaceful routine with the
girls and their life together. After the year was up,
Bryson received his million-dollar inheritance, which
he'd promptly split up into three equal portions. He
donated a third of the money to a charity for abused
and neglected children. Then, he started a scholarship fund for young black men interested in pur-
suing a science degree. Then, he'd donated the
remaining funds to the legal defense fund for women
so that no woman would ever be strong-armed into
giving custody of their children to overbearing and
abusive fathers.

Jordan had been right. He did do good with the
money, and she was proud of him. And they'd turned
that house into a loving home. Bryson had success-
fully beat Senior at his own game, and they were
happy in *their* home, with *their* family.

"Baby, I need you to step out of that dress and
bend over," he murmured, as he unbuttoned her
dress.

"Bryson," Jordan said, a smirk on her face.
"They're expecting us."

"I'll be quick."

She raised a brow. "Really?"

"Okay, I won't be quick."

And he never has been. "We'll be done soon enough, and then we'll come back here." She kissed his chin. "And I'll show you how happy I am to be your wife."

He bent lower to kiss her. "Promise?"

"Promise. I love you," she said.

He wrapped his arms around her waist, and smiled down at her. "I love you, too, Mrs. Wells."

DON'T MISS THE FIRST BOOK
IN THE WELLSPRING SERIES

TOUCHED BY YOU

Enjoy the following excerpt
from *Touched by You* . . .

Chapter 1

The ground was wet. Cold.

But Carter Marshall couldn't bring himself to move, to walk away. He clutched the weathered copper ornament in his hands. It was the only thing he had left of his old life, the only tangible reminder that they both existed. Everything else was gone, charred beyond repair.

"I'm not sure how to do this," he mumbled to himself. He knew he had to let the anger go now. It had consumed him, filled him to capacity and pushed him to keep going. He wondered what would take its place, or if he'd even be able to let go of the hate he had in his heart for the man who had taken away everything.

The rain pounded on his head, drizzled down his face. It had been an hour since he'd arrived, but he couldn't bring himself to complete his task. Instead, he'd sat there, his expensive Tom Ford suit soaked and his Cole Haan shoes muddy. Nothing mattered anymore. Not his wealth, not his name, not his work.

Everything that he'd once held dear seemed like a curse now.

"I'm sorry," he muttered. "I'm sorry I wasn't there. I was too obsessed with work, too driven, too focused on my damn money. I thought if I just worked hard enough, I could give you the life you deserved. I only wanted to make you happy."

His eyes welled with fresh tears. As if he hadn't cried enough already. The loss of his beautiful wife and daughter had devastated him to his core, weakened him. Even now, almost two years later, he could still smell the gasoline, taste the smoke in the air, hear the screams of the neighbors as the fire burned. He recalled the determination on the firemen's faces as they worked to put the blaze out, and he remembered the exact moment they all realized that it was too late.

You're the best part of my day, my hero.

Her words still haunted him. *Her hero.* His wife of three years, his college sweetheart, had told him he was her hero. Only he didn't feel heroic. What was the opposite of hero? Coward. Loser. Nobody.

Instead of being home with his wife and newborn daughter, he'd been working. Late. It seemed his work had eclipsed everything in his life, despite his denials. Krys had told him time and time again to live a little, to enjoy life. But the lure of the prestige, the money, the connections that his business guaranteed was important to him. He'd worked too hard, too long to let it go. He'd been distracted, meetings all day and projects to finish. When the phone rang, he'd moved it to voicemail with a little text that said, Give me a minute.

To think that was the last thing Krys heard from

him . . . He'd been so busy he couldn't even pick up the phone and answer. Was she scared? According to the arson investigators, the fire had started around seven o'clock. The call from her came through a little after seven. What if that one phone call could have changed something? Countless hours in therapy, numerous assurances that he couldn't have known, did nothing to quell the guilt he felt every time he looked at her response to his text. The worst part was that he hadn't even seen her response until hours later, after he'd been ushered from the scene of the crime. It read, I love you. Always remember.

Even in her last minutes, she'd been thinking of him. And he'd been thinking of his next project, his next dollar. *What good is all the money in the world without her, without them?*

Closing his eyes, he willed himself to move, to do what he came to do.

He scanned the area around him. It was *their* spot. Krys had insisted they visit as often as possible since it was the place where he'd proposed.

Today would have been their wedding anniversary. Remembering her beautiful face on the day he made her his wife made his heart ache. Krys was beautiful, in a classic "Clair Huxtable" kind of way. She was a good woman, believed that taking care of the home, being a wife and mother was the best job in the world. They'd been so young, so full of hope.

People had questioned him about the choice to marry so soon after college graduation, for even being with the same woman for so long. Even his best friend and business partner, Martin Sullivan, had been wary. And he'd known Krys for as long as he'd known Martin. Carter couldn't explain it, though. He wasn't an impulsive person. Everything Carter had done in life had been carefully planned. It was the reason he and Martin had been so successful. Neither of them played around when it came to business.

Marrying Krys, though, was his destiny. At least, he'd thought so at the time. She'd supported him through some of the worst times of his life—the death of his youngest sister and his grandmother and his parents' subsequent divorce. Krys never wavered, never wanted him to be anybody but himself. She'd never complained when he traveled for work or forgot to take the trash out. She was perfect, and he didn't deserve her. He'd broken the promise to love and to cherish, to have her and to honor her. If he had, he would have answered her call. He should have been there. Especially since she'd always been there for him. Krys had given him the best gift he could ever have—her heart, her body, her soul. He'd promised to protect her, to be there for her. *Except I wasn't, not when she needed me the most.*

Time hadn't made this wound better, hadn't healed him like they told him it would. He'd started to resent them—his parents, his friends, his employees . . . everyone. The questions were becoming unbearable. The sad looks infuriated him. Most of all, when people told him *It will be okay,* he wanted to slap them. Because he was not okay, and wasn't sure he would ever be okay again. He knew he had to try, though. For them. For Krys and for his baby girl, Chloe.

Carter closed his eyes and inhaled the wet, night air. It was too late to be the father Chloe needed. She wasn't even a year old. He'd never heard her say

"Da Da" or had the pleasure of watching her toddle into his waiting arms for the first time. *It's not fair.*

The tears fell freely down his cheeks and his stomach lurched into his chest. *I failed.* Carter looked down at the glass Christmas ornament in his hand. It was shaped like a heart, personalized with their names and their wedding date. Krys had purchased it for their first Christmas as a married couple. Sighing heavily, Carter dropped the ornament into the small hole he'd dug, next to the tree where he'd dropped on one knee and proposed to his first love, his only love.

"I made them pay, Krys."

Within days after the fire, the Detroit Police Department had arrested the young men that were responsible. But pressure from city officials had them backtracking on the investigation. Of course they did, because one of the men, the main culprit, was the college-aged son of one of the most influential business owners in the city.

The McKnight family was well-known in the Detroit area. Carter had effectively launched a smear campaign, blasted them on every social media site. Through his own computer skills and those of his partner, they'd crippled the McKnight business. Revenge was best served with a depleted bank account. A guilty verdict wasn't enough for him. He'd just been awarded a settlement in the civil lawsuit he'd brought against the city and the family for hampering the investigation.

Money wasn't his motive, though. He wanted them to lose everything, just like he had. Those young men had destroyed his life on a whim, because of a bet. They'd targeted his house because it was on the corner lot in a mostly African American neighborhood—because they could.

"I donated most of the money to the burn unit at Children's Hospital and set up a foundation to help burn victims and families who've lost everything to a fire."

It would never bring them back. He knew that, and he'd certainly paid the price of the personal vendetta he'd waged against the culprits, with his family and his work. The criminal and civil trials had taken a lot out of him. Now, it was time for him to let the anger go, let them go. That was the hard part.

He covered the glass ornament with mud and stood to his full height. By all rights, he should be celebrating. He'd won. His mother had set up a family dinner, and his brothers had mentioned a hookup he had no intention of taking advantage of. What would be the purpose? Sex? Because that's all it would be. He was empty, a void that would never be filled.

"Everyone wants me to move on, but how? Is it even okay to love someone else?"

And now he was officially crazy, talking to the night air, to Krys like she could actually answer. At the same time, if he had a sign, maybe he could let go fully. His wife and child died, but his love never would. That much was certain. *I don't have room for anyone else.*

"I love you. Take care of each other."

Sighing, he made his way back to his car and, after one last glance at the tree, sped off.

A houseful of people awaited him when he arrived at his mother's place about an hour later. There were old friends, cousins, and more cousins.

The smell of fried chicken wafted to his nose, and his stomach growled.

"Carter, get your butt in here."

Iris Johnston was a loud, formidable woman. She pulled him into her strong arms and squeezed tightly. Carter wasn't an overemotional person, rarely gave out hugs, but he couldn't help but wrap his arms around her plump waist and relax into her embrace.

"Ma, I thought it was only going to be family." He pulled back and kissed his mother on her cheek. "You promised not to make a big deal about this."

Iris shrugged and gestured to the table of food in the corner. "Eat. You deserve this. You've had a tough few years."

His stepfather, Chris, joined them and patted him on the shoulder. "She's right, Carter. Have a seat and relax yourself. This is the least we could do for you."

Carter walked through the house, greeting the people who'd turned out for him. One by one, they hugged him, gave him sad glances before they offered more congrats and condolences. *Shit.* It was like Krys and Chloe had just died. His thoughts flashed back to all the food his mother insisted be dropped off to the house, all the stares.

When he finally made it to the kitchen, he grinned at the sight of his brothers.

"Carter, I'm glad you're finally here," Kendall said, giving him a quick man-hug. "Mom has been worrying the shit out of us." Kendall was the baby brother, and officially a college graduate as of two months ago. It had been a happy day when he'd walked across the stage, because they all thought he wouldn't make it.

"Yeah, man. She was a nightmare." His brother, Marvin, leaned against the sink. Carter reached out and clasped his hand in their signature handshake. Marvin was the middle son, the lawyer of the family.

"Well, I'm here. Not sure how much longer, though. I told her I didn't want a party."

"Baby brother, if you leave, we're all going to have to pay for it." Carter turned to see his older sister, Aisha, standing behind him. "And let me tell you, I'm sick of y'all fools leaving me behind to clean up your messes."

Carter pulled his sister into a tight hug. "I'm sorry, sis. But you know crowds are not my thing. I'm getting antsy just listening to the chatter."

Aisha's expression softened, her brown eyes wide with unshed tears. "I know. But you have to start living again. You know Krys would want that." She rubbed his cheek. "You can't die with her. You're still here for a reason."

Carter blinked and prayed for an intervention, anything to stop the pain in his sister's eyes. She was worried about him. Being the oldest of five siblings, Aisha had been a sponge her whole life, taking on their emotions like they were her own.

"I don't want to talk about this," Carter said, leaning down and kissing his sister on the forehead. "Where's the food?"

Aisha's shoulders fell, and she nodded. "I'll fix you a plate."

Moments later, he was sitting at the small table in the kitchen, eating while the party roared on in the other room. Aisha sat across from him, watching him eat.

"I've been calling you. When are you going to

come back to the office?" she asked. Aisha worked as the chief financial officer of Marshall and Sullivan Software Consulting Inc. She basically kept the company up and running while he and Martin traveled the world. His sister had been calling him for weeks, every single day. "Martin needs you back in the office."

Carter knew he'd been a lousy business partner. Martin had basically picked up all the slack in the last two years. It wasn't right for him to continue this way. And with his best friend recently tying the knot, Carter wanted to be able to step up again to let him be a happy newlywed. "I know, Aisha. I plan to go back soon."

"Soon? The office has been inundated with calls, requests for proposals. You're on the verge of something bigger than you ever dreamed, especially with the Wellspring offer. Don't give it all up."

"Aisha, please shut up!" he snapped. His sister's mouth closed in a tight line, and he immediately regretted his outburst. "I'm sorry. It's just . . ." *Forget it.* She wouldn't understand. Work was the last thing he wanted to do, because work was what he'd allowed to get between him and his wife for too long.

"I get it," his sister said, picking at the table with her thumbnail. "You're hurting, and I don't want to take that away from you."

He was such an asshole. Aisha had only been trying to help, to take care of him like she'd always done. It wasn't her fault he was incapable of being social. He had never really been the type of person that enjoyed being around a lot of people. Carter had always been more solitary, preferring to be by himself than go to the club.

"I didn't mean to yell." He dropped his fork on his plate. "But Krys is gone, Aisha. She's dead, and so is my baby girl. It takes a huge effort for me to get out of the damn bed in the morning. I just . . . I need some time."

"I know Krys is gone, Booch. I get it."

Carter rolled his eyes at the use of his childhood nickname. Only a few people still used it, but it always reminded him of being a kid. He wasn't a child anymore. He wasn't going to conform to everyone's ideas on how he should handle his grief. Shit, he was the one that had to go home every night to an empty house, an empty life.

"No, you don't get it, Aisha." Carter pushed away from the table and stood, pacing the floor. "Please stop pretending you do." He pointed at his chest and whirled around to face her. "I'm the one that has to deal with the fact that some ignorant prick decided to set fire to my freakin' house. With *my* family inside. I'm the one that has to look at myself in the mirror every day, knowing that my wife was scared and needed someone to talk to her and I didn't answer the phone."

"You can't be everywhere at once, Booch. You were working. Krys understood that about you."

"How do you know what Krys understood?" The anger that rose up in him was irrational and directed solely at the one person who didn't deserve it. "She needed me." Bile rushed up his throat and he fought to control it from coming out, spewing over his mother's hardwood floor.

Aisha stood and approached him, fire in her brown eyes. She gripped his chin and twisted it downward to meet her gaze. "You want to know how I know? Krys called me."

Carter's eyes widened. "What?"

"I didn't want to tell you because I knew it wouldn't help you at the time. You had the trial and then the lawsuit. It was keeping you going. Now that it's over, I need you to hear me, Carter."

He swallowed roughly, clenched his hands into fists.

She sighed. "Krys called me that night. She knew she wasn't going to make it." His sister's eyes filled with tears. "She needed to talk about some things. One thing she made sure she said was that she loved you. Carter, she loved you. Everything about you. But she knew you. She knew that you'd let her death consume you, she knew you'd let this ruin you. Your wife, my sister-in-law, wanted to be sure that you didn't. She wanted you to live, to have a life even though she wasn't here. She made me promise to tell you when the time was right. I'm telling you now."

Exhausted and emotional, Carter gave in, letting the tears that had filled his eyes spill. He fell back into the chair. His head bowed, he whispered, "I don't know how to do this, Aisha. How can I live without her?"

Aisha pulled a chair in front of him and sat down, tilting her head to meet his gaze. "It won't be easy. But you have to. You deserve to live. That's what she wanted for you. God didn't keep you here so that you can die a slow death, in your grief."

"What else did she say?" His voice cracked. "Was she scared?"

Shaking her head, his sister squeezed his knee.

"Krys cried, but not because she was scared for herself. She didn't want Chloe, your baby girl, to suffer. She was scared for you, for the family she'd leave behind. I, on the other hand, was hysterical with tears."

Knowing that Krys wasn't scared for herself didn't surprise Carter. His wife was never scared. It was something he'd always loved about her. During labor, she'd refused to take pain meds. But she'd squeezed the shit out of his hand. So bad, he'd needed it iced afterward. "I can imagine you bawling. You're such a big baby."

"Hey, I'm still the oldest."

The room descended into silence as they sat there. Finally, he said, "I miss her." The admission was probably obvious to his sister, but it was the first time he'd said it out loud to anyone. It was like he'd been walking in a haze, refusing to show anyone that he was affected. Only the people closest to him could tell, and that was because they knew his routine, his personality. Everything about him had changed that October night.

Aisha pulled him into a strong hug. "I know."

They stayed like that for what felt like an eternity, him being held by his big sister. They'd grown up, but remained close. As children, they were joined at the hip. Only two years apart, Aisha had dragged him everywhere with her, to all the parties. She'd been taking care of him since they were toddlers, when she would sneak him cookies under the kitchen table.

When he pulled away, he brushed her tears away. "Thank you," he mouthed.

She gave him a wobbly smile. "Always."

"What's going on at work?"

"So much. Martin is handling everything, but I don't want him to get burned out. He's finally settled with Ryleigh and they're happy. They deserve some time to just be newlyweds. Traveling to Wellspring, Michigan, is not ideal for him right now."

Carter thought about Aisha's plea. She was definitely right. Martin did deserve to enjoy his new marriage. And he had to step up and let him.

"Who was scheduled to go with Martin to Wellspring?" Carter was so out of touch he couldn't even remember the Wellspring project particulars.

"Walt." Walter Hunt was the new software engineer they'd hired a few months ago. "He's not strong enough to handle point on this project. Handling a project of this magnitude is too much for him."

Carter rolled his eyes. Parker Wells Sr., president of Wellspring Water Corporation, had hired Marshall and Sullivan because they were the best in the state, and they'd designed an excellent Enterprise Resource Planning system. And his sister was a big part of that. *Aisha is right. This is too big a job to trust to anyone other than me or Martin.*

"So what are you going to do?" Aisha asked, a mixture of worry and challenge lining her face. "Someone is supposed to be in Wellspring on Monday to meet with the players. We've pushed the date back already. If we don't do this—"

"Calm down, Aisha." Carter had the perfect solution—one that would give him time and space from the emotions that surrounded him in Detroit. "I'll go. I'll head the project myself. And I'll leave in the morning."

Carter and Aisha talked for several more minutes,

working out the details of his trip. Aisha also gave him updates on a few other issues with the company. He would leave first thing in the morning and drive to Wellspring, which was approximately a three-hour drive from Detroit. A hotel had already been booked for Martin, so Aisha was charged with switching the reservations to Carter's name.

"Aisha?"

His sister turned toward the door. "Hey, girl!" Aisha stood and hugged the woman who'd interrupted their conversation. "Long time, no see. Carter, remember Ayanna? We went to high school together."

Carter smiled at the woman. He definitely remembered Ayanna. The woman standing before him, with her light skin and light eyes, was still as beautiful as he remembered. Instead of the trademark braids she'd rocked in high school, her hair was wavy and flowing down her back. But the attraction he once had to her was long gone.

Ayanna was also his "first." And judging by the way Aisha was singing her friend's praises, his sister didn't know. There were rules, after all. Back then, Aisha had banned him from ogling her friends. Little did she know or even realize, her friends weren't exactly shy when it came to him. Carter might have been a one-woman man when he met Krys, but he hadn't always been that way.

Aisha was yapping away, catching up with her friend. And Ayanna was checking him out. The heat in her eyes told him exactly what she was thinking.

"How have you been, Carter?" Ayanna asked, batting her long lashes. "You've been in my prayers."

"I'm good. And you?"

"I've been enjoying life." Ayanna inched closer

to him and wrapped her arms around him in a tight hug.

Carter inhaled Ayanna's scent. She still smelled the same. It would be so easy to take it to the next level. The look in the woman's eyes when she pulled back and shot him a sexy grin was an invitation. Any other man would have run with it. All Carter felt was cold. But this could be what he needed to move on. He just wasn't sure he believed that.

"I didn't know you were coming," he said, wondering if Ayanna was the "hookup" his brothers had told him about. Only Marvin knew of their dalliance all those years ago.

Ayanna folded her arms over her breasts. "I actually was in the neighborhood, saw the cars and decided to stop. Your mother sent me in here to give you best wishes."

Aisha piped up. "You should totally stay. There is plenty of food, and we'll be playing cards later. It'll be good to catch up."

"I'd love to," Ayanna said. "It's a shame that we grew up together and barely see each other."

Detroit was a large city, with a population of almost seven hundred thousand people. Plenty of people he'd grown up with still lived in the city, but seemed so far away. Many of the kids he went to school with had left, though. Some had moved to the suburbs, and others had left Michigan altogether.

Growing up in Detroit was a good experience for Carter. His parents both worked good jobs, and their neighborhood was a safe haven for him. Everyone knew each other and looked out for each other. He remembered block parties and going to the skating rink with friends. No matter what the outside world thought of his city, it was his home. Although he'd had plenty of offers from different companies, he'd never considered moving. It helped that Krys was also from Detroit. They'd actually grown up fifteen miles away from each other, but had never met.

Thinking of Krys brought him back from the walk down memory lane. Even if Ayanna was giving him "the eye," he had no business even considering it. Especially today.

Taking a deep breath, Carter grabbed his still-full plate and tossed it in the waste bin. "I'm going to go out and talk to Mom before I leave," he announced to the two women. "I'll call you in the morning, Aisha—before I leave."

Even if he hadn't believed it was a good idea before, he was sure that taking on this project was the perfect solution—a new town, a new opportunity where no one knew him. Wellspring might be the welcome change of pace he needed.

Chapter 2

Brooklyn Wells hated charity functions. *But I love chocolate*, she thought.

She snatched a chocolate éclair from the tray as the waiter passed her, and stuffed it into her mouth. Moaning in delight, she chewed the piece of heaven as if it was the last one she'd ever eat. Damn, that was good.

"If you don't slow down, you're going to turn into an éclair, Brooklyn."

Rolling her eyes, Brooklyn assessed her stepmother as she walked by with a wealthy benefactor. The sound of her fake, monotone laugh echoed in the massive ballroom. The woman was as stiff as a board. Or was it boring as a stiff? She snickered to herself. It wasn't funny, but she'd been forced to amuse herself all night. Between countless handshakes, fake smiles, and polite nods, she'd had enough. But her father, the almighty, had mandated that she attend—for the family. Never mind that the charity was in the top twenty-five of America's worst charities. Despite her countless emails and pleas to donate to a more deserving charity—one that didn't line its executives' pockets with cash and one *not* connected to her father—her domineering father dismissed her requests and told her she'd better "shut up and show up."

"Can I talk to you?"

Sighing heavily, Brooklyn looked at her ex. Sterling King used to send a shiver up her spine with one look from his startling gray eyes. But the puppy-dog look he was sporting at that very moment only made her want to shove him into the tray of caviar right behind him.

"I have nothing to say to you," she hissed. "We've been through this so many times, Sterling. If you—"

Her words were cut off by his hands pressing urgently against her back as he guided her toward the back of the room, away from the stares of Wellspring society.

When they were tucked away from the crowd, behind a pillar, she jerked out of his hold. "What are you doing?" She folded her arms across her chest. "I told you I didn't want to t—"

Before she could finish her thought, he was on his knees. In his hand was a box holding a solitaire marquise-cut diamond. Absolutely stunning. But not her style.

"Brooklyn, I love you. Will you marry me?"

She glanced behind her, hoping her father wasn't lurking in the shadows. It would be just like Parker Sr. to have planned this entire thing. For all she knew, he'd purchased the ring himself. Her father had been trying to get her to marry Sterling since she'd graduated from college. Something about building an alliance between the King and Wells families.

Brooklyn could care less about the business and her father's interests, so she hadn't intended to follow her father's directive when it came to Sterling and marriage.

"Um . . ." It wasn't like her to be rendered speechless. But she couldn't seem to find the words—well, the one word she needed to say. "I-I have to . . . pee." She turned on her heels and dashed through the ballroom without a backward glance.

Brooklyn breezed past a group of investors, lifted a glass of champagne from a moving tray, and headed straight to the private bathroom in the hallway. Once inside, she locked the door and gulped down the sparkling drink.

Gazing at herself in the mirror, she turned on the water and pulled out her cell phone. When her brother picked up, she whispered, "Parker?"

"Sis, where are you? Didn't I just see you?"

"I need you," she pleaded.

"What is that in the background? Water? Where are you?"

"I'm in the private bathroom."

"Um, you're crazy. Why are you calling me from the bathroom?"

Brooklyn knew he was on his way to her. After their mother died, her older brother took care of her when her father never bothered. He took her everywhere with him, introduced her to all of his friends. He'd threatened all his fellow football teammates with bodily harm if they even dared to approach her. So, she ended up with twenty brothers and no boyfriends.

Even now, as adults, she recognized that they didn't have the same philosophy in life. Parker was all about the family business and name, being the guaranteed Wells heir, and she couldn't care less about her trust fund or the perks her last name provided. But she never doubted her brother would be there for her, no questions asked. She heard him greet someone, excuse himself from another person, then . . . There was a knock on the door.

She rushed to the door, unlocked it, and swung it open, pulling him inside with her.

"What the . . . ?" he said, brushing off his charcoal-gray designer suit and straightening his tie. Parker crossed his arms over his chest. "You've really flipped out this time, sis. Why are you holed up in the bathroom?"

"Sterling proposed," she blurted out.

Instead of the fury she'd half expected in her brother's eyes, she was shocked to see the light of amusement in his brown orbs.

"Are you . . . Parker, did you hear what I said?"

Then, a smirk? Her dear brother thought her predicament was funny.

Clearing his throat, he said, "Sis, calm down." He gripped her shoulders and squeezed. "You had to know this was coming sooner or later."

"Sterling and I haven't been together in years!" she yelled. "I can't even stand him, let alone want to marry him. What was he thinking?"

Although she and Sterling had grown up in the same circles, and were great childhood friends, their attempt at a relationship went up in flames after three months. Unfortunately, his handsome—almost perfect—face and physique weren't enough to keep her interest. Not only was he as boring as glue, he was horrible in the sack. As if that wasn't bad enough, his incessant need to call her "Brooksielynsie" made her want to throw up. God, she hated stupid pet names with a white-hot passion.

"You know this is all Senior, right?" Parker told her. Her father had insisted that they call him "Senior" instead of Dad, although Brooklyn was the only one that could get away with calling him Daddy at times. She guessed it had a lot to do with her father's need to be superior to everyone else in the world. "Just tell that idiot hell no, and keep it moving. This isn't the end of the world." Her older brother barked out a laugh. "I can't believe you locked yourself in a bathroom. Get it together." He shook her gently for emphasis. He wiped the corner of her eye with his thumb. "Fix your face, baby sis. You are looking rough."

"You get on my nerves." She pouted, turning to the mirror and pulling out her compact. She eyed her brother through the mirror. "I panicked, okay? I'm allowed to panic. We can't all maintain control like you, big brother."

Parker stared at her and gave her a small smile. "You remind me of Mom."

Averting her gaze, she busied herself with her makeup. "I can't add tears to this night, Parker." She missed her mother, Maria, with everything in her. Her mother had been dead for fourteen years, but the grief was still just under the surface. Especially since her death was so tragic. "Let's just concentrate on getting me through the night without killing Sterling."

He placed a kiss on the top of her head. Her brother had more than a few inches on her in height, but he never made her feel small, like some of the other people in town. "Point taken. Stay clear of Sterling for the night. We can't have a scene. But tomorrow, make it clear that you'll never be Mrs. King. No matter how our father has conspired with his father to make it happen."

Her father had been cultivating a business relationship with Sterling's family for years. When Sterling's father was elected to the state senate, Brooklyn's father practically salivated with glee. Although Brooklyn wasn't involved in the daily business of the family company, she knew her father thought that having political allies would further strengthen his hold on the town and the state. For years now, Senior had been attempting to buy land in several counties to tap into the springs, and expand the company. It was obvious Senior had something up his sleeve, but Brooklyn would not be a pawn in any game her father wanted to play.

Parker picked up her empty champagne flute and opened the door. He held the glass up to her. "You need another of these. And go find that man with the chocolate puff things you love so much. It's going to be okay."

She waved at her brother as he strutted out of the small bathroom and followed him a few minutes later. Spotting a cute server with a tray full of those yummy chocolate eclairs, she grabbed one and smiled at him as he strolled by. When he returned her smile with one of his own and a wink, she averted her gaze and pretended to look for someone in the crowd. She was not in the mood to be propositioned or hit on.

"And please try not to get drunk tonight, Brooklyn."

Senior's fifth wife stopped right in front of her and scowled. "This is a charity event, not a Super Bowl party."

"Leave me the hell alone," Brooklyn muttered under her breath.

"I heard you," Patricia hissed with a hard roll of her eyes. The woman, barely ten years older than Brooklyn, smoothed a hand over her messed-up blond wig.

"I'm sure you did. Did I stutter?" Brooklyn said between clenched teeth.

"Look, I'm not playing with you," Patricia snapped. "Be good."

"You are not my mother, so stop acting like it."

"Well, I married your father."

"So did his last few wives, before he dumped them."

Patricia grumbled incoherently before she stomped off, probably in search of Brooklyn's father. At any minute, Senior would come over and berate her for daring to talk to his child bride that way.

Shrugging, Brooklyn scanned the room, looking for her brother. Parker was standing with one of her father's board members. They were talking in hushed tones, probably about some business deal. Parker was always talking about business, always trying to please their father. For the life of her, she couldn't understand why. It's not like he didn't loathe him as much as she did. Unlike her, though, Parker thrived on business and he was good at what he did. One day, he'd run the company—Wellspring Water Corporation.

The music faded and the chatter dimmed. Parker Sr.

approached the podium, Patricia close to his side and . . . Sterling right behind him. Dread coated her insides as she watched the trio on the stage. *What the hell is going on?* When she met Parker's concerned gaze across the room, she guessed he felt the same way.

"Hello, ladies and gentlemen," her father's baritone voice greeted over the microphone. "I'm so glad that you've joined us tonight. We're on target to meet our fundraising goal for such a worthwhile organization. But I hope you don't mind me taking a few minutes to make an announcement and a toast. The servers will be around to make sure your glasses are filled."

With a smile, Brooklyn took the offered glass of champagne from a short server and waited for her father to speak again. Something told her that what was coming next was a game changer.

With his glass held high, her father smiled and wrapped his arm around Sterling. "I've watched this young man grow into quite a remarkable young man, capable of greatness."

Brooklyn gulped down her champagne.

"I want to congratulate him and my beautiful daughter on their engagement."

Brooklyn choked on the champagne and it sprayed out on the woman in front of her.

"Congratulations, baby girl," her father announced before turning to Sterling. "You will be a fine addition to the Wells family, son."

She glared at her father, standing in front of the crowded room with a satisfied Sterling. That son of a—

"Brooklyn, come here," her father commanded from the stage.

Before she could stop herself, she shouted, "Hell, no!"

Gasps from the crowd filled her ears as her gaze met her brother's across the room. Parker started toward her, but she backed away. Out of the corner of her eye, she saw appalled older women frowning at her. But she couldn't care. She didn't care.

I have to get out of here. But her legs didn't seem to want to work right. As she stumbled toward the door, as if she was stepping in quicksand, she tried to block out the loud whispers from the guests. Focused straight ahead, she finally took off at a sprint, intent on getting as far away as possible. Vaguely, she heard Parker calling her name, but if she stopped to look at him or speak to him, she'd never make it out of there.

The cold, bitter temperature smacked her in the face when she made it outside. She hugged herself, rubbing her arms. Glancing back to see if anyone followed her, she shuffled down the street. Her dress was long, her toes were bare, and the snow was coming down, but she had to keep going. To where, she didn't know.

Grabbing her phone, she tried to dial her friend Nicole. No answer. She typed a quick 911 text to her friend. Distracted, she started across the street. She heard the blaring horn before she saw the truck heading straight for her. She tried to run, but slipped and fell on her side. Opening her mouth to scream, she frantically searched for someone. The street was empty. Bracing herself for the impact, she prayed for mercy and forgiveness for being such a bitch sometimes.

Only there was no pain. Instead she felt like she was wrapped in a warm, heavenly cocoon surrounded by trees and ginger and . . . Gain detergent? Was she in heaven?

"Are you okay?"

Her eyes popped open and she was met with beautiful, brown, unfamiliar ones staring back at her. Her mouth fell open when she realized that she wasn't sitting at the Lord's feet. She was still, in fact, outside in the brittle Michigan cold, lying underneath a stranger. She bucked up and the man stood to his full height.

She peered up at him and back at his waiting hand. Sliding her hand into his, she let him pull her to her feet.

"Are you okay?" he repeated, surveying her face with a worried expression. "You were . . . I thought that truck was going to . . . I picked you up and pulled you out of the way, but slipped on ice and we both went down."

"It's . . . okay." Suddenly, she felt warm again and it wasn't because the man had taken his own coat off and wrapped it around her shoulders. She had a strong feeling it had something to do with the man himself standing before her. Brooklyn had never seen him before, but she was immediately intrigued by him. Maybe it was because he'd saved her life? Or maybe it was because he was fine as hell. Either way, she wanted to find out more about him.

He swayed back and forth on his feet and scanned the immediate area. "Do you need me to call anyone?" he asked, shoving his hands into his pockets.

She shook her head and waved a hand in dismissal. "No, I'm just going to head over to my friend's place. It's right around the corner. I'm . . . I can't thank you enough for saving my life. I thought for sure that truck was going to take me out."

"No worries." His full lips held her attention as he asked her . . . Lord, she didn't even hear what he'd said. Was it weird that she was focused on some strange man's mouth after she'd barely escaped death?

Shaking herself from her haze, she asked, "What did you say?"

He chuckled. "Just that I'm glad you're okay."

"I'm sure I have a few scrapes and bruises from the fall. But I feel okay."

"Good to hear," he said, glancing at his watch.

"Thanks again. I wasn't paying attention. I was distracted," she babbled on as she brushed the snow off her dress. "I don't know what got into me. It's just . . . I was trying to get as far away as I could, but I didn't bring my coat, and Nicole didn't answer her . . ." The rest of her sentence died on her lips when she looked up and realized she was talking to herself. The mystery man was gone.

Connect with U s

Visit us online at
KensingtonBooks.com
to read more from your favorite authors, see books
by series, view reading group guides, and more.